Cypress Whisperings

By Phyllis Hamilton

Indigo is an imprint of
Genesis Press Inc.
315 3rd Ave. N.
Columbus, MS 39701

Cypress Whisperings

ISBN: 1-58571-027-X

Manufactured in the United States

First Edition

Prologue

Three years earlier. . .

"Man, I don't know how much more of this I can take. For the past week, all we've done is sit around this stuffy van waiting for this joker to show."

Fully appreciating Stan Richie's comments, Jack glanced out the window. The three of them, himself, Stan, and friend, Robert Petain, had been assigned to a drug task force.

"I tell you," Robert began with a loud yawn, "when I joined the FBI, this is hardly what I imagined."

"Yeah, we know what you imagined." Stan playfully threw a gum wrapper in Robert's direction. "Ladies coming out of the whazoo. You figured that the badge would be icing on the cake."

Whenever they started up with this kind of banter, Jack usually sat quiet. He wasn't the sort to kiss and tell. And even if he was the type, there wasn't much that he could contribute that Robert hadn't already told or tried.

Looking at his friend disgustedly, he couldn't help thinking of Sandra, Robert's wife. Only last week, Robert had claimed a change of heart. For the nth time he had vowed to walk the straight and faithful. He was going to become a 'home body,' even went as far as to surprise his wife by screening in their back porch.

"Can I help it if I got the smooth charm and good looks?" laughed Robert. "The women come to me, I don't go chasing."

"Man, who are you fooling? You're nothing but a dog.

I've watched you, as recently as last night. You don't care if a female is married or single. Don't get me wrong, I ain't mad at you, but how do you sleep at night after taking another man's woman?"

"My philosophy is simple. If he can't keep her, he must not be making her happy." Feeling Jack's eyes burn a hole into his back, Robert felt himself becoming irritated. Turning to Jack, he asked with a smile that didn't quite meet his eyes, "Ain't that right?"

"What are you asking him for," laughed Stan. "You know that Jack's not like that. He has scruples, he thinks with more than just his..."

"Hey, hey!" Cutting him off, Robert warned, "Don't go there, man. Besides, none of us is beyond reproach." As he returned his attention to Jack, Robert narrowed his eyes. "Old Jack here has done his round of tasting another man's honey."

Jack, long used to Robert's deft ability to shift focus off himself, shook his head. "Don't put me in your mess."

Undeterred, Robert pointed a finger first at himself, and then at Jack. "The only difference between the two of us is that I'm honest."

"Yeah, we know all about honor among thieves." Purposefully misquoting the adage, Jack coolly stared his friend down.

"Thief? What the hell. Just who's calling the kettle black?"

Knowing exactly what Robert was implying, Jack, with more than a bit of smugness, calmly replied, "You can't steal what's been given."

"Hey guys, I hate to break up your little 'love fest' but it looks like the informant convinced Bartles to go ahead and make the deal now."

Their conversation already forgotten, Jack and Robert followed Stan out of the van. All three knew their roles. Stan was to approach the men from the left, Jack and Robert from the right. Crossing the street to stand behind the Desire Theater, the three agents approached the suspects. Just as Stan neared Bartles, the second man took off running. Robert, working on adrenaline, immediately took off after him.

Assured that Stan had Bartles, Jack quickly followed his partner around the corner of the theater. Just as he reached the front of the building, he saw the suspect wrench Robert's service revolver from his hand and fire. As Robert dropped to the ground, Jack immediately aimed his pistol at the shooter who now had his gun pointed at him. Firing first, Jack's bullet found its target.

Taking out his radio, he called for an ambulance and ran to the aid of his fallen friend. Applying pressure to the wound, he refused to believe that Robert had been fatally injured. But the dying agent knew otherwise.

With a firm grip, on Jack's arm, Robert gave a short dry chuckle. "All kidding aside, man. About Sandra, you know my heart... And all of my empty promises... Sandra and you, it's all right, I'm cool with it. You two have waited long enough. Tell her how you feel." Sensing himself slipping, he patted Jack's arm one last time. "It's all right, man, tell them that I love them."

"Jack, I don't mean to be rude, but did you come over to give me the third degree, or do you have a specific reason?"

Rising, he stuffed his hands in his pockets and in a controlled voice commented, "Do I have a reason? Now that's sweet. Let's see, is taking the kids biking specific reason? Or coming over to cut the grass? How about fixing the leaky faucet you mentioned the other night. I can go on if that's not specific enough for you. Or, maybe this is the answer you're looking for..." With a roughness born of anger, unrequited love, and penned up frustration, he cleared the space between them in one stride and grabbed her shoulders. Pinning her against the counter, he captured her lips with his own.

Chapter One

"All right you two, stop that jumping around up there and get back to bed," yelled Sandra for the third time. As she listened to the scrambling of small feet, she tapped the balustrade at the foot of the staircase and waited for complete silence. A full thirty minutes had transpired since she first tucked the children into bed.

Waiting for what she knew was to follow, Whitney almost as if on cue yelled, "Mom?...I love you." Shaking her head in frustration, Sandra grudgingly smiled as she listened for the sleepy voice of her eight-year-old son and wondered-as she did every evening, when if ever, the night was going to come when the kids would go to bed without a fuss. Several seconds later, Jesse hollered, "I love you, Mom." Softly chuckling, she climbed half way up the staircase and acknowledged their calls with both firmness and love. "I love you all too. Now for the last time, go to bed."

When she was satisfied that the children had finally settled down, she descended the stairs and turned her mind to the dishes that were waiting for her below. Stopping first in the den, she picked up a stray drinking glass and carried it over to the dishwasher. Usually, she found the late evening chores pleasantly relaxing. As the children grew older, the evenings became busier, leaving the hour or two before she turned in as the only time to replay the day's events, think through problems or simply muse. But tonight was different. Voices from her past were annoyingly screaming just as loudly as the children had been earlier.

With a furrowed brow, she stared vacantly out the Priscilla-dressed window that hung over the kitchen sink and forced her mind away from the source of her emotional discord. Sighing heavily, she returned to the task at hand and began to angrily position the silverware, glasses and dishes into their prescribed dishwasher niches. The letter that was sitting unopened on her nightstand upstairs was weighing heavily on her mind. Sandra had been unconsciously expecting it, for her mother-in-law mailed a letter every year at this time, and every year its contents left her unhappy and depressed. Having finished her chores, she clicked on the dishwasher, turned off the kitchen lights and slowly ascended the stairs. Wanting to put off having to read the letter a little while longer, she quietly walked into the bathroom that connected Whitney and Jesse's bedrooms. Not to her surprise, the room was in need of some minor straightening. Even though the children, as part of their daily chores, were responsible for making sure that the room stayed clean, they often overlooked refolding the sloppily hung towels and wiping off the mirror.

After cleaning the last small handprint from the oversized mirror, Sandra stepped back and critically assessed her appearance. Dressed in jeans and a baggy sweatshirt, she looked at least five years younger than her 32 years. Her 5'3" curved frame was attractively crowned with curly, shoulder-length dark auburn hair. Tonight its curls were tamed with a calico scarf.

Despite the mirror's reflection of a beautiful woman, Sandra felt very plain and ordinary. Undoing the scarf, she shook her heavy hair loose and silently debated whether to give her tresses a radically short cut. Wearily deciding that it was best to leave well enough alone, she turned off the light, checked on the children, and walked to her bedroom.

Having ignored the letter for as long as possible, she settled against the pillows and in irritation ripped the envelope open. Ignoring the check that fell onto the comforter, she took a deep breath and promised herself not to allow what she was about to read to upset her. With detached emotion, she quickly read the handwritten sheets, noting the subtle barbs and veiled innuendoes that were masterfully hidden between her mother-in-law's seemingly loving and caring words. Dorthea Petain, over the last three years, had made it quite clear that she held Sandra indirectly responsible for her only child's "unfulfilled life, and tragic, untimely death." The older woman constantly told friends and family that if her daughter-in-law had not been so eager to marry, Robert would not have been compelled to drop out of dental school and take a job that was not only below his station, but one for which he was obviously ill suited. Thus, he would still be alive and carrying on his father's dental practice.

Sandra knew that Dorthea's argument was that of a grieving mother and illogical. Her mother-in-law's only way of coping was to place the blame on someone else. Like mother, like son, Sandra thought with irritation as she let out a heavy sigh. Regardless of how Dorthea chose to remember her sainted son, Sandra could only remember him for what he was...a self-centered, irresponsible, womanizer...a costly mistake, pure and simple. The only reason he dropped out of dental school was that he didn't posses the discipline to cut it. With cavalier nonchalance, Robert Petain denied her almost eight years of happiness, joy, self-confidence and peace of mind. Whitney and Jesse were the only good to come from their relationship. Ironically, they were the reason she just couldn't shove her deceased husband completely out of her mind.

Stuffing the letter back into its envelope, she thought of the coming summer. The season would mark the three-year anniversary of Robert's death and Sandra, as she did every year, would take the children out to his grave. Regardless of how poorly Robert treated her, he had been a loving father. Due to their age, Whitney and Jesse had few memories of their dad. They, her son especially, knew only of his sense of humor, playfulness and smile. Realizing that it was important not to do anything to disparage his memory, in their presence, Sandra only spoke of their father in the fondest of terms.

Despite the fact that she was raising the children alone, she was relieved that she no longer had to live life as if on a roller coast. During her marriage, there would be months when life was very pleasant, almost idyllic, followed by months when life could only be described as hell.

Before replacing the envelope on the night stand, Sandra picked up the check that had fallen out earlier. Grimacing at the amount, $2,000, her thoughts turned to her mother-in-law once again. Realizing that Dorthea thought no more of the large amount than if she had written it out for $20, she read the brief note that was paper clipped to the draft.

Since you took away my only child, the only pleasure that I now have left in this lonely old life is sharing my money with my grandchildren. Treat Whitney and Jesse to a shopping spree on me. I am sure that there are quite a few things that they have had to do without, items that Robert would have seen to them having, that is if he were still alive. Also, my offer to have the children spend a portion of their summer break with me still stands. A visit from them would brighten this old lady's life. Besides, it will give the children an opportunity to eat a home cooked meal for a change. I know that your little "shop" is the most important thing to you. I'll give you a call soon.

Dorthea

Cautioning herself to view the older woman's note objectively, and not get sucked into Dorthea's trap of guilt, Sandra decided to split the money in the same manner she had done for the last three years. She would allow the children to spend $50 each, and deposit the remainder into their college fund. The kids had all the "extras" that they needed. "Lavender and Hops," her small shop, was doing quite well. So, despite how her mother-in-law felt about the business, she was self-sufficient and more than able to take care of the children's needs. As for the summer, Dorthea's request was not entirely unreasonable, perhaps they could work something out.

Picking up the letter and the check, she dropped them into the nightstand drawer. As she reached over to turn off the lamp, her eyes caught sight of the heavy gold wedding band that adorned her left hand. The band, as well as the beautiful engagement ring that sat on top of it, had been offered as symbols of undying love and faith. But she often likened them to expensive props in a complicated and tragic farce. With a momentary hesitation, she sighed heavily and pulled off first the diamond engagement ring, and then the gold wedding band. Staring down at them in the palm of her hand, she felt a weight lift form her shoulders. Opening up the drawer once again, she deposited them unceremoniously into the envelope and turned off the light.

Enveloped in the comforting darkness of the room, Sandra enjoyed the feeling of relief, wondering why she had taken so long to take off the rings. Would she now be able to put the past firmly behind her? But as she drifted off to sleep, her dreams were not filled with portents of a bright future, but with the broken heartened chastisements of a familiar figure from the past. He sadly admonished that her courage was ten years late in coming and that she was fast running out of time.

Chapter Two

The next morning began as it did every morning. Whitney didn't want to wear the dress that they had selected the night before, and Jesse found cartoons more interesting than putting on his shoes and socks.

Drying her hands, Sandra rounded the tiled kitchen counter and walked into the den. Turning off the television, she reprimanded her son. "Jesse, how many times have I told you that the television stays off until all of your clothes are on and your bed is made up? This isn't a new rule..."

"Mommy, I'm wearing this," Whitney firmly interrupted.

Stifling a smile, Sandra assessed the appearance of her five year-old daughters and took in her solemn expression. The little girl was definitely her own person. Very head strong and opinionated.

Bending down to her level, Sandra matched her daughter's serious tone, "I guess you didn't like the dress?"

"Uh, I feel like leggings."

"Leggings?"

"Leggings." Whitney's stance brooked no argument.

Smoothing the girl's clothes in place, Sandra smiled as she studied her daughter's little face. Whitney's beauty was oddly mature. The dark auburn hair and satiny nutmeg complexion were identical to her own, as well as her large chestnut brown eyes and dark features.

Playfully pinching the girl's nose, Sandra observed, "It's obvious that your mind is made up, and I have to admit that you did match your outfit up quite nicely...I suppose it'll be fine."

As their eyes met, Whitney unexpectedly reached up and gave her mother a hug. "Mommy, I love you."

"I love you too sweetie," Sandra chuckled as she returned her daughter's hug with a kiss.

Jesse, oblivious to his mother's and sister's tender moment, entered the room and badgered, "Hey Mom, where's my lunch?"

Sighing, Sandra straightened and glanced over in his direction, "It's sitting on the counter. Where's your backpack?"

"Um..." Jesse slowly answered as he headed towards the television.

Not giving him time to think of an excuse, Sandra interrupted, "Go find it."

"But, there's this cartoon..."

"Now!" insisted Sandra. Looking over at her son's scowling face, she bit back a smile. Even when upset, Jesse was a handsome child. His dancing eyes, quick wit, and playful manner usually made him good company, but this morning he was bent on having his way.

Hearing a horn blow outside, the kids grabbed up their gear, ran out the den and into the front foyer, towards the door.

"Don't forget, Mom, Uncle Jack's picking us up from school," yelled Jesse.

"Yeah, he's taking us to the monster truck rally," chimed his sister.

"I know all about it. Have fun, and don't give him a hard time." Again the horn blew. "You all better hurry," she urged, giving each child a quick kiss. Taking a moment to wave to the mom driving car pool, she stood on the porch and watched the van back out onto the street. As she closed the front door, she noted the time on the grandfather clock, and scrambled up the stairs to her bedroom.

She didn't have to open the shop until a little before 10:00, but the two hours after the children departed was seldom enough time to prepare dinner, do chores, a quick yoga routine, and properly dress. Today, as usual, she had a little over 30 minutes to shower and change. Choosing a simple sarong denim skirt and a short-sleeved white blouse, she stood before the cheval glass to determine which accessories would complement her outfit. She kept her look elegantly casual, and this morning was no exception. Opening the drawer that held much of her jewelry, she picked up a delicate sterling silver and turquoise choker and matching pair of drop earrings. After slipping on a pair of low-heeled leather sandals, she remembered her plan to deposit Dorthea's check. Hurriedly, she grabbed up the check from the nightstand. Spying her engagement ring and wedding band, she gathered them up and decided to place them in a simple navy blue velveteen box that lay in her jewelry drawer.

It had been quite some time since she last opened the box, but she remembered its content very well. It was a beautiful silver watch given to her years earlier during another lifetime. Before snapping the box shut, she fingered the watch that her rings now joined. Hesitating briefly, she gently slipped it on her wrist and fastened the clasp. As Sandra caressed its delicate filigree, her eyes misted. The timepiece, still as beautiful as it was when she received it almost eleven years previously, evoked a flood of memories.

Irritated at her wave of sentimentality, Sandra silently reminded herself that she had to remain honest and objective about the past and keep it in the correct perspective. She had already wasted enough time. Sighing heavily, she attempted to slip the watch off, but despite all of her efforts, the watch's clasp refused to open. Glancing over at the walnut tambour clock that sat alongside the bed, she realized that she had little choice but to wear it to work. Quickly grabbing up her handbag and keys, she hurried out the door.

As she turned into the shopping district, Sandra was pleasantly surprised to find a parking space relatively close to her shop. After maneuvering the minivan into the spot, she decided to walk several doors down to her favorite coffee klutch.

"Hi Sam," she greeted the weathered, but friendly smile of the rotund shop keep. Inhaling the tempting aroma of freshly brewed coffee and hot pastries, she sighed, "Um, it always smells so good in here."

"Sandra, always as cute as a button. What will it be this morning...wait, let me guess. Pecan or raspberry cream decaf?" teased the older man.

"Am I that predictable?" laughed Sandra. "I'll take a pound of pecan."

Chuckling, Sam quipped, "No, you're not predictable. You just have the sense to stick with a good thing."

"Well Sam, that's not hard to do. Everything in your shop is wonderful. Including these chocolate almond croissants here," complimented Sandra as she pointed to the fresh pastry display. "I think that I'll have one of them as well."

As the older man rang up and bagged her purchases, he inquired, "How are my babies?"

"Oh, they're fine. I'll try to bring them by when I come in on Saturday."

As she paid what was due, the affable shopkeeper handed her a white bakery bag filled with treats. "These are for Jesse and Whitney. Tell them that Sam sends his love."

Smiling thanks, she waved good-bye and headed over to her shop.

Not knowing whether it was the light balmy weather, typical of mid-spring in New Orleans or the quaint facades of the store fronts, Sandra found herself thinking back to the numerous times she and Robert would window shop along the street. Before their marriage, the two of them would spend hours browsing through the art galleries, jewelry and antique stores. They often wound up eating at one of the cozy little restaurants that were tucked along the row.

Once while basking in the area's bohemian atmosphere, she promised herself that one day she would own a shop in the district. When she shared her goal with Robert, he simply laughed and predicted that she would give all of her merchandise away and be out of business the first week. Looking back on the conversation, she remembered feeling irritated with his response. Now, it was obvious that those feelings were in fact her instincts trying to warn her of the trouble that lay ahead.

As Sandra entered her store, she turned on the lights with a proud smile. How surprised Robert would be at her success. Lavender and Hops was in its second year of business, and was doing quite well. Due to good planning, creative marketing and lot of hard work, it was fast becoming a haunt for the local health afficionados. The location of the store enhanced its popularity. It sat in the midst of a rejuvenated section of New Orleans, in an area that enjoyed a perfect mix of tourists and locals. Through the aggressive efforts of the local chamber of commerce, the district was fast becoming a regional cultural mecca as well. Along its streets were restaurants, antique stores, art dealers, avant-garde boutiques, bookstores, and an array of unusual shops.

Greeted by an intoxicating mix of botanical scents, she made her way to the back storeroom. As she walked down the main aisle, she automatically took note of the bins of dried botanicals used for making potpourri, healing and beauty treatments. The shop's space was attractively stocked with large, brimming apothecary jars of herbs and dried florals, and rows of small amber vessels filled with essential oils.

Sandra had been successful in giving the store a Victorian aura. Displayed amongst the herbal products were "hand fashioned" gift items and proven turn-of-the-century health aids. Even before signing the lease, she had known instinctively how to decorate the unique space. She loved Victoriana, but knew it could easily overwhelm. So, with care not to go overboard, she had managed to strike a wonderful and appealing balance. The hand-hewn wooden floors and walls made a wonderful backdrop, as did the intricately plastered ceiling. The great expanse of front window was dressed with lace curtains and offered wonderful lighting. Wanting to fill the store with splashes of rich color, Sandra had tastefully adorned the overhead light fixtures with stained glass shades, and strategically placed Tiffany style lamps throughout.

The overall visual effect was soft and inviting. The botanical scents made the atmosphere very heady. Customers would often spend hours browsing through the stocked armoires and tables reading calligraphic cards and literature that described the store and its contents.

Surveying her quaint shop, she was struck once again by the irony of it all. If it hadn't been for Robert's death, Lavender and Hops would in all likelihood still be only a dream. As she turned on the coffee maker, the bell that hung over the front door rang out announcing her first customer of the day.

"Well, hello Mrs. Gladstone."

"Hello Sandra," greeted the very tastefully dressed

woman.

"I see you're out early as usual. What can I do for you?"

Beaming, Mrs. Gladstone reached out and patted Sandra's arm, "I don't know if you remember, my daughter is expecting her first baby sometime next week."

Nodding, Sandra was well aware of the woman's bit of information. Once a week, she made a point of stopping by and bringing Sandra up to date on the progress of her daughter's pregnancy.

"Finally I'm going to be a grandmother, and I'm getting just as big of a kick decorating the nursery as the mother. When I was here the last time, I noticed your sleep pillows."

Guiding the woman over to the display, Sandra handed her several. "I have moms who come in and swear that their fragrance calms even the most colicky baby. I fill them with chamomile, hops, lavender, and a bit of oak moss as a fixative. Depending on the child, you can even add several drops of eucalyptus oil to help relieve stuffy noses and other sinus ailments.

"They are just beautiful. How do you wash them?"

"Here, let me show you." As Sandra slipped the fabric cover from around the potpourri, its relaxing fragrance wafted throughout the air, urging the woman to make a purchase. "How much are they?"

"This one is $15. Now there's a matching one..." Poking through the filled chifforobe, she held up a larger matching pillow. "This one would make a thoughtful gift for the new mom. It'll help her to get back to sleep after all of those late night feedings, and it's $20."

Admiring the set, Mrs. Gladstone quickly made up her mind. "Oh, they're both so-o darling...I'll take both. Sandra, your merchandise just sells itself."

Taking the pillows, she thanked the woman, and offered to gift-wrap her purchases free of charge. "It'll take a few minutes, so why don't you look around while you wait." As she measured out the wrapping paper, she couldn't help noticing that Mrs. Gladstone picked up several complimentary items. Remembering Robert's chaffing prediction of her giving away the store, she derisively wished that he could see that sometimes it made good sense. The local shopkeepers called the complimentary extras 'lagniappe'. She called it good business.

Just as she was putting the finishing touches on the last bow, Mrs. Gladstone carried several bags of potpourri over to the vintage cash register, as well as a bottle of shampoo base, several vials of essential oils, and ingredients for an herbal face cream.

Softly smiling, Sandra teased, "Oh, I see you found something else."

Reaching for the reading glasses that hung around her neck, the woman laughed. "Like I said, Sandra, your store sells itself. I had promised myself that I was only going to buy the sleep pillows today, but once I picked up one of these little botanical "recipe" cards you have displayed all around the shop, I just had to try my hand at making my own face cream. I imagine you could browse in here for hours."

Both complimented and pleased, Sandra continued chitchatting as she bagged the lady's purchases and gently reminded her to keep the pillows out of the baby's reach. As she said her good-byes, she put several generous samples and mail order forms into a small floral sack, and urged the woman to return soon.

The rest of the morning saw a steady stream of customers, mostly tourists commenting on the shop's unique flavor and merchandise. The morning literally blew by leaving her surprised to see that it was well past lunchtime. Usually she closed the shop for 45 minutes while she grabbed a bite to eat, but today had been so busy that she had hesitated to do so. Her mom and close friend, Jack Thibodeaux, constantly urged her to give Millie Caesar, her part-time clerk, more hours.

From a practical standpoint, it was a good idea. Not only would her presence keep the store better staffed, but she was also a walking storehouse of botanical knowledge and experience. Constantly she found herself amazed at the plethora of information the woman contained in her head. All one had to do was to mention an herb or ailment, and Millie was a ready reference. But until she was sure that Lavender and Hops was a financial success, she was determined to keep strictly to her budget and save Millie for the shop's busier days, or when she had to be away because of the children.

A lull in the steady stream of customers finally came around 1:30. Seizing the opportunity, she quickly walked across the street to pick up a sandwich from a small deli. Crossing back over to Lavender and Hops, she spied the figure of a square-shouldered man knocking on her shop's door as he peered into the window. As she grew closer, she immediately recognized the neatly barbered, coarse black hair.

"Jack!" Turning around, the man greeted her with a friendly hug and quick kiss on the cheek. Taking her key, he opened the door and teased, "Do you always keep your valuable customers waiting?"

Jokingly Sandra retorted, "It keeps them appreciative." As they entered, Jack glanced around with sincere interest and asked about business.

"Oh, it has been great! In fact, today's been so busy that I'm just getting around to eating lunch." Placing the deli bag on the counter, she headed for the back room. "Jack, can I get you something to drink? I have sodas in the fridge."

"Sure, a Coke would be fine."

Unconsciously, Jack allowed his gaze to appreciatively followed Sandra's retreating figure until she was out of sight. He had always admired her shapely legs and softly rounded hips. With a startling clamor, the sharp ring of the telephone brought him back to reality. Reaching for the receiver, he hollered, "I'll get it. Hello...just a minute..." Placing the caller on hold, he yelled back to Sandra, "Someone named Carl." Hearing Sandra pick up the other line and speak, his curiosity peaked, but he forced himself to ignore a sudden temptation to listen in on his friend's conversation.

Several minutes later, Sandra returned to the counter and apologized.

Smiling, Jack responded. "Business comes first." He studied her face, he hoping for some hint as to the purpose of the call. But to his irritation, she did not attempt to explain.

Oblivious to his thoughts, she handed him the soda can and asked, "What brings you over?"

"Nothing really. I had to see a client down this way and had a little time to kill before I'm due to pick up the kids."

As the two enjoyed a comfortable silence, Sandra unwrapped her sandwich. "Jack, I know I don't say it enough, but thanks."

Caught off guard and embarrassed, Jack brushed her acknowledgment aside, "Sandy, you know how I feel about you...and the kids. I probably enjoy spending time with them more than they with me."

Briefly their eyes held as the old schoolhouse clock overhead moodily ticked away the afternoon. As Sandra lifted the soda can to her lips, he noticed her unadorned left hand. Not quite knowing how to inquire about her absent rings, he carefully cloaked his observation in a light-hearted comment, "Whitney and Jesse must've had you running behind schedule this morning?"

Chuckling softly, Sandra nodded. "As usual...but how did you know?"

"Oh...you forgot your rings."

Self-consciously, Sandra withdrew her hand from sight and placed it in her lap. Quietly she explained, "I didn't forget them. I...I just thought that it was time to put that part of my life behind me, for good."

Without comment, Jack simply nodded. Just as the schoolhouse clock sadly chimed the hour, the shop's door clanged opened, breaking the melancholy mood. As Sandra prepared to wrap her sandwich so that she could greet her customer, Jack motioned her to finish. "Go on and eat your lunch, I'll show her around."

With the afternoon sunlight filtering in through the lace curtains, Sandra thoughtfully watched Jack usher the middle-aged woman from display to display. It was rather obvious that the customer had quickly warmed up to his slow and easy smile and unassuming command. Jack's whole persona was an interesting contradiction. While his rugged chiseled features were decidedly handsome, a quick glance often left the impression of someone hard and cold. But when he favored you with a smile, his face transformed into one that was warm, friendly and open. His 5'10" well-knit golden brown frame often appeared a good deal taller. It must be the lines of his clothes, she thought, as she took in his elegantly tailored navy blue suit.

With considerable ease, Jack rang up the older woman's merchandise and made the customary offer to gift wrap any of her items. After the woman left the store, Sandra gleefully commented, "How did you talk her into spending over $75? Are you sure that you don't want to leave your law practice and hang out with me?"

Laughing, Jack begged off. "No thank you. I don't exactly picture myself selling potpourri and herbs to little old ladies."

Displaying mock chagrin, Sandra raised her chin defiantly and asked, "Is that how you describe what I do?

I'll have you to know that I am a holistic purveyor."

Jack chuckled and affectionately rubbed her arm. "I think that you're a bit wacky."

Continuing to smile, she commented, "Jack, I'm glad you stopped by."

Reaching for the two empty soda cans, Jack gave her a good-natured wink, "I'm glad that you're glad." Changing the subject he asked, "Any instructions for tonight?"

"Yes, don't let the kids talk you into buying a lot of junk food."

"What do you consider junk food?"

"You know, hot dogs, soda, candy..."

Looking at Sandra with simulated dismay, he cried, "Hey, that's dinner. But I'll tell you what, I'll try to throw in something nutritious like popcorn, nachos..."

"You all just have fun, and try not to think about me here tonight, slaving away."

Jack, with lines of concern apparent, purposefully asked, "Isn't Millie coming in to help out?"

Shaking her head no, she immediately wished that she had not mentioned her evening plans. "Jack, I know that I said that I would consider it, but it just wouldn't make sense. Tonight, I'm only giving a facial to Maggie."

"But I thought that we agreed..."

Cutting him off mid sentence, Sandra did little to hold back her annoyance. "Jack, I never agreed to anything. You said that I should give Millie more hours."

"Well, why don't you at least consider scheduling your sessions during the day. It'll be safer, more conven-ient. What sense does it make to be down here at night, alone? You're only asking for trouble..."

As Jack continued, Sandra walked away and began to refill the various containers of botanicals. It was obvi-ous that she was only half listening.

When he had finally spoken his mind, she glared

over at him and commented, "Listen to yourself. You're still thinking like a 'G-Man'."

"I'm thinking like a man who's seen a lot of innocent people get hurt...and worse."

Sandra studied Jack's face as he absently thumbed through a supplier's catalog that had been left on the counter. She could tell by his darkened expression that Robert, along with who knows whom else, had entered his mind.

She crossed over to him, ran a conciliatory hand across his back, and in a compromising tone said, "Listen, I promise to be very careful. What you're saying makes perfect sense. If it'll make you feel better, I'll only schedule established customers after hours. Maybe I can work something out with Millie, perhaps give her a few more hours.

Jack looked deep into her eyes and possessively took her hands into his. "Sandra, you are right, this is your business. I have no right telling you how to run it, but I can't help but worry about you." Lowering his eyes to her hands, he fingered her watch. Recognizing it, his dark hazel eyes quickly shuttered.

Noticing the change, Sandra quickly withdrew her hands from his and abruptly commented, "You better get going, school will be out soon. You know how traffic can be."

"It is getting late."

Despite the acknowledgement, Jack made no movement to leave. Instead, with unhurried control, the umber eyes studied her face. It was obvious that his thoughts rested on matters far more complicated than just traffic. "Don't forget, I have my pager turned on if you need anything." Whatever he had been contemplating, he kept to himself.

Following him to the front of the store, Sandra quietly accepted his usual kiss and closed the door gently.

But, for reasons unclear even to her, she quickly reopened it and ran towards his retreating figure, reaching him just as he was getting into the car.

"Jack...?"

Caught off guard, he flashed a faint shadow of his usual warm smile as he turned.

Sandra, in response, felt suddenly foolish. "Jack...I...I...just tell the kids that I love them."

With a momentary hesitation, Jack reached over and gently caressed her chin with the back of his hand. "Don't forget to lock up."

Walking back to the shop, her hand unconsciously sought out the antique band of the silver watch.

Chapter Three

As the afternoon wore on, the steady stream of customers eased considerably, giving Sandra an opportunity to prepare for her evening client. Thinking back on her conversation with Jack, she had to admit that although she felt that her decision not to extend Millie's hours was prudent, deep down she appreciated Jack's display of concern. Over the years, his protective nature had always been a great source of comfort, but even more so since Robert's sudden death. He had been particularly helpful in easing her and the children through the painful months that followed the fateful night her husband, also an FBI agent, was killed in the line of duty. Closing her eyes, Sandra remembered how Jack, along with several of her husband's superiors, came to the house to break the news. It seemed that a convicted felon whom Robert and Jack had under surveillance for drug trafficking had gotten wise to their cover. In the confrontation that followed, the suspect managed to wrestle Robert's service revolver from his hand and shoot him at point blank range. He died before medical help could arrive.

For quite a long while, Jack blamed himself for not being able to prevent the murder of his partner and college friend. Despite the fact that he had managed to kill the felon before either he or any of the other agents present were fired upon, he often second-guessed every decision made that fateful night.

Looking around the shop, she sighed heavily as she wondered about the peculiarities of life. Robert, seldom supportive of her dreams and wishes, in death provided for them. His death benefits and insurance were more than sufficient to pay off bills, the house and start the business. In a very real sense, it was the seed money for her new beginning.

The phone, breaking her train of thought, loudly pierced the store's quiet.

Even before picking up the phone, she had a very good idea as to who was calling. "Lavender and...."

Hi Sandra, Maggie."

With a friendly laugh, Sandra teased, "Let me guess. You're running late."

"This time I have a good reason. Do you think that I could push my appointment back a half hour?"

"Don't worry about it, get here when you can."

Sandra, now conscious of the evening shadows, locked the front door before heading to the rear room to prepare the facial. She thought of her amusing friend. Perpetual tardiness was part of Maggie's make up. She had met the effervescent woman the first day she opened shop and had taken an instant liking to her. She quickly became one of her best customers, and they began to socialize on a personal basis. Quite fond of Maggie's husband and three children, Sandra considered her one of her dearest friends.

With practiced skill, she measured out the natural ingredients, aromatic tinctures, and essential oils that were used for the aromatherapy portion of the treatment. Just as she finished laying out the floral crochet-edged towels, she heard a loud rap at the front door.

Puzzled, she noted the time. It was too early for Maggie. She knew that it would take her at least 30 minutes to get from her location over to the shop. You're only asking for trouble...hopefully Jack wouldn't be proved right, but just in case, she picked up the cordless phone before heading towards the front. As she neared the door, she could make out the figure of a tall, wiry man rapping on the door.

"We're closed," she mouthed as she gestured to the sign hanging on the door.

Undeterred, the man loudly explained, "I'm supposed to meet Maggie Doucet here. I'm her brother."

Sandra, with understandable hesitation, took in the man's friendly face and expressive eyes and sensed that he was telling the truth. "Maggie didn't tell me that anyone was meeting her here," she explained as she unlocked the door.

"Well, you know Maggie," grinned the stranger. "Along with always being late, she tends to leave out important little details. She probably thought that she would beat me over here, I am a bit early."

"Well, you've just proved that you're her brother. She called no more than ten minutes ago, and you guessed it, she's running late. You're more than welcome to come on in," Sandra offered while pulling a stool from around the counter.

As he slipped off his well-worn denim jacket, she took stock of his lean build. In the direct light of the store, the resemblance between him and Maggie was very striking. They both shared the same dark eyes and beautiful mahogany complexion. But, physically, that's where the similarities ended. Whereas Maggie wore her dark hair sleekly cut, it was obvious that Lee preferred to wear his long and pulled back in well-kept dreadlocks. While quickly appraising his appearance, she remembered that Maggie had indicated in previous conversations that he was an artist.

"By the way, I'm Lee Chienier," he warmly smiled and offered his hand.

Returning the smile, she accepted his proffered

hand. "It's nice to meet you, Lee, I'm..."

"Sandra," supplied the easygoing man. "Maggie told me. Say, don't feel bad about not opening the door right away. The way things are nowadays, you can't be too careful."

More than a little curious as to why he chose to meet Maggie at the shop, Sandra commented as casually as possible, "Your sister didn't mention you wanting a facial."

With a self-deprecating laugh, Lee dryly remarked, "I'm quite sure that she didn't; if you haven't already noticed, I'm not exactly what you would call the facial type."

Noting his rolled up shirtsleeve and fitted jeans, she silently agreed as she wondered what type he was.

"My jeep has been giving me a little trouble, so I took it over to my mechanic a couple of blocks from here," Lee explained as he left the counter area to explore the shop's jars and bottles. "Maggie's giving me a lift home." Sniffing the contents of an apothecary jar, he bluntly asked, "What is this stuff?"

Walking over to where he stood, Sandra giggled, "Well..."

"Wait, let me guess. The area's wizards and witches patronize here for their brew and hex provisions. So where do you keep your oversized ladles and cauldrons?"

No longer able to control her laughter, Sandra objectively surveyed the shop. She had to admit that under the soft lighting, the jars and dark vials were perfect fodder for anyone with an imagination. "Most of what you see are botanicals, herbs, and oils that are used for potpourris, herbal treatments, and aromatherapy." As Lee picked up an amber bottle of tincture, Sandra supplied, "I'm also a licensed esthetician."

"Esthetician?" Lee smiled down at the lovely woman,

as he made no effort to hide his ignorance.

Sandra, instinctively responding to the man's affable charm, lowered her voice and added a mysterious timbre. "You know...a modern voodoo madam!"

"Voodoo madam." Playfully nodding his head in agreement, Lee flirtatiously remarked, "I can see it. Those brown eyes of yours would have no problem casting a spell."

Unable to keep from blushing, Sandra drew her eyes away.

Finding the woman's ingénue charm quite appealing, Lee continued their conversation. "Some of this stuff seems a bit "new age."

Sandra, relieved that their conversation had become more neutral, responded with a great deal of interest, "On the contrary, the use of herbs and botanicals dates back to the Bible, and in most cases, it can be proven scientifically. In fact, shops similar to this in Europe and the Far East are as common as our American pharmacies."

"So then, you're not into the power of crystals, past lives, voodoo gris gris, and all of that?

"No, not personally. But, I do have customers that seem to feel that those things work for them."

With a shrug, Lee remarked, "I've never understood any of it. People tend to make life way too difficult. Oftentimes the answers to our dilemmas are staring us right in our faces." Looking around the shop, the interesting stranger complimented Sandra. "But this is nice...it's natural, back to the basics."

As she guided him through the store, Lee picked up one of the little "recipe" cards and asked, "So, I'm a new customer coming into your store for the first time, the only thing I know about herbal is tea. How would you get me started?"

"Well, it depends, I would first ascertain your needs.

You can start with something as simple as mixing up your own potpourri blend for use in your office or home. I have some customers who simply enjoy the various fragrances, while others carefully select and blend the oils for synergy purposes."

Interrupting, Lee asked with genuine interest, "Now is this proven or just psychological flim flam."

"Oh, it has been documented." Pointing to a book display, Sandra continued, "I've put together a pretty thorough reference center to assist those who are interested in the field."

"Now you mentioned something called synergy...."

Flattered by Lee's interest, Sandra beckoned him to follow her over to a display of "recipe cards." Choosing one, she offered an example. "For instance, let's say you were looking for a blend to stimulate creativity. This card suggests adding the essential oils of rosemary and grapefruit to a room diffuser." As she handed the card over to Lee, his strong hand lightly brushed hers, causing the fine hair on her arms to rise.

"Let me guess. For your customers' convenience, you sell several makes and models of diffusers, in a variety of price ranges no doubt."

"But of course," she sweetly answered as she pointed to yet another display.

"Why is it that I'm not surprise?"

Before Sandra could comment, a light rap interrupted their conversation. Hurrying over to the door, she remarked, "I bet that's Maggie."

"Hi Sandra, I'm sorry I'm so late, but..." Maggie's melodious voice pleasantly filled the room.

"That's all right." Sandra cut her friend off with a sisterly hug. "I've been talking to your brother."

Waving to her sibling, Maggie scurried over to the stool where Lee had settled and gave him a quick kiss. "I'm glad you found the shop. How long have you been waiting?"

"Oh, about 30 minutes or so, but Sandra here has been filling the time quite nicely."

Maggie, with a look of obvious satisfaction, turned and mischievously winked at Sandra. "Good, I'd hoped that you two would hit it off."

Suddenly it struck Sandra that Maggie had intentionally planned for Lee to arrive early. Her devilish friend was playing 'Little Miss Matchmaker'.

Flushed with both irritation and embarrassment, Sandra took Maggie's elbow and directed her to the rear room. "It's getting late, so we better get started." Hoping that Lee hadn't caught on to his sister's matchmaking attempt, Sandra avoided making direct eye contact as she offered him a choice of refreshments, "It'll take us about a hour, so feel free to browse around. If you're thirsty I have coffee, herbal tea, soft drinks..."

"Better yet..." piped Maggie. "Come on back and keep us company."

Sandra crossed her fingers and hoped that Lee would be content with staying up front. She found him quite appealing, but just the thought of being set up...well, she wasn't going to be a willing partner.

"Naw, you go on. I'm fine." Lee, catching Sandra's eye, gave a flirtatious wink before continuing. "In fact, I've enjoyed browsing so much that I've already decided to give something a try."

Sandra, quickly picking up on what he was suggesting, felt her skin grow warm. Self-conscious, she offered a weak smile and fled to the back of the shop.

Settling into the comfortable chair that Sandra had positioned next to the workstation, Maggie, unaware of Sandra's discomfort, chatted on about her day's ups and downs. Without comment, Sandra readied her supplies and kept her displeasure to herself. Even though they were the best of friends, she forced herself to treat the woman no differently from any of her other customers. The purpose of the facial treatment was not only to clean and tone, but to relax as well. Almost as if Maggie was reading her mind, the gregarious woman sank back against the soft cushion of the chair, propped her feet on the matching ottoman and gave out an appreciative sigh.

With a gentle touch, Sandra draped one plush pink towel around her neck and protectively wrapped her hair with another. As music softly played in the background, Sandra expertly applied the scented ingredients. Sighing once again, Maggie closed her eyes.

It was not uncommon for some clients to fall asleep. While decorating, Sandra had gone to great lengths to make the salon area of the shop as attractive and peaceful as possible. An eclectic mix of English Country and Victoriana, its pink and lavender floral scheme was picked up in both the floral chintz that dressed the window and table skirts, as well as on the hand-painted porcelain fixtures.

After ten minutes had passed without a further peep from Maggie, Sandra's irritation began to fade. Allowing her thoughts to drift back to the man who was waiting up front, Sandra slowly ran his image through her mind.

Catching Sandra totally off guard, and in turn causing her to knock over a container of cotton balls and a bottle of astringent, Maggie loudly piped, "So what do you think of my brother?"

In spite of the mess that she now had to clean up, she smiled as she dryly remarked, "I thought you were asleep."

Maggie, with a shake of the head, ruefully admitted with a grin, "I was giving you time to work out some of your anger."

"So you were playing 'Little Miss Matchmaker'?"

Not too convincingly, Maggie admitted, "I just saw an opportunity and thought that it would be fun to see if the two of you would hit it off." Grabbing a towel, Maggie helped her friend wipe up the spill and again persisted, "So what do you think of Lee?"

Conscious of not encouraging her oft times over-zealous friend, Sandra carefully searched for the right words, "Well...he seemed very nice."

Maggie, teasing Sandra, indignantly mocked, "He seemed very nice. For crying out loud, Sandra, you sound like someone's dear old aunt. You can't tell me that you didn't notice how attractive he is?" Without waiting for a reply, Maggie prattled on, "Did I tell you that he's an artist?"

"Maggie, I don't..."

"He's what you call a folk artist...you know...he designs and builds primitive wood furniture," her pride very much apparent.

Interest piqued, Sandra, despite common sense warning her not to comment, found herself asking, "Has his work been shown in any of the galleries, or does he only do commissioned pieces?"

In her usual effervescent style, Maggie bubbled, "He does both, and I might add, he's in high demand."

"So why does he need you to set him up?"

Maggie, eyes twinkling at the prospect of Sandra being interested in her brother confided, "It's just that he needs to meet someone from outside that superficial jet set that he hangs out with. You know the types."

Chuckling Sandra remarked," Not really. Maggie, your brother hardly needs me to save him from his inevitable demise."

"Why, that's gracious of you," came a low, smooth voice. Startled, the two women turned to find Lee standing in the doorway.

Indignantly Maggie turned towards her brother and demanded, "How long have you been eavesdropping?"

"Oh, long enough to see that you're up to your usual

tricks." Lee, seemingly unruffled by his sister's scheme, offered a good-humored chortle as he perched himself on a stool.

Now, determined more than ever to pair the two up, Maggie continued undaunted, "I was just telling Sandra that..."

That you need to shut up and keep quiet, Maggie annoyingly thought to herself as she interrupted her friend with a stern admonishment. "Maggie your masque isn't going to set if you keep talking." Picking up a small timer, Sandra set the dial to the appropriate mark and turned to Lee, "She's not allowed to speak until the buzzer sounds."

"It's going to take more than a buzzer to shut her up," Lee appreciatively laughed. Returning his comment with a warm smile, Sandra began to prepare for the next phase of the facial. Even though her back was turned, she was very much aware of Lee's presence and now regretted silencing Maggie. Desperately searching her mind for a cute or clever comment, she nervously drew a blank. Just when she had decided to bring up his art-work, Lee broke the silence with a casual compliment.

"You know, this little shop of yours has a charming quaintness about it. Sort of an herbal pharmacy and spa all rolled up into one."

"Thank..."

Maggie, ignoring Sandra's furrowed brow, called over to Lee. "Do you know that more and more men are now enjoying facials? Not only are they great for the skin, but also they're very soothing. Why don't you make an appointment with Sandra?"

Feeling her face warm once again, Sandra, this time no longer able to find the humor in Maggie's matchmak-ing efforts, turned to Lee, "I'm sure that you have better things to do with your time. Besides..."

Maggie, recognizing what she considered the perfect

opportunity, once again interrupted. "He's coming right past here next week to pick up his jeep. He could stop by then."

Lee, obviously used to his sister's meddling cheerfully quipped, "Hey, don't I get any say in this?'

"Sure you do. So brother dear, why don't you take Sandra up front to the appointment book, and give her the day and time."

Sandra feeling more embarrassed than she could ever remember, refused to allow the conversation to continue. "Lee, listen, that really isn't necessary."

Amused by Sandra's predicament, Lee stopped her short with a sincere smile. "Any man in his right mind would be a fool to pass up what my sister so eloquently describes as a soothing evening with you. While Maggie lets this mud thing do whatever it's supposed to do, let's go back up front and take a look at that appointment book."

Picking up the timer, Sandra resisted the temptation of using it to give her dear friend a sound clunk on the head. Usually she would have offered Maggie a relaxing cup of chamomile tea or some other refreshment while she sat and waited. But for obvious reasons, she decided to forego the offer and instead followed Lee out the door.

It had been a long while since Sandra had felt such shy hesitancy. Lee seemed nice enough, and he certainly had a good sense of humor, but there was an unsettling sense of familiarity. Up at the counter, she slowly opened the appointment book as she tried to assure him that her feelings wouldn't be hurt if he wanted to change his mind.

"You know, you don't have to do this..." Her voice quietly trailed off as she caught his dark eyes assessing her.

"I know," Lee replied simply.

Something about those eyes, Sandra thought to herself as she flipped through the book. "When is your jeep going to be ready?"

"Tuesday, I think that's the 15th."

Aware that there was an opening available on that date even before she turned to the page, Sandra reached for her pen. Choosing to ignore what she had promised Jack only a few hours earlier, she asked, "Is there any particular time...I'm the only one here on Tuesday evenings...I mean I usually schedule clients after I close up the shop, so..."

"What time do you usually close shop?" Lee gently interrupted.

"5:30."

"5:30 sounds good to me."

Jotting his name in the book, she asked, "Is there a phone number? I mean, just in case something comes up?"

As Lee patiently gave out the information, he impulsively reached over and touched her antique watchband. "There's a small antique store out where I grew up that specializes in vintage jewelry. If you like, I'll bring you their card next week."

"That'll be nice." Sandra, all at once relaxed by his thoughtful gesture, looked up and met his eyes. "As you can probably gather from the shop, I love just about anything old." The loud buzz of the timer signaled Sandra back to the salon and cut short their conversation. "Well, that's my cue to get back to work. I shouldn't need more than another 15 minutes, so feel free to finish looking around the store."

Maggie, unable to check her curiosity, glanced around for her brother as she innocently asked, "So did you two get everything all squared away?"

Unable to further ignore her friend's feigned act of innocence, Sandra rinsed off the mud masque in stony

silence. In turn, Maggie, well aware of her friend's per-
turbation, decided to refrain from pressing the question
and instead changed tactics.

In a voice dripping with well-intentioned concern,
Maggie attempted to cajole Sandra into appreciating her
efforts. "Don't be angry with me, I just thought that you
and Lee would hit it off. So..."

"So you decided to play 'Little Miss Matchmaker'."
She wasn't going to let her friend from off of the hot seat
just yet.

"Well, so what if I did?" This time it was Maggie who
was annoyed. "What's the big deal anyway? It's not like
either one of you is involved with anyone else. You live
the life of a hermit, tied to this archaic turn -of-the-centu-
ry shop. You remind me of some forgotten character
from...from the 1890s!"

"Maggie, just what do you know about the 1890s?"
Sandra in spite of her irritation, found herself amused by
her friend's penchant for the dramatics.

"Enough to know that pretty soon your customers are
going to start referring to you as the Widow Petain."

Sandra had long ago discovered that tact and sensi-
tivity were definitely not Maggie's strength. To enjoy a
friendship with her, you had to have a thick skin. But she
also knew that her friend was without pretense or super-
ficiality, and that her concern and love were genuine.

Certain that Sandra's good mood was restored,
Maggie continued with added enthusiasm, "I know that
you don't see it, but the two of you have a lot in common." Noting Sandra's skeptically raised eyebrows in
the mirror, the exuberant woman continued, "For starters,
you're both gorgeous, and..."

Taking in her friend's reflection as she listened,
Sandra hastily folded several towels and dryly remarked,
"Thank you for the compliment, but looks do not a match
make."

"Oh, stop being such a stick in the mud. I know that I'm his sister, but you have to admit that he is good looking."

Sandra, handing Maggie her purse, replied, "Didn't we have this conversation earlier?"

"All right, all right, I'll drop it. But, when he asks you out, don't turn him down."

As Maggie prepared to pay the bill at the register, Lee stepped forward and pulled out his wallet. "Sis, my treat."

Accepting his offer with a playful hug, she asked, "Thanks, but what did I do to deserve this?"

With a mischievous glint, Lee's magnetic eyes took in Sandra's, "I have a feeling that you've done quite a bit."

Certain that there was a double meaning behind his words, but unwilling to accept its hidden compliment, Sandra felt her cheeks grow warm as she forced her attention back to writing up the sales slip for the platinum credit card that he had handed her. As she ran the card through the register, she wondered about the man who was standing in front of her. He was definitely a mixed bag. Despite the fact that his dress was that of a starving artist, his choice of credit card made it obvious that he was doing better than barely eking out a living from his profession.

"Thank you, and I'll see you next Tuesday." Sandra, giving what she hoped was a nonchalant smile, handed him the carbon receipt and walked the pair over to the door. Just as they were leaving, Lee turned towards Sandra, "If you put together some of the items that you were showing me earlier, enough to get started, I'll pick them up on Tuesday."

"Sure, but...I wasn't...earlier...I wasn't trying to hard sell you into buying anything."

Softly Lee replied, "I know."

Never one to waste an opportunity, Maggie took in

the chemistry between the two. "Sandra, do you want us to wait around while you lock up?"

"No, I have to tidy up before I close. You two go on, I'll be fine."

As she went about the routine of preparing to leave, Sandra's thoughts never completely left Lee. Vainly she searched her mind to find a phrase that would aptly describe his good looks. Despite his affable manner, she had an unsettling feeling that a trip with him would take her down a road familiar, but not necessarily easy.

Chapter Four

Thank you, Jack. His thoughtful ritual of leaving the porch light on when he had the kids and she was due to come in late, was only one of many thoughtful things that she had come to appreciate and expect during their long friendship. Sandra, smiling as she pulled into the driveway, noticed that the light's soft cast made the cottage styled home even more warm and inviting than usual. The moss roses and purslane that she had planted several weekends earlier, added wonderful splashes of color as they flowed profusely from the window boxes.

As she entered the empty house, she instantly thought of Robert. Right after his death, it felt so strange coming home alone. In the silence, she would half expect to hear his voice, or see him walk in from another room. But now, the quiet was a pleasant welcome. From the hands on the gold celestial face of the grandfather's clock, she quickly calculated that she had about an hour and half before Jack was due back with the children. If she hurried, there was just enough time to get in a workout on the stationary bike. Running up the stairs to her bedroom, she quickly changed into a pair of Capri leotards and a cropped T-shirt. Between the bike and her early morning yoga routine, she was able to keep her figure trim. Without it, she feared that her often-admired soft curves would turn into wiggling jellyrolls. But exercising also offered an additional bonus as well; it gave her mind an hour to drift and unwind.

With a brightly colored scrunch holding her hair away from her face, Sandra ran down the stairs and padded across the polished wood floor into the den. Quickly flipping through her collection of audiotapes, she pulled out one of her favorites, an old Bobby Womack cassette. Within a few minutes, she was lost in the rhythm of the whirring bike and the soulful strands of the music. With her adrenaline pumping, she was on her own natural high. As she fell into the pulsing beat, her mind drifted to the extremely sexy Lee Chienier.

Giving way to the mood of the music, she allowed her imagination to run rampant as she contrived a mental scenario of the upcoming Tuesday evening. In her no-holds-barred dream fantasy world, she held the role of a seductress. Dressed in a sexy little black dress, she gently massaged Lee's handsome face and neck. With music softly playing and candles romantically lit, her fingers worked their way down his neck and shoulders as he sensually groaned at the delight of her touch.

So caught up was she in her musings, that several seconds passed before she recognized the fading ring of the door bell, followed by the sound of a key turning in the rear French door. Hopping off the bike, she glanced over at the clock sitting on the fireplace mantle and realized that she had been riding for nearly an hour. Just as she reached the door, Jack stepped in with the sleeping Whitney resting in his arms. Close behind, in a zombie-like state, was her equally tired son, Jesse.

"Hi," Jack leaned forward and gave Sandra a quick kiss on the cheek. "You must not have heard us drive up. What were you doing?"

"Here, let me take her." Sandra reached up for the sleeping child. "I was working out to the music. How was the truck rally?"

Placing a brown bag on the tiled kitchen counter,

Jack smiled down fondly at the children. "We had fun. After we get the kids to bed, I'll tell you all about it."

"C'mon buddy, don't get comfortable yet." Jack, urged the boy up from the sofa. With Sandra leading the way, the two of them headed up the stairs.

As Sandra was pulling off Whitney's clothes, Jack gently patted her forehead, whispered good night, and sealed her dreams with a kiss.

Whitney, waking at his words, groggily murmured, "Good night, Uncle Jack. I love you."

With an adoring gleam, Jack softly returned, "I love you too sweetie, now go back to sleep."

"Go ahead and hang up her clothes, I'll make sure that Jesse hasn't gotten into the bed with his clothes still on."

"Sounds good to me, I know how he gets when he's sleepy," whispered Sandra. "You are a glutton for punishment."

Sandra, picking up Whitney's discarded shoes and socks, softly smiled as she listened to Jack cajoling a sleepy Jesse into his pajamas. His voice, low and pleasant, emanated feelings of solace and security. Over the years, Jack had become like a comfortable old shoe. Always there when she needed him, seldom letting her down.

Gently closing Whitney's door, she quietly tiptoed into Jesse's room and planted a good night kiss on his cheek. The young boy, already fast asleep, snuggled deeper under the blanket. With the children happily well on their way to dream land, she switched on the bathroom night light before heading towards the stairs.

As they walked into the kitchen, Sandra playfully grabbed Jack's arm and asked, "That wouldn't be ice cream in that brown bag by any chance?"

"Un-uh, not so fast, you know the rule, first things first." Snatching the bag, Jack tantalized her by holding it just out of her reach. "You get the bowls, while I take out the spoons."

Dutifully obeying, Sandra quickly did as she was told. This was a ritual the two had played out many times over the twelve years of their friendship. The one who brings the treat, serves. As Jack began scooping out the chocolate and coffee flavored ice cream, she expressed her approval. "Oh good, Mississippi Mud! I love this stuff, but you know that I need this like I need a hole in my head." Picking up the lid, she let out a low whistle as she read the calorie and fat content of one serving. "Well, Jack, all I can say is that it's a good thing that I put in an hour on the bike this evening."

"Hey, lady, you don't have a thing to worry about. Trust me, you still have all of your wiggles in the right place." Out of the corner of his eye, while placing the ice cream into the freezer, he appreciatively took in not for the first time, how she pleasingly filled out her T-shirt and workout leotard.

Sandra, oblivious to both his compliment and interest, handed him the fullest bowl and quipped, "That's just it, I don't want wiggles."

As if reading the other's mind, they both headed for the back porch to enjoy the warm spring breeze. Settling into their usual seats, Jack in the chaise lounge, Sandra curled up on the swing, and they ate in comfortable silence. The balmy night was perfect. The scent of the roses, along with the soft rustling of the cottonwoods and the rhythmic creaking of the wooden swing in concert, all made for a relaxing backdrop. Sandra, breaking the quiet commented, "From the looks of things, I take it that the kids enjoyed the truck rally. I hope that they didn't give you any trouble."

"They, or should I say 'we', had a blast. This was my first time going, so I didn't know quite what to expect. But it turned out pretty nice. I think all three of us got a kick out of it. We had some time before, so I took the kids over to Mario's for pizza."

Pleased that they had enjoyed themselves, she attentively listened as Jack described the goings on of the truck event and the evening. When he asked about her evening, she came very close to mentioning Lee. But not quite knowing why, stopped short of relating how Maggie tried to play matchmaker. Instead, she changed the subject.

"Hmm," Sandra sighed in appreciation as she gingerly ate the frozen confection. "All of this caffeine is going to keep me up."

"Well, we'll just have to talk until you get sleepy. Besides, I'm sure this night air will have you fast asleep in no time."

Inhaling, Sandra suspired, "It does smell good, doesn't it." Once again they lapsed into a comfortable silence, the thoughts of both, miles away. Unbeknownst to the other, they each were remembering the summer Robert built the screened porch as a surprise for Sandra. It would be his last summer. Sandra was out of town with the kids visiting her mother-in-law. While she was gone, Robert, with the enlisted help of Jack, worked feverishly to get it completed. In fact, Jack had just finished putting on the last coat of paint when Robert, back from the airport, pulled into the driveway with Sandra and the children.

In so many ways, it seemed like only yesterday. Glancing over at Sandra's face, his mind flooded with the memory of her joy. She had always wanted a screened in porch, but it was evident that she was surprised that Robert had cared enough to fulfill her wish. During the short weeks leading up to Robert's death, he hoped that she understood, as he did, that Robert offered the porch as atonement for his past indiscretions.

Throughout the Petains' marriage, Robert enjoyed

the company of other women. As his best friend, he knew that attractive women were Robert's Achilles heel. In college, he loved to play the field, but had appeared to be quite taken by Sandra. For a while, he seemed to have settled down, but soon after marriage, his proclivity for playing the paramour resumed.

Being close to both Robert and Sandra, Jack often found himself placed in an awkward position. At first, he used to try keeping silent when he would stumble onto one of Robert's affaires d'amour. He reasoned that it was best not to take sides, but to let things take their natural course. But gradually over time, it became evident that Robert was not willing to do anything drastic to improve his marriage, and Sandra showed no indications of seeking a divorce. Throughout much of their marriage, she remained stoically quiet. With only few exceptions did she seek out his comforting shoulder. On one of those rare occasions, Jack, frustrated by her willingness to stay in a relationship that was obviously making her unhappy, suggested that she consider getting a divorce.

Her heartbreaking response not only garnered her greater respect, but also moved him to speak to his friend. Apparently, Sandra, putting the happiness of her children above her own, recognized that Robert, despite his other faults, was a good father. His love for his children was obvious and genuine. Therefore, she did not want the problems of their marriage to interfere with Whitney's and Jesse's happiness and sense of security. In essence, she was willing to sacrifice her own joy.

After his conversation with Sandra, Jack, out of concern and with love, spoke to Robert regarding his callous treatment of his wife. Laying it out in black and white, he called his philandering friend a fool for jeopardizing his marriage and family for a few hot moments with the local cop groupies -'fender lizards' as they were disparagingly referred to by his fellow agents. He also warned Robert that if he did not immediately make a change, he would do everything in his power to encourage Sandra to get a divorce.

Their discussion, which started off very calmly and rationally, soon escalated into a horrible and highly charged argument. Robert, full of bitterness, refused to accept that he was coming to him as a friend. Bringing up incidents from their college past, he accused him of wanting his wife, saying that from the very start of their marriage, he had always suspected that there was something more going on between the two of them than just simple friendship. Adding to the accusations was also the humiliating acknowledgment that Sandra had blurted out during one of their arguments that if she had to do things over, she would have never married him, that even before their wedding vows, she had already given her heart and soul to someone else. With anger hotter than hell, Robert demanded to know if he was that someone else.

In response, Jack, temper flaring, caustically rejoined with a smirk, "What do you think?" Knowing that they both already knew the answer, Robert blindsided him with a punch to the jaw. The force behind the hit was so hard that Jack found himself on the ground. As they rolled around, pounding years of anger and frustration out of the other, Jack made his friend realize that Sandra made her choice as to whom she "truly" gave her heart to on the day she said, "I do." He also pointed out how ironic it was that the only man who honestly had the right to love her was throwing away the opportunity.

In the end, Robert admitted that despite his insecurities, he had no right to treat Sandra as shabbily as he had. He promised to give their marriage an earnest try, to make amends. Building the porch was the first step, but unfortunately time ran out too soon. Sandra never fully understood her husband's poor treatment of her. Several times Jack had been tempted to tell her of that fateful conversation, but the timing was never right. Bringing it all up would open a Pandora's box of painful memories, emotions and regrets, so until the time was right, he kept it to himself.

While lost deep in thought, Jack wasn't aware that his eyes had fixed on Sandra, that is, until she playfully brought him back to earth, "Jack, earth to Jack!"

Stirring from his reverie, he reached over towards Sandra and helped himself to a generous spoonful of her ice cream.

Nudging him away, she asked, "Where were you a minute ago?"

Thankful for the shadowy veil of darkness, he casually shrugged his shoulders, "Oh, I was just thinking..." As his words melded with the mournful creaking of the porch swing, she quietly finished his sentence.

"You were thinking about Robert." Not waiting for a response, she continued, "You needn't feel uncomfortable telling me. I understand. Robert was such a major part of our lives, it would be abnormal not to think about him." Issuing a disparaging laugh, she joked, "I know that I think of Robert and his two-timing ways whenever I answer the phone and there's no one on the other end."

Jack, looking a bit taken aback by her candor, had not heard her refer to Robert's infidelity in quite some time.

Noticing his continued silence, Sandra felt the need to explain her remark. "I can't live my life looking at the past through rose-colored glasses. I have to keep it in proper perspective. It's time for me to move forward."

"Is that why you have stopped wearing your rings?"

"In a word, yes."

Thoughtfully perusing the face of the lovely woman that sat across from him, he debated whether to share the conversation that had occupied his mind earlier. Choosing his words carefully he began, "Sandy, I know that Robert regretted the way he treated you. Building this porch was his way of telling you that he was sorry. He..."

Not caring to hear any more, she rose to her feet and sharply cut him off, "Now I've heard everything. This porch was supposed to erase over nine years of hell? Good Lord, please!!" Without waiting for an answer, she grabbed up the empty bowls and stormed into the house.

Thinking it best to give her space and time to calm down, Jack remained seated. In the still night, it was easy to remember the real reason why he had joined the FBI. It was the quickest, surest way to get out of Louisiana and away from Sandra, or so he thought.

At the time, the hurt in his heart was as vast as the night sky. Walking to the edge of the porch, he stared up at the stars. God-Destiny-Fate, whoever-whatever, made it impossible for him to walk away from love. Eight years later, who did the United States government choose as his partner? None other than Robert Petain. Life couldn't have worked out more serendipitously than if he had planned it. Serendipity...Happenstance...Fate, different names but still the same disquieting face and Pandora's invariable partner in crime.

Once again, his thoughts turned to that distant but ever present summer. The image of his best friend dying on the cold, hard pavement forever etched in his mind. They both knew that he wasn't going to make it. Resolutely accepting his fate, Robert made only one request. He gave his permission for Jack to tell Sandra that he loved her. "You two have waited long enough. Let her know how you feel," he whispered.

As simple as it sounded, it was a request that Jack once again likened to Pandora's box. Remembering how the mythological tale ended with Hope being the only thing left inside the box, he let out a weary chuckle. Hope often times had a way of becoming a mixed blessing. It could offer him all of the reasons that he needed to pursue a relationship with the only woman that he had ever loved, just as easily as it could deceive him into believing that he had a real chance at recapturing her heart.

Chapter Five

As she studied the catalogs and order forms that lay strewn across the counter top, Sandra marveled at how quickly three days had passed. Monday, usually one of the slower days of the week, was surprisingly busy with tourists. Her weekend, while not entirely spent at Lavender and Hops, had been equally busy.

Saturday morning, she and the children woke early and headed for the shop. Whitney and Jesse assisted Millie with restocking the apothecary jars, sweeping and dusting, while she gave a facial. After leaving, the three of them spent the remainder of the day grocery shopping, running errands and enjoying dinner with Sandra's mother. On Sunday, Jack accompanied them to church and treated them to an early dinner. The remainder of the afternoon was spent helping Whitney and Jesse complete science fair projects.

It would not be an exaggeration to say that her weekend had proven to be just as busy as her workweek. But, despite all of the activity and running around, Sandra found her mind constantly preoccupied with Mr. Lee Chienier's impending appointment. Now, with less than hour to go, she found it difficult, if not impossible, to concentrate on the task at hand.

"What's the use," Sandra mumbled to herself as she slammed the catalogs shut and irritatingly stacked them under the counter. Feeling thoroughly foolish, she grabbed up a feather duster and paced her way around the shop. At an armoire mirror, she stopped and admonished herself to calm down. She was fast becoming a nervous wreck, even before Lee showed up. What was the big deal anyway, she told herself. Lee Chienier was no different from any other customer coming in for a facial.

Despite all of her recriminations, she found herself scurrying back to the salon area. It was the fourth time in the last twenty minutes that anxiety prompted her to check on the setup. After making sure that all of the necessary oils and towels were in place, she tinkered with the preset music volume. "Come on, Sandra, get a grip," she chastised as she once again studied her reflection in the mirror. She must have changed her clothes at least three times that morning, switching first from a pants outfit to a skirt and sweater. Still not satisfied, she finally settled on a soft silk cream-colored poet's blouse and a navy, slim-fitting linen skirt, which she topped off with a delicate gold locket.

Smoothing her loose waves into place, Sandra decided to recheck the aromatherapy starter kit that Lee requested. Normally when assembling the kits she would meet with the customer beforehand and ascertain their needs. But with her nerves as frazzled as they were, she thought it best to have the kit already in place before he arrived. Pouring herself a cup of chamomile tea, she tried to calm herself as she waited out the final minutes.

As the school clock on the wall slowly ticked off the last ten minutes, the door clapped open, causing the bell to ring out. Faking a casualness that she far from felt, she smiled and blurted out the first thing that came to mind. "You're early!"

"Hey, not a hello, or a glad to see you?" Lee chuckled as he shrugged off his jacket. Walking over towards

Sandra, he explained his early arrival. "My buggy was finished a little sooner than I expected. So, I headed on over. But if you're busy with your coffee, I'll..."

"I'm drinking tea, chamomile tea," corrected Sandra. As soon as the words left her lips, she realized how silly she must've sounded. Why would he care what she was drinking?

Still smiling, Lee placed on arm on the counter as he leaned in close towards Sandra. Locking onto her gaze, his smooth voice teased, "I stand corrected. If you prefer, I can come back when you're done, or maybe just sit here, right across from you and just browse a bit."

Not quite knowing how to comment on Lee's flirtatious remark, Sandra took a long sip form her mug. This relative stranger had a disturbing habit of scattering her emotions. As she frantically tried to pull her thoughts together, she was saved by the proverbial bell-the ringing clamor of the telephone.

Quickly rising from the stool, she excused herself. "Hello, Lavender and Hops. How may I help you?"

"Hey beautiful," Jack chimed.

"Jack..." usually delighted when she heard from him, Sandra at the moment was hardly in the frame of mind to hold a phone conversation. What's up?"

"Oh nothing. I was just about to leave the office for a meeting and I remembered you mentioning something about having to work late tonight. So, I thought it best to give you a call, just to make sure that you're OK."

Sandra, very conscious that Lee was sitting only inches away, glanced over in his direction.

"Jack, that's very sweet, but like I said before, there's really no need to worry, I'm fine. Listen, I have a customer waiting for me, so I'm going to have to call you back later this evening. But thanks for calling."

Fully expecting him to simply bid her good-bye, Sandra became somewhat piqued as Jack pressed the conversation. In a voice that echoed his concern he asked, "Is this an old customer or..."

Sandra, desiring nothing more than to get him off of the telephone, abruptly interrupted and supplied the information she knew he was angling for, "Jack, if you must know, it's Maggie's brother."

"Brother?" Isn't that a bit odd?"

Sandra, inexplicably annoyed by the wary tone of his voice, cut him off. "No, it's not. Listen, I'm going to have to talk to you later."

Silently cursing Jack for being so overprotective, she replaced the receiver and smiled up brightly at Lee. "Ready for your facial?"

Despite her calm smile, upon entering the salon area, Sandra could feel her heart racing as she nervously suggested that Lee change out of his shirt and into one of the sage green smocks that were hanging in the small dressing room.

Lee, attracted by Sandra's discomfiture, slipped off his denim shirt, "What, nothing with flowers?"

"Oh, so you're a floral man. Which would you prefer, something in orchids or sunflowers?" Finally feeling herself relax, Sandra directed him to lean back while she gently positioned his head against a set of thickly rolled towels.

"Oh no, green suits me just fine," grinned the wiry man as he settled his long-legged frame.

While Sandra explained the facial process, she smoothed a towel around his shoulders. In response, Lee closed his eyes and exhaled deeply as she began to cleanse his face. It was obvious from his breathing that he was quite comfortable and thoroughly relaxed.

As she gently massaged the strong dark muscles that made up Lee's attractively weathered face and neck, Sandra allowed her fingertips to instinctively take their cues from the lay of his skin. Just from its texture, it was apparent that he spent quite a bit of time outdoors. She wondered if his sport was fishing or hunting. Taking in his jean clad body, and well worn, but high quality hiking boots, Sandra had no trouble imagining him sloshing through the dark waters of one of the nearby bayous.

Just as her deft hands began to travel down his strong neck to his shoulder blades, Lee broke her train of thought with an appreciative moan, "God, you feel good...I understand why Maggie faithfully keeps her weekly appointment. All of this time I thought that facials only entailed cleaning the skin with sponges and soap, and maybe a little mud."

Pleased that Lee was enjoying her efforts, Sandra softly chuckled as her pliant fingers bestowed their magic. The intoxicating fragrance of the herbal cleansers, oils, and ointments permeated the room and mingled with the soft music that drifted throughout the shop. As the hour progressed, the room became charged with an exciting undercurrent.

Sandra, despite all of her efforts to redirect the course of her thoughts, found herself fantasizing as to what it would feel like to be kissed by Lee. She imagined his embrace to be unyielding and the kisses to be hungry, urgent and full of passion.

Lee, as if reading her mind, instinctively covered one of her hands with his and gave it a momentary tight squeeze. Startled by the familiar gesture, Sandra quickly withdrew her hand, and busied herself over the sink.

"I wasn't expecting the facial to be quite so sensual. I'm surprised that you don't have men queuing up at your counter for appointments. With those limber fingers of yours, you could start a whole other business."

Sandra, realizing that the best way to deal with Lee's forward manner was to make light of it, with mock indignation, pointed a reproving finger in his direction. "I'll have you to know Mr. Chienier, that I run a very professional and reputable establishment. I've 'soothed' dozens of clients, and not one of them ever commented on the sensuous nature of my hands."

"That's only because all of your clients are women. Which, I'm sure is a fact that your boyfriend finds quite comforting."

"Boyfriend?"

"Isn't that what they are calling them these days?"

Immediately realizing that Lee had drawn his conclusion by listening to her phone conversation with Jack, Sandra's eyes sparked in a good-natured twinkle. "Now, I figured you out to be the type that would be a bit more straight forward. If you want to know if I'm seeing someone, why don't you just ask?"

Embarrassed, but still very much at ease, Lee explained his assumption. "I just assumed that Jack was your boyfriend."

With a hint of a smile creasing her mouth, Sandra placed her hands on her hips, "So you were eavesdropping on my conversation?"

"No... at least not purposely. I would've had to be deaf not pick up on the fact that someone named Jack appeared to be very interested in your well being."

As Sandra gently smoothed a yogurt, yeast and marshmallow leaf masque onto his face, she attempted to explain their relationship. "Well, for the record, Jack is not my boyfriend. He's a very sweet and dear friend, more like a brother."

"I wonder if ol' Jack views you so platonically. Most men wouldn't like to hear a beautiful woman refer to them as being 'like a brother'."

Cutting him short, Sandra slathered on the last of the botanical concoction. "Shh!...you're as bad as your sister. Sit tight, and close your mouth and eyes. I'll be back to rinse off the masque in a few minutes."

Without either being aware, both Lee's and Sandra's

thoughts were turned to the other. It was fast becoming obvious that there was a chemistry that warranted exploration. Lee found Sandra beautiful as well as charming. He had realized from the start that Maggie was trying to set the two of them up, and deciding to be a good sport, he had gone along. But as the week progressed, he sincerely looked forward to revisiting the shop. And now he was certain that Sandra Petain was definitely worth getting to know better. Her coquettish feistiness did more than just spark his interest. He had a feeling that she could be just as feisty between the sheets.

Breaking into his train of thought, Sandra gently patted Lee's shoulder. "We're almost done. Thanks for being so patient, I know that Maggie put you up to coming."

"My sister means well. Maggie's always plotting and planning. It's as if she's on some sort of personal mission to save me from either the social abyss of the woods where I have my studio or from my 'wild friends'."

"Maybe she's caught you talking to the trees one time too many."

Lee, returning her quip with an amused smile, reached out and took hold of the oversized mirror that Sandra proffered and studied his reflection.

"Do you see a difference?"

"Boy, do I. Never knew that I could get this rough old face of mine looking and feeling this good. Those hands of yours are wonderful."

Rising, Lee slipped off the green smock and walked over to the louvered dressing room not far from where Sandra was busy stowing away her facial supplies. Sandra's pulse rate quickened as she purposely kept her eyes diverted from Lee's bare mahogany torso. His upper chest and arms were defined with well-cut muscles, and his forearms were sturdy and strong.

As if fully aware of Sandra's observations, Lee casu-

ally brushed past her as he reached for his shirt. Slowly
shrugging it on, he positioned himself a few short inches
from where she was standing. "About this boyfriend of
yours..."

"Are we back to that again?" Looking into Lee's
intense black eyes, Sandra felt dangerously drawn.
Despite her instincts warning her to be wary, she found
herself unable to release herself from his gaze. "As I
explained earlier, Jack is not my boyfriend."

"All right, your brother then...he's not the over-pro-
tective sort is he? I mean, the two of you don't have
some sort of understanding?"

"No, there's nothing like that between us. Are you
going somewhere with this line of questioning?"

"It depends. How would you like to accompany me
to an art show next Friday night?"

Playfully, as if she had to take a moment or two to
consider, Sandra demurred, "Well..."

Moving closer towards Sandra, Lee impulsively
reached out and smoothed a wayward lock into place. "I
come with references; Maggie can vouch for my character."

"That she can. So, I guess it's Friday then."

A jarring rap at the front door startled the pair, forcing
Sandra to break from Lee's steady gaze. As she hurried
towards the source of the commotion, she immediately
recognized the figure and undid the lock. "Jack? I
thought I told you that there was no need to..."

"My meeting lasted a bit longer than I expected, so I
decided to swing on past. I thought that you might want
some help closing up."

"That's very thoughtful, but like I told you over the
phone, I'm fine."

Jack, making no move to leave, made himself comfortable. "Well, I'm here now, so I'll just wait. Maybe we
can stop for a cup of coffee on the way home."

Her thoughts totally contrary to her words, Sandra feigned a smile. "OK, but I'm still with my customer."

"Oh? I don't mind..." Or so he thought, for at that moment, Lee, with his shirt still unbuttoned, entered the room.

Not quite sure as to why she would rather not have the two men meet, she made the introductions. "Um...Lee, this is my good friend, Jack Thibodeaux. Jack, this is Maggie's brother, Lee Chienier."

As the two men briefly shook hands, Lee offered a friendly and open smile. Jack, on the other hand, was cordial but definitely guarded. It was obvious that he was rather suspicious of the other's presence.

Lee, breaking the heavy silence, walked over to the cash register and took out his billfold. "Well, Sandra, it's getting late. I've thoroughly enjoyed myself, maybe a bit too much. I have a feeling that those hands of yours are going to be an impossible habit to break."

With a beguiling wink, she teased, "Well, isn't that the whole idea?"

The pair's conversation sustained Jack's suspicions. It was obvious that he had interrupted something more than just a simple facial. Lee's smooth candor was not only irritating and dubious, but as he sized the honey-tongued talker up with a practiced eye, Robert was immediately brought to mind.

As he leaned on the far end of the counter, he took in Lee's long dread locks and lean build, and wondered what he did for a living. His clothes, though casual, were definitely of an expensive cut, as well as his leather boots and wallet. From the looks of things, he was pretty well heeled.

Accepting his credit card, Sandra tallied up his bill. "Were you still interested in the aromatherapy items?"

"Sure, do you have them ready?

"They're right here," Sandra pointed to a bag. "I

wasn't sure how much you wanted to spend, so I kept it pretty basic."

Jack, more than ready for the man to leave, interrupted the cozy conversation and at the same time, marked his "territory" by using his friend's pet name. "I see Sandy has hooked you into buying up half the shop."

In response, Lee's dark eyes caressed Sandra's face, "Oh, I don't mind. It'll give me the perfect excuse to drop in often."

This was definitely not what Jack wanted to hear. Watching as Lee and Sandra settled up, he impatiently tapped the counter top. When the transaction was finally completed, Jack rose and walked over to the front door.

Lee, although aware of Jack's obvious desire for him to leave, refused to be hurried. Instead, he asked Sandra several lengthy questions regarding his purchases before finally making a move towards the door. Just as Jack opened the door to usher him out, Lee stopped short and turned towards Sandra, "I guess we'll see each other on Friday. Between now and then, I'll give you a call." Bidding them good night with a flirtatious wink to Sandra and an unreturned nod towards Jack, he finally left.

If Jack expected Sandra to shed some light onto what he had just witnessed, he was disappointed. She didn't even offer a glance his way as she went about her routine of closing shop. He could stew all that he wanted, but if he didn't soon make his intentions clear, she could quite easily and happily enjoy a life without him. In other words, de ja vu all over again.

Sandra, a quiet beauty almost ethereal under the dimmed light, brought back sensual memories for Jack. The soft glow of the scattered Tiffany lamps backlit her sensuous figure and prompted Jack to liken her dark auburn waves to a radiant halo. Each time Sandra moved her head, her silver and amethyst earrings gently jangled. All of this, along with her attire, gave her an almost Victorian quality. Against the dark wooden shelves laden with apothecary jars and florals, Sandra looked as if she truly belonged to another era. It was as if she was biding time waiting for that someone special to come along and sweep her off of her feet.

Sandra, her mind still on Lee, moved about the shop quite unaware of Jack. It wasn't until the old schoolhouse clock chimed away the hour that she turned her attention to the man who sat silently at the counter. Walking over, she teased, "So you couldn't resist playing big brother?"

Fully expecting him to reciprocate with a bit of his usual playful banter, instead she was surprised to see his forehead furrow. Before she could comment, he brusquely asked if she was ready to lock up.

"Sure, all I need to do is turn off the lights..."

"Good, I'll walk you to your van. If you don't mind, maybe we'll do coffee another time."

"OK, if that's what you want." Somewhat relieved that he was reneging on his invite for coffee, she casually shrugged and followed him out. "Jack..."

"Hmm?"

"Is there anything wrong? All of a sudden your mood seems...I don't know, a little distant."

Gently removing her car keys from her hands, he opened her door and shrugged. "I'm just a little tired, that's all." Planting a light kiss on her cheek, he surveyed her face and instructed her to drive carefully, "Give me a call when you get home."

Looking through her rear view mirror as she pulled away, she gave a quick wave good bye.

Chapter Six

Further thought to giving Millie more hours definitely had to be considered. The weekend had arrived and the tourist season was in full swing. Between the shop and the kids, Sandra didn't know if she was coming or going. She hadn't spoken to Jack since Tuesday, which was highly unusual, for he normally called or stopped by every day. Sandra hated to admit it, but she was increasingly becoming more dependent on her dear friend, both as a baby-sitter and as chauffeur for the kids. His eager hand certainly made her life easier. Somehow, in the midst of the bustle of the week, Sandra did manage to find a sitter for Friday evening. Since Lee hadn't called yet, she purposely refrained from thinking about the planned evening out beyond arranging for someone to watch the children.

Not surprisingly, Maggie had called earlier in the week to discuss Sandra's upcoming date. During their conversation Maggie casually made mention of all of her brother's attributes. Thanks to her friend's proud praises, she discovered that Lee Chienier held a doctorate in fine arts, was a full professor at Tulane University, as well as a highly celebrated artist.

As if reading her thoughts, the phone rang. "Lavender and Hops..."

"Hello Sandra, Lee."

Without giving her time to respond, his deep voice hurried on, "Are we still on for tonight?"

Keeping her voice cool, Sandra answered, "As far as I know."

"Good, the showing is scheduled for 7:30, and I thought that we could enjoy dinner afterwards."

"That sounds lovely."

"All I need is your address, unless you prefer that I meet you at the shop."

"No, my home is fine. It'll give me a chance to kiss my kids good night." She hadn't told him she had children, or for that matter, had been married. But Sandra was sure that Maggie had brought him up to speed on all of the details regarding her life. Quickly she gave him directions to her house and exchanged home phone numbers.

Upon hanging up the telephone, Sandra—like a schoolgirl, gave a twirl and looked into a mirror positioned over a chest laden with miniature topiaries. "Girl, get a life," she admonished her reflection with a disgusted shake of the head. "It's only a date."

After watching the wall clock all afternoon, Sandra flipped over the closed sign, and was opening the door by the time the clock chimed 5:30. If she hurried, she had 45 minutes to collect the children from her mother, who thankfully would have them fed. That would give her all of 15 minutes to change clothes and freshen her face.

Just as she was pulling the shop's door closed, the telephone rang. Debating whether to answer it, she decided to allow the answering machine to screen the call.

"Hello, Mrs. Petain? This is Shaun..."

Recognizing the voice as that of her baby-sitter, she ran over to the phone and grabbed up the receiver. "Shaun, what's up? I'm just on my way out the door."

After a flurry of sneezes, the teenage girl continued, "Mrs. Petain, I'm sorry, but..."

Even before Shaun could finish her sentence, she

had a sinking feeling that the young woman was canceling.

"I waited until the last minute to call, hoping that I'd feel better. But I think I've come down with a bug of some sort. So I..."

Sandra flatly echoed her fears, "You can't baby-sit." Squelching her disappointment, she forced a bit of cheerfulness into her voice. "That's all right. You get in bed and take care of yourself. I'll work something out."

After bidding farewell, she slowly hung up the phone. Rapidly running out of time, she assessed the situation and weighed the alternatives. As she mentally ran down the list of names she could call on to baby-sit, she finally decided that it was too late to ask anyone to fill in. Ordinarily she would have asked her mother, but Friday nights were "club night." Even before her dad's death, she always played bridge every Friday.

With a heavy sigh, she rifled through her purse for the slip of paper on which she had just written Lee's phone number. Right as she was about to pick up the receiver, the phone rang once again.

Making no effort to hide the irritation she now felt, she answered with a gruff hello.

"Boy, who burnt your grits?"

Surprised to hear Jack's voice on the other end of the line, she quickly apologized as she explained her ill temper. "I didn't mean to answer the phone quite so sharply. It's just that up until five minutes ago, I had plans to go out this evening."

Without thinking, Jack quipped, "What happened? Lee cancel out?" As soon as he had spoken the words, he wished that he could retrieved them, for the exasperation that tinged Sandra's voice suddenly turned terse.

"No, Lee didn't 'cancel out', as you so flippantly put it. It was my baby-sitter. Anyway, how did you know that I had a date with Lee?'

Shooting out a short laugh, Jack answered, "He made it a point to let me know when I was last down at the shop, remember?"

"How could I have forgotten? You didn't exactly make an effort to be friendly."

"What are you talking about? Any friend of yours is a friend of mine."

"So you're saying that you like Lee?"

"No, I haven't spent enough time with him to form an opinion one way or the other. And I might add, neither have you."

Filling the line with a heavy sigh, Sandra lamented, "Well, that was the idea behind us going out tonight."

Is this where I'm supposed to offer to baby-sit?"

With her fingers crossed, she pulled at Jack's heart-strings, "Only if you want to..."

In the past, her relationships seldom got past the first date. But he had seen the likes of this Lee character before, Robert being one of them. Figuring it best to keep close to the fire, Jack played along and volunteered, "What time do you want me over?"

Looking up at the clock, Sandra quickly calculated how much time remained. "Let's see, I still need to get over to Mom's. In fact, I should be over there right now."

"Sandy, I don't know why I'm so good to you, I'll pick Whitney and Jesse up from Maureen's. You go on home and change or whatever you have to do."

"Thanks, you are a lifesaver. Now, Mom's already fed them so..."

Laughing, Jack interrupted, "I know what to do. You just go and try not to have too much fun."

Thoroughly unaware that she was the one who had just been manipulated, Sandra's excitement was restored. Things were back on schedule. Before leaving the shop, she called her mom to let her know of the change of plan and to talk to the children. As expected, they were thrilled at the prospect of spending an evening with Uncle Jack.

Sandra, who had arrived home with barely 20 minutes to spare, found her thoughts turning back to her son and daughter. It struck her that the events of the evening had worked out for the best. Even though Whitney and Jesse knew that she was going out on a date, it was better that they weren't there when Lee called for her. Despite the fact that the kids had adjusted to their father's death, they still had reservations regarding her going out with other men. In fact, the few other times she had gone out, Sandra had always made it a point not to introduce the children.

Remembering a comment that Whitney had made the previous night as to why she had to go out with someone else when Uncle Jack could take her anywhere she wanted to go, Sandra sighed. It seemed a lifetime since she too once believed the same thing.

Putting on the finishing touches of her makeup, Sandra glanced over at the clock on the nightstand. Only five minutes left. Frantically, she searched the closet for her navy pumps with the string tie. After finally finding them, she noticed a snag in her hose. Letting out an oath, she pulled on a second pair, slipped into her shoes, and stood before the cheval mirror to assess her appearance.

The elegant burgundy ankle length chemise complimented her figure and nutmeg complexion wonderfully, as did the long floral chiffon scarf that she gracefully knotted at the base of her hairline and arranged with an Audrey Hepburn-like flair. To complete the look, Sandra adorned her ears with antique pearl and gold drop earrings matched with an antique locket watch. Grabbing up several hair pins, she first piled her heavy locks on the top of her head, thought better of the idea and allowed her hair to hang loose in a gleaming mass of waves and curls. Finally she was satisfied with the image that stared back, satisfied but nervous.

Hearing a car pull into the driveway, she looked out her bedroom window and recognized Lee getting out of a gleaming black Range Rover. Just seeing him, dark muscles taut under his crisp white cotton shirt, made her blood run a bit warmer. Unaware that he was being observed, Lee brushed down his navy slacks before shrugging into his relaxed fitting linen jacket. Out of his jeans, Lee with his dreadlocks pulled back into his signature ponytail, mustache groomed and neat, looked the picture of sophisticated urbanity. His image left her feeling very excited and caused her to anticipate the evening turning deliciously dangerous.

As she made her way down the stairs, the front bell rang. C'mon girl, calm yourself. She took a deep breath, waited for the bell to ring a second time and then opened the door.

With a broad smile, Lee stepped into the foyer, "Just what I like, a woman who can manage to be both beautiful and ready on time."

Responding to his compliment with a simple thank you, she bit her tongue to keep from blurting...and you're just what I like, a man who smells as good as he looks. "So would you like to sit down, or should we be going?"

"I'm in no rush, we can sit and talk for a few minutes."

She was quite conscious of the heat that radiated from his body as she led the way into the living room. It made the space between them feel a lot smaller. Very rarely did she entertain in the cozy, eclectic styled room. Its furnishings were an interesting and appealing mix of Victorian and new. Lee had immediately mentioned the beautiful, hand rubbed wood floors that ran throughout the room, as well as the rest of the house and how wonderfully it offset the room's color scheme. "Sandra, you have a great eye for color and light. Everything around you always seem so appealing; it's almost as if you bring with you an ...aura."

"Wow, what does one say after a compliment like that? Thank you." Thrown by his unexpected compliment, Sandra self-consciously smoothed the skirt of her dress. "Um...would you care for something to drink?"

"A glass of water would be nice."

Surprised to find Lee following her out of the room, Sandra forced herself to relax and to go with the flow. Once in the kitchen, the tall man casually leaned against the counter top and surveyed his surroundings as she took a glass down from the cabinet and poured the refrigerated water.

"What I've seen of your home, I like. Everything has your touch. You'd be surprised how many people are afraid to give into their whims when decorating. They think that they have to be held to someone's decorating canon on style. But you are definitely your own person—warm and inviting."

Snapping the refrigerator door shut, she found herself growing surprisingly annoyed with his smooth, easy familiarity. "Isn't it a little too soon to tell what kind of person I am? After all, you've only recently met me."

Lee, not in the least bit put off, took in her large dark chestnut brown eyes and disarmingly concurred. "You're right, we've only recently met, but I feel as if we've known one another for a long time."

As he reached for his glass, Lee's hand brushed against hers, and despite her wariness, she felt an unconscious wave of desire wash through her body. Sandra, withdrawing her hand as if she had touched fire, glanced up at his face. It was then that she knew that he would kiss her.

Bong, bong...reverberated the grandfather clock, its disruptive sentry welcomed by Sandra.

"Look, at the time. We better get a move on it before

it gets too late. Just give me a minute to run upstairs to collect my purse."

Just as her shapely figure left hearing distance, Lee chuckled, "Don't worry, I'm not going anywhere. For you, I have all of the time in the world."

Chapter Seven

As Lee maneuvered through traffic, Sandra settled back onto the Range Rover's buttery black leather upholstery. Its scent, along with Lee's deep resonant voice made for quite a mix. It seemed that Lee was taking her to an exhibit at the Sol Galerie. Sandra surmised that the featured artist must be extremely accomplished. The art gallery, which was located on Julia Street in the Warehouse District heading uptown, had long been the bastion of New Orleans' sophisticated elite. For an artist to have his work shown at such a gallery was a validation that he had 'arrived'.

As they pulled up outside the stylish late 1890s structure, two valets came forward. One opened the passenger door and assisted Sandra, and the other took charge of the vehicle. Inside the former, but still beautifully appointed home was an impressive assemblage of art aficionados, critics and artists.

Sandra, who had enjoyed several openings of lesser-known collections, was both excited and overwhelmed at the prospects of the evening. Within minutes, she determined that Lee was obviously well known amongst this circle of affluence. Despite the fact that he was constantly hailed, he never stopped to speak to anyone, opting instead to simply smile and nod.

Taking hold of Sandra's hand, he softly whispered in her ear, "I thought that we'd view the exhibit before I introduce you around." Leaning in a bit closer, he briefly placed a hand on her waist, "Oh by the way, you look delightful."

Before she could say thank you, he placed a finger gently up to her lips, "Shh!" His easy, playful manner made her feel very comfortable and relaxed.

Just as Sandra was about to comment on a sculpture, a woman's rather loud and indulgent voice cut in. "Lee darling, you made it after all."

Turning, Sandra discovered a statuesque woman in her early forties had captured Lee's attention. The woman's sleek black dress and hose gave her the appearance of a couturier's model, as did the jet-black hair that was pulled into a tight chignon. While the woman gushed over Lee, Sandra took in her expertly made up face which was highlighted with a deep red lipstick, and noticed how her pearl ornamented shoes perfectly matched the heavy gold broach and earrings that adorned her outfit. Just as Sandra decided that she made a very striking picture, the woman flashed a cursory glance that left the younger woman feeling extremely gauche. Slipping between the couple, she possessively took hold of Lee's arm.

"Lee darling, I thought you weren't going to show. What made you change your mind? Oh, never mind, it doesn't matter. I'm just glad that you're here."

Gently extracting his arm free, Lee smiled over at Sandra. "Aileen, I'd like you to meet someone."

"Who darling?" With obvious disregard for Sandra's presence, Aileen casually glanced around.

Reaching for Sandra's hand, Lee pulled his date to his side, "Aileen, I'd like you to meet Sandra Petain. Sandra, this is Aileen Soileau-Braishear, both proprietress of this very fine salon and my industrious agent."

Sandra was not surprised when her polite hello was met only with a tight smile. Without even a perfunctory attempt at conversation, Ms. Braishear once again returned her attention to Lee. Leaning in close, with familiarity, she playfully tapped Lee's chest with a manicured fingertip, "I thought I told you to dress."

The woman's comment was not lost on Sandra. She was well aware that Aileen's words were directed more at her than at Lee. Mentally assessing her own appearance against that of the haute couture and avant garde dress around her, she refused to feel second best.

As she wondered how to best deal with Lee's friend, she watched as Aileen draped herself onto Lee's arm and cooed, "Love, there's some people on the other side of the room that you must meet."

Grabbing up two glasses of white wine from a passing waiter, Aileen handed a flute to Lee, forcing him to release Sandra's hand, and took a sip from the other. Lee instantly recognizing Aileen's faux pas, handed his glass to Sandra, and gave the pretentious woman a glare impossible to ignore. In response, Aileen offered a mock apology, "Oh, Sandra darling, how silly of me. I didn't mean to ignore you, I just totally forgot that you were standing there."

Lee noticed his date's pinched expression, and made what Sandra considered a half-hearted attempt at getting rid of the haughty woman. "Aileen, Sandra and I were about to view the ex..."

"I don't mean to interrupt, darling, but there are several people who have been asking for you all evening." In a tone that was more of a statement than a request, Aileen asked Sandra, "You don't mind do you? It'll only take a few minutes, and we'll be right back."

Sandra, thoroughly fed up with both Aileen's snooty behavior and Lee's unwillingness to brush the woman off, handed the wine glass back to Lee. "You two go and enjoy yourselves, I'll view the exhibit on my own." Dismissing the pair, Sandra turned and walked in the direction of a collection presented in a second gallery opposite where they had been standing. As far as she was concerned, the two could have one another. She'd be damned if she was going to tag behind as if she were Lee's little mutt.

As she made her way around the second gallery, she found herself thoroughly enjoying the exhibit, and gradually her thoughts were distracted from Lee and Aileen. The portion of the collection that appealed to her the most was an arrangement of pieces primitive in design, and held a certain note of whimsy. She knew enough about art to recognize the style as being folk art; a stylizing that was based on the unique reality of the artist. She had gotten halfway around the room when she noticed a collection of furniture that consisted of a rocker, several chairs, headboard and end tables. There were two groupings, one of a delicate willow twig and the other of the much sturdier cypress, both trees indigenous to the surrounding swamp area. All of the pieces were breathtakingly beautiful. The thought that a human could fashion branches and hewn wood into such graceful and intricate art was talent to be admired. Preparing to pick up one of the placards positioned in front of an especially beautiful rocker, Sandra heard a low, smooth voice.

"So, beautiful, what do you think?"

With a jump, she half turned to find Lee standing behind her, hands casually stuffed in his pockets.

If he thought that he was just going to slide his way back into her good graces, he had another thought coming. So, she knitted her dark brows and flatly commented, "Oh, it's only you."

If he caught her sarcasm, it was impossible to tell, for he amicably smiled as he ambled on. "I always thought it a little crazy to pass furniture off as art. Furniture serves a practical purpose..."

"Well, so does art. Besides, how can you define what's art and what isn't? It's in the soul of the creator and eye of the beholder."

"That was very eloquently stated, Ms. Petain, and refreshing." As Lee rested on her large chestnut eyes, he continued. "You obviously have an appreciation and good understanding of this field. That's more than what I can say for most of these 'patricians' wandering around here."

Sandra, still smarting over Lee and Aileen's earlier treatment, offhandedly commented, "You seem to fit in quite well with these 'patricians'."

Throwing his head back, Lee laughed outright, "Touché! You have made your point." Moving in close, his black eyes sensuously slipped over hers, melting away her resolve to remain angry. "I apologize for my insensitive behavior." With an arm around her waist, he pointed to the display before them and asked, "So which of these is your favorite?"

"That's an impossible question to answer, everything is so beautiful. There's almost a serene beauty to it all. When I gaze upon the lines, there's an eerie stillness, as if I'm frozen in time with the hands that fashioned each curve. I feel an urge to reach out and touch the wood; I'm drawn to it. It's almost as if it has a soul. In fact, when I look at the rocker, I get the feeling that if I sit in it, I can close my eyes and actually talk to the craftsman who fashioned it." Feeling self-conscious, Sandra chuckled, "You must think that I'm crazy."

Shaking his head no, Lee encouraged her to continue. "After having said all of that, which would you choose?"

In a slow manner that suggested such a decision was too great, she answered, "If I had to choose, it would be a toss up between the trellis headboard and the rocker...but, the rocker I think.

"Then it's yours," Lee announced.

"Mine! I think that it's time for a reality check here."

With amusement lighting his dark eyes, Lee asked, "You like it, don't you?"

"Like it, love is a better word. But I couldn't afford a salt shaker from this room, let alone something as priceless as..." Stopping mid-sentence, she shook her head, "I bet this rocker alone is a small fortune."

"It is," Lee agreed. "But don't worry. It's my gift to..."

"Your gift?" Pulling away, Sandra firmly declined his generous gift, "Lee this is much too extravagant." Reading the placard she continued, "See, it says here the artist is asking $14,800."

Offhandedly Lee asked, "Who's the artist?"

"I don't know, let's look at the card. Lee Chienier!" Totally thrown off guard, she looked up at Lee and demanded, "This is your work?" Without giving him time to answer, she rushed on, "Why didn't you tell me that you were taking me to see your work? You have no scruples whatsoever, to let me go on like some ninny..."

With her new found knowledge, she surveyed the art pieces with fresh appreciation. Knowing that they were crafted with Lee's hands, she was even more in awe of the work. "Lee, you are truly talented."

Cognizant of the sincerity behind her praise, he took her hand. "Thank you, I could not have received a lovelier compliment from a better person. You really do appreciate the time and love that goes into my work. That is why I want you to accept my gift."

" Oh Lee, I couldn't...besides, isn't the whole purpose of a showing to sell..."

Quieting her lips with his finger, he walked her over to the rocker. "Do me a favor and sit."

"Lee, I couldn't, it's on display..."

"It's mine and I'm giving you permission. So go on."

Bemused by Lee's insistence, she self-consciously obeyed.

Taking several steps back to assess the image

before him, Lee softly commented, "Sitting in the rocker, wearing that beautiful dress, with the overhead lights catching the soft red tones of your hair, all make for a rather lovely picture. You're any artist's inspiration..."

"Lee, you are stoned out of your mind." Quickly standing, she offered a compromise. "I tell you what, if you give me your word that you will not embarrass me like that again, I'll 'think' about accepting your gift. But, I'm not making any promises."

"That's fair enough." Changing the subject he glanced down at his watch, "Do you want to see the rest of the exhibit, or are you ready to make the great escape?"

Just as Sandra was about to answer, Aileen's unmistakable drawl dripped across the room. "Lee, Lee..."

With their backs turned, he whispered in Sandra's ear, "Don't turn around, maybe she'll go away."

No such luck. Before they could turn around, Aileen had already planted a hand on Lee's shoulder. "There you are, dear. You are a positive hit." Sandra smiled, amused at the affected manner in which Aileen jabbered.

"You won't believe this, but Dixie Rhoades of *The Times-Picayune* wants to do another feature article on you, and Mrs. Girard is interested in you doing several commissioned pieces for her beach house in Pass Christian." Aileen sped on without catching a breath. "She saw the rocker, loves it, wants it, as well as the settee, and any other pieces that you can dream up. Says she may even want you to work with her decorator when she redoes her home here in the city."

Unaffected by his agent's report, Lee gave a blasé shrug. "That's great, Aileen, but the rocker is already spoken for."

Sandra, despite the fact that she had waffled over accepting the chair, was pleased that Lee refused to part with it.

"Someone spoke to you about purchasing the rocker?" Aileen groaned as she flipped through several pages of a small leather notebook.

Lee playfully winked at Sandra and answered, "No, not exactly. I'm giving it to Sandra."

"Sandra?" Aileen pealed, as if the idea was beyond belief. With a fake smile, she gritted between clenched teeth, "Nothing against you, dear, but I really must talk to Lee."

"Sure, go right ahead," chuckled Sandra as Lee followed the woman, wickedly mimicking her affected mannerisms.

When Aileen was certain that they were out of hearing range, she demanded, "Since when do we pass out $14,000 gifts?"

"$14,800," Lee corrected with a smile. Then with a firmness that brooked no argument, he made it clear that the woman had overstepped her boundary. "Aileen dear, to whom I pass out gifts is none of your business."

More than just a little piqued by his gilb manner, Aileen retorted, "Lee dear, this is business, and it pays the bills, mine anyway."

Lee, genuinely appreciative of Aileen's efforts, tried to placate the irritated woman. "Listen, I know that you take this gallery nonsense a lot more seriously than me, so let's work out a compromise. Go ahead and make a date with old money bags, I'll meet with her and get a feel for what she likes. You can tell her I insist on designing an entirely new piece just for her. That should appease her. Besides it's the way I like to work anyway."

Aileen, more than satisfied, beamed as she curled her arms into the crook of Lee's and kissed him affectionately on the cheek. "Thank you dear, you truly are a genius."

Smiling Lee gently extricated her arm and turned back to where he had left Sandra. To his vexation, she was gone.

"It looks like she got tired of waiting, dear," Aileen grinned like a Cheshire cat. Indeed, Sandra had. After watching the two for several seconds, it became obvious to Sandra that Aileen was not going to leave them alone. She understood that Lee viewed the woman as something of a necessary evil, but she refused to graciously stand and watch Aileen flirt with her date. She had been down that road too many times with Robert. Deciding to investigate another gallery, Sandra headed for the opposite end of the building. Half way across, she felt a tap. Turning, she was met by the friendly hug of her friend, Maggie.

"Where's Lee?" Maggie demanded bluntly.

Instead of answering directly, Sandra replied, "You didn't tell me that your brother was so talented."

"I didn't want to lay it on too heavy. I thought that you might get scared away." As she glanced around, she repeated her original question, "So where is that brother of mine?"

With irritation that smacked of real anger, Sandra veiled her answer under a layer of feigned sweetness. "Ms. Aileen has attached herself to his sleeve."

Smirking, Maggie grabbed up a champagne glass from a passing waiter. "That woman! She is hardly his type. Ms. Aileen has been trying to get her claws into him for years."

"She seems to be doing wonders for his career."

"Oh, she is good at what she does, and that includes being a real bitch."

"Who are you gossiping about this time?" With a start, Sandra and Maggie turned around to find Lee standing behind them.

Maggie, not missing a beat piped, "I was warning Sandra about 'Aileen Dearest'. You know she would love to sink her claws into you." Laughing, the outgoing woman playfully swatted her brother's shoulder. "I bet she got a kick out of seeing you with Sandra."

"My darling sister, I can take care of Aileen." Chuckling, he nodded in the direction of the object of their conversation. She was across the room, artfully schmoozing with an unsuspecting patron. "Even though she can be a bit overbearing, you have to give her credit for being a damn good agent."

As another waiter passed with a tray of wine, Lee lifted two glasses and offered one to Sandra, who hesitated briefly before accepting it. Long tired of both the art exhibit and Aileen, she was more than ready to leave.

When she forced her thoughts back to the conversation, Maggie, still continuing with her attack on Aileen retorted, "Overbearing, that's putting it mildly. That woman is...is...tumid and turgid! In fact, Sandra's been telling me..." pausing she imitated the agent's rather affected style, "That Ms. Aileen has been monopolizing you the entire evening."

Stifling a laugh at her friend's rather dramatic commentary, Sandra flushed as she made a futile stab at toning down Maggie's comments. "Monopolize wasn't quite how I put it...I don't mind, really. I understand that this is business."

Furrowing his brow, Lee looked Sandra directly in the face. "Sandra, it's not your place to apologize, it's mine. After all, I am the one who invited you here. In fact, why don't we leave right now?"

"That's fine, but we don't have to go on my account. I'm sure your sister doesn't want to be stuck here alone."

"Go!" interrupted Maggie. "I'm going to leave soon myself." With a mischievous twinkle she added, "But first I want the pleasure of giving Aileen your regrets."

Briefly kissing his sister's face, Lee affectionately tickled her chin, "Sis, now promise you'll be nice. I'll give you a call later."

Once settled in the Rover and on their way, Sandra quietly asked, "Don't you think that you should have been the one to tell Aileen good-bye?"

"No, she knows that I usually only make an appearance at these doings. Believe it or not, it adds to my appeal, as well as to the price!"

As they drove in silence, Sandra perused Lee's profile. There was something about his nonchalant manner that was quite unsettling. On the surface, his unconcern came across with a certain appeal—a charm almost. But upon closer examination, it was a bit too practiced, too deliberate.

Breaking into her thoughts, Lee spoke from the darkness of the opposite side of the vehicle. "You certainly are a different kind of lady. Any other woman would be venting holy steam by now. I take you out on our first date, abandon you in a room of strangers, am 'monopolized' by another woman, and you just sit there with the most amicable expression on your face."

Out of the blue, Robert came to mind, causing Sandra to flash, "It's just that over the years, I've learned how to make the best of a bad situation."

"I get the impression that you're comparing me with someone from your past."

"I wouldn't say that I was comparing you...it's just that you remind me of someone."

Lee, seemingly unfazed by her remark, reached over and gently took hold of her hand. "Well, hopefully dinner will shake any misconceptions you have about me."

"I don't know, this dinner will have to be pretty good." Curious as to where they were headed, but content to be surprised, Sandra noticed that they were leaving the city and approaching the toll bridge that crossed Lake Pontchartrain

"We're going to a very special place. The chef serves the best gumbo and bread pudding in the state. It's not a place I usually take my dates, but I think that you'll get a kick out of the ambiance, as well as the cuisine.

Chapter Eight

The traffic across the 26-mile causeway was light, the sky was clear, and there was a soft breeze blowing in off the lake. Relaxing, she found herself looking forward to the rest of the evening.

After they crossed, Lee continued on the main interstate for a short while, and then turned down a narrow state highway. With any other first date, Sandra would have felt apprehensive about going so far out, especially at night, to a place that was obviously remote. Somehow, though, without entreaty, he had put her qualms to rest. Feeling very comfortable, she listened as he caricatured some of the local celebs that had been present at the art gallery.

The pleasant drive seemed far shorter than 68 miles, for before she knew it, they were pulling up to a very beautiful turn-of-the-century home. Sandra didn't know what to expect, but it certainly wasn't this. When they turned onto the state highway, she assumed that they were headed to some local fish fry. With Lee and his contradicting personality, it wouldn't have surprised her. Therefore, she was not prepared for the elegant and charming Victorian bed and breakfast that sat before them. Against the night sky, the pristine white and lavender structure stood out in stark contrast to the bayou that formed its backdrop. It was almost as if someone had taken oil to canvas and painted the scene from the imaging of a prolific writer.

"Why Lee, this is beautiful," Sandra gasped. "How did you ever find this place?"

Containing his pleasure at her delight, Lee did not directly answer her question, but instead whetted her interest. "If you think this is something, just wait until we get inside."

Inside? Sandra was still soaking up the beautiful wooden wraparound porch, wooden swings, and gas lamps.

Just as they approached the front door, an attractive older woman appeared. "Lee, I thought that was you," she greeted in a distinctive Cajun accent. "How's my boy?" Holding open the screen door, she patted him on the side of his face and gave him a motherly hug and kiss. "Perfect timing, dinner is just about ready."

Smiling at Sandra, she beckoned them to enter, "C'mon in." Pointing to several lengths of cotton ribbon hanging from the doorframe, the woman explained, "Even though I have the lavender up, we're still bothered with mosquitoes."

Sandra, who was attracted to the woman's ready friendliness, found herself thinking that anyone who used lavender oil as an insect repellent must be OK.

As they stepped into the foyer, Lee fondly placed an arm around the older woman. "Miss Lavania, I would like for you to meet Sandra Petain. Sandra, this is the love of my life, Lavania Fontenot."

"Nice to met you, Mrs. Fontenot."

"Just call me Lavania like everybody else," corrected the friendly woman. Smiling, Sandra tried to puzzle out her relationship to Lee as she took in the woman's beautiful butter toffee complexion and regal stance. Other than the warm friendliness, there was little resemblance between the two.

"I hope that we didn't keep you waiting, I know how you like your guests on time."

"You're not holding up anything. We're quiet this weekend. Our next guests aren't expected until Sunday sometime. Besides, where do you get off calling yourself a guest? As often as I have had to just about take you over my knee, you're family." Dimming the hall light, Lavania directed the pair into the parlor. "Lee, make Sandra feel at home while I go let Al know that you're here. He's back in the kitchen brewing up a pot of chicory."

As she followed Lee out of the dark entry hall into the softly lit room, Sandra was met with an esthetic treat. In keeping with the Victorian exterior, the parlor's walls were done up in muted shades of lavender, cream and rose, as were the coordinated floral-dressed upholstery and windows. Rich mahogany furnishings pleasingly filled the room's floor, nooks and crannies.

Fluffing a silk, gold-fringed pillow, Lee made himself comfortable on a burgundy damask sofa and watched with interest as Sandra slowly walked around the beautifully appointed room.

Turning towards Lee, Sandra spoke in a reverent whisper, "You can literally feel the history of this home. It is almost as if time has been captured."

Lee, whose arm was casually draped along the back of the sofa, watched with amusement as Sandra gently caressed the dark furniture and stroked the ornate silver picture frames that were informally placed around the room.

Impulsively, she stopped in her tracks and closed her eyes.

No longer able to contain his curiosity, Lee chuckled as he asked, "What are you doing?"

"Hush," she chided. "It's just that the feel of this room is so wonderful, that I want to etch it in my memory."

Flushing at Lee's soft chuckle, Sandra found herself giggling as well, "I know that I sound absolutely crazy.

You must take me for some kind of ninny."

"No, no, on the contrary, I find you rather refreshing and quite delightful."

Bending over a ceramic jar of moist potpourri, Sandra gave an appreciative sigh as took in the rich scent of the brandy-cured rose petals and Victorian mix of chamomile, heliotrope, lavender, rosemary, myrtle and oils. "Um, this smells simply wonderful. The fragrance literally greets you as you enter the room."

As Sandra looked up, an oil portrait of a rather dour-looking gentleman prompted her to ask, "Do you think that Mrs. Fontenot would give us a tour later?"

When Lee didn't immediately answer, Sandra turned around and noticed the grin spread across his face. Suddenly feeling quite unsophisticated, she retracted the request, "I guess I'm being too presumptuous..."

Quickly allaying her concerns, Lee shook his head. "No, quite the opposite. I'm sure Miss Lavania will get a kick out of you asking." Hoping to put her at ease, Lee continued, "You know, I don't usually drive dates all the way out here. But after observing you at Lavender and Hops, this seemed like the natural place to bring you."

Before Sandra had time to respond to Lee's remark, Lavania's stately gait echoed down the hallway. Impulsively reacting with childlike quickness, Sandra hurried across the room and quickly sat down next to Lee.

Expecting only their hostess, Sandra was caught off guard when an elderly gentleman followed close behind. The slender man's appearance immediately captured her attention. He was at least 6'5" tall and extremely thin. His bright copper complexion drew her eyes to his sharp features, and shaggy brow and beard. Heavy gray eyebrows hung over his penetrating topaz-colored eyes like burgeoning purslane.

Sandra imagined that over the years, his mere appearance probably scattered many a child from their play. It was impossible to guess his age; he could have been anywhere from 60 to 100. The manner in which he wore his clothing was akin to an artist's rendering. The plaid shirt and blue denim cover-alls despite their casualness were heavily starched and sharply creased.

So absorbed was Sandra in her study, she didn't realize that the gentleman was perusing her as well. That is, until he sat down the tray he had been carrying with a rather loud thud, leaned over the coffee table towards Sandra and blurted, "Young lady, I'm 69 and not a day older!"

With a start, Sandra colored. Without thinking, she glibly smiled, "Really? I had you pegged for 65." To her relief, the room filled with laughter.

Giving Sandra a friendly wink, the elderly man turned to Lee and remarked, "You got yourself a sassy one here."

"Alphonse!" Lavania admonished, "Stop teasing Sandra. You haven't even been properly introduced and already you're giving her a hard time."

Lee, now standing, gave the man a warm hug as he smiled down at Sandra. "Don't you mind Mr. Al. He only teases if he likes you. Otherwise, he just gives you an out-an-out hard time."

As Mr. Fontenot reached down to take Sandra's hand, Lee made proper introductions. "Sandra, if you haven't already guessed by now, this is Miss Lavania's other half, Mr. Alphonse Fontenot, or Mr. Al. Mr. Al, this is Sandra Petain."

Slowly sitting down, Alphonse gave her shoulder a friendly pat. "You're the gal my little "Mag-Pie" rattles on about. Just from listening to her, I know your life's story." To prove his statement, Al began ticking off Sandra's personal profile, counting off each tidbit of information with his fingers. "Let's see, you have two children, a boy and a girl, been widowed for a couple of years. Your husband was a 'G-Man', murdered." Shaking his head, he editorialized, "Nasty business."

Lavania, who had just finished pouring the hot brew, fussed, "Alphonse, leave the girl alone. She came out here for a good time."

Pushing his wife's comments aside the way only older couples can do, Al waved away her concerns and turned back towards Sandra. Looking deeply into her eyes with a penetrating stare, he remarked, "Ain't nothing wrong with speaking of the dead. Especially if you've never done them any harm and have made your peace." Squinting his eyes a bit, he held his gaze steady, "This old place is full of ghosts, you know. They'll talk to you if you listen. But you've got to listen...real hard."

"Old man, I said to hush," Lavania interrupted. "Drink your chicory."

"Psst...,"Alphonse laughed, elbows on knees, his slender sinewy hands dangling, "She likes to give me a hard time." As he handed Sandra an antique bone coffee cup, he gave her a second wink. Speaking to Lee, but still looking directly at Sandra, Mr. Fontenot cryptically pronounced, "Yup Lee, you have yourself a fine woman here, but I wouldn't assume that she's yours to keep."

Not knowing quite what to say, Sandra turned her attention to the hot cup of chicory. The drink, popularly known as New Orleans style coffee, was simply called chicory by the locals. In traditional Louisianan manner, adding 6-7 ounces of chicory to a pound of coffee stretched the coffee grounds. The chicory added a rich, biting flavor, as well as doubled the yield.

Sandra gingerly took a sip and commented, "Um...this is good."

"You're tasting my secret ingredient," smiled Alphonse.

Laughing, Lee joked, "You mean liquor ingredient."

"Da...," grimaced Al. "Only a drop."

Sandra, feeling quite comfortable, turned to Lavania, "Mrs. Fontenot, your home is very beautiful. I was wondering if perhaps you wouldn't mind giving me a tour. In fact, I'm surprised that you're not swamped with guests."

Sitting back, Lavania laughed, "I'm glad we're not. We get our fair share of regulars, just enough to keep us busy."

"Then I gather you don't advertise?"

"Naw, word of mouth," answered the older man. "We only want those who appreciate the bayou and understand its charms."

"Well, I haven't done much exploring of the swamps," admitted Sandra. "They've always seemed a bit mysterious, even a little scary."

Laughing, Fontenot remarked, "That's because you haven't been out in them. But I guarantee that if you hang around here long enough, that will soon change...and I have a feeling that you'll be back."

Again, not quite knowing how to respond, Sandra sipped her coffee. Al, turning his attention to Lee, tactlessly observed, "This is the first time in a very long while you brought a girl around. The last one was that agent friend of yours, Miss Aileen Bitch."

"Aileen Braishear," Lee good-naturedly corrected.

Dismissing the correction, Al replied, "Aw, I said it right the first time."

"I take it that you didn't like her," Sandra surmised as she did her best not to laugh.

Alphonse shrugged his shoulders, eyes sparkling with animation. "What was there to like? She just came along to size up the place. You should have seen her adding up how much everything was worth. She has a mind like a cash register." Al, imitating the sound of an old register, began pulling an imaginary lever back and forth, "Ching...chang...ching...chang. On her way out, I asked for the grand total and a receipt."

Not able to contain her amusement, Sandra unsuccessfully choked back a giggle.

Alphonse took his wife's hand, "C'mon Lavania, my stomach is starting to grumble."

"Do you need any help?" offered Sandra.

"Don't be silly," answered their hostess as she waved for the younger woman to sit back down. "Just make yourself a home. Lee will give you that tour after supper. It'll give you a chance to work off my file' gumbo and whiskey bread pudding."

After they left the room, Sandra turned to Lee. "Mr. and Mrs. Fontenot sure are sweet. How did you ever meet them, let alone find this place?"

"Maggie and I used to live right up the road. The Fontenots and Chieniers go a ways back. We used to come over and play as kids. Soon after I started grad school, our parents were killed in a car accident. So, Maggie came to live here until she went off to college. After that, we both would come back here for semester breaks and holidays."

Quickly thinking of Maggie's personality and Al's proclivity towards bluntness, Sandra smiled.

Lee, noticing the slight upturn of her lips, asked, "What's so funny?"

"Oh, I'm just picturing Maggie going toe to toe with Mr. Fontenot."

"All that I will say is that it's not very pretty. But you know, the old man means well. There was a time when the Fontenots were just about the wealthiest people around these parts. They were, still are, landowners. Back then, they grew nothing but rice. Al's great-grandfather, a freeman, worked this land back in the 1850s. Even back then, unlike a lot of the 'haut monde' here, they always took the time to care for their neighbors, as well as the people that worked for them."

"Do I hear someone talking about me," Lavania

teased as she entered the room.

Upon hearing the woman's voice, Lee's face lit up with affection as he chided, "You shouldn't eavesdrop Miss Lavania."

Lavania, leading the way into the dining room shot back, "Humph! How can I eavesdrop in my own house?"

As Lee gave the older woman a quick peck on the cheek, he confided, "If you must know, I was telling Sandra that Maggie and I used to live up the road."

"What's this about my little "Mag-Pie?" asked Al as he walked over and poured wine into each glass.

"What did I tell you about eavesdropping?" Lavania scolded her husband. "If you must know, I was just about to ask Sandra how..."

Confused, Al interrupted. "Weren't you listening earlier? Sandra knows all about our little Maggie." Exchanging smiles, Sandra and Lee listened to the couple barb back and forth.

"Listen, I know that Sandra knows Maggie. If you had given me a chance, I was just about to ask Sandra how Maggie managed to introduce her to Lee."

"Well, Maggie is a client of mine, and...," started Sandra.

"Client?" Alphonse interrupted. "You're not one of those lawyers are you?"

Laughing, Sandra searched for the right words to describe her line of business. "No, far from it. I own a..."

"She owns a herb emporium," Lee mirthfully supplied.

Confusion written all over their faces, the Fontenots frowned as they passed platters of food around the table.

"Lee, don't put it that way. You make it sound like I sell illegal drugs or something," chided Sandra. "I own a small shop named 'Lavender and Hops' where I sell dried herbs and flowers, potpourris, essential oils and tinctures, as well as related gift items. I'm also a licensed esthetician, so I can also offer advice on herbal treatments and remedies. That's how I met Maggie. She comes in once a week for a facial."

The older man nudged Lee as he commented, "Sorta what old lady Foster used to do around here."

"Old lady Foster?" Sandra asked curiously.

"She was the one person who had a cure for anything that ailed you," explained Lavania. "People swore by her remedies. Some even went to see her before they'd go to see a regular doctor."

Pointing towards the window, Al piped, "She had a use for every plant out there." The older man smiled but shook his head from side to side, "Eventually she latched on to one that killed her old crazy butt."

And so the evening went. Between Alphonse's colorful conversation and Lavania's wonderful meal, dinner proved to be quite an experience. After they had finished eating, Sandra offered to help clear the table, but Lavania insisted that Lee give his date the 'grande tour'.

As Lee gave a brief history on each room, he confirmed Sandra's suspicions that the house was filled with much of its original furnishings. Each room was a gorgeous example of all that personified the Victorian era. Lee showed her the chamber of rooms on the other side of the foyer, away from the parlor and dining room. They began the tour in the smallest sitting room.

Sandra enjoyed listening to Lee as he furnished interesting tidbits about each room.

Lee, once again, watched Sandra under the soft light, as she slowly made her way around the room. He took notice of how she occasionally picked up a bibelot that caught her attention, or admired one of the crystal and enameled inkwells, crystal decanters and pewter picture frames. A smile crossed his face each time she would murmur at the beauty and charm of it all.

As he sat settled into an armchair, a mischievous

thought ran across his mind as he observed his date. He wondered what Sandra's response would be if he crossed the room, took her unto his arms and kissed her. It had been years since he had dated someone so 'wholesome'; he had forgotten what a turn on it could be.

Sandra, totally unaware of her date's thoughts, gently roused him, "Lee, I understand why Miss Lavania doesn't want to open her home up to just anyone. Every single thing in here deserves to be appreciated."

"Yes it does, yes it does." Lee softly agreed.

With no clue as to which lines his thoughts were running along, Sandra completely missed the double meaning in his response.

"Do you think that we can see the upstairs?"

"I'm waiting for you. There are five bedrooms to work our way through."

As her hands caressed the intricately carved balustrades, Sandra noticed the display of aged photographs and daguerreotypes that ran along the wall. Quite a few of the subjects possessed the Fontenot trademark eyebrow, sharp nose and piercing eyes. Commenting on this, Sandra asked Lee if the photos were of family members.

Sinisterly arching an eyebrow, his voice took on a hushed tone. "These are some of the ghosts that are said to wander the rooms and bayous."

"Ghosts? I assumed that Mr. Alphonse was only teasing earlier."

With what Sandra took as mock seriousness, Lee responded, "No, no, no. For those who have listened, they have been known to soothe and speak to the soul."

Making light of his comment, Sandra joked, "Well, I guess it's cheaper than going to a therapist."

At the head of the staircase, the highly polished wood floors led off into two directions. "There are five bedrooms on this floor, with a sitting room adjoining the two larger rooms. I'll show you the bedrooms that are used for the bed and breakfast guests first."

Pointing upward, Lee continued, "As you can see the stairway continues on up. At one time, the servant's quarters were upstairs on the third level. The Fontenots only use the rooms if they're booked down here. Also there's storage space and..."

"Ghosts! finished Sandra

"No," teased Lee as he played along. "Remember, they live in the walls, better to see and hear." At that very moment, a book sitting on a wall shelf fell over on its side, causing the couple to double over with laughter.

The bedrooms proved to be just as beautiful as the rooms that comprised the first level. The beds were all dressed with Lavania's 'real lace' - beautiful handmade lace. Each bed was either canopied or draped with a cornice positioned right above the headboard.

Letting out a playful laugh, Sandra aroused Lee's curiosity. "What's so funny?"

"Oh, I just got a picture of you sleeping in one of these beds."

"You don't see me as being one of those refined types?"

"Well, it's just that I imagine you in a more masculine setting. You're not what they would call the ruffles and lace sort."

"No, I'm not the ruffles and lace sort." As he opened a door, Lee beckoned her in. "Is this more of what you had in mind?"

Stepping into the bedroom, Sandra took in the decidedly more masculine room. It was a bit smaller than the others were, but it boasted an alcove with a floor-to-ceiling window. A heavy wooden four poster bed and matching chifforobe filled much of the space, and the look was no longer Victorian, but more of an eclectic 'arts and crafts' motif. The railroad memorabilia that filled the shelves, the hand-hewn lamps, cedar chest, desk and chair, made Sandra think of the American West.

"Now this looks more like you." Running her hands across the desk, she commented, "The furniture is absolutely beautiful."

As she spoke, Lee walked over to the alcove, pulled back the drapes and caught her hand as he drew her close. "Do you hear the trees? Close your eyes and just listen."

Doing as instructed, Sandra shut her eyes.

"They have a way of making you listen to your heart," he whispered.

She didn't know about the trees, but being so close to Lee, she could hear the rapid beat of his heart, which in turn caused hers to quicken. Unconvinced that her heart knew what was best, she hurriedly opened eyes only to find herself turned on by the pleasing contrast that his strong mahogany hands made against the white linen drapes. With all senses heightened, she found herself unprepared for the window's view. Placing her hand upon Lee's chest, she took in mile upon mile of trees and snaking roads. The waters of the bayou glistened in the moonlight, splaying like fingers out across the rice fields.

"This is the kind of beauty that inspires, that whispers," she sighed. The quietness of it all was almost overwhelming.

Lee, not much caught up in the beauty of the view as in the reflection of it upon Sandra's face, felt himself drawn to her rose-scented perfume. Its fragrance beckoned him to move closer, the enticing bouquet urged him to find its hiding place. As his dark hands touched the delicate fabric of her dress sleeve, she turned and tilted her head towards his. Their eyes met and held as he slowly lowered his lips to hers. Recognizing the lust buried in his loins, Sandra braced herself for the kiss that she knew was to soon follow.

"Lee!" Lavania Fontenot's voice drifted in from the hall.

Caught off guard, Sandra and Lee, neither looking at the other, quickly parted.

"Looks like rain," Lavania forecast as she entered the room. "You better run down and roll up the windows of that Jeep of yours."

Smiling, Sandra remembered how Lee also referred to his $60,000 Range Rover as a Jeep. As if confirming the woman's suspicions, a crack of thunder pealed across the sky.

Lee, headed out of the room, but stopped to put an affectionate arm around the older woman, "Miss Lavania can hear rain hitting rice paddies over 100 miles away!"

"I don't know about 100 miles, maybe 50." Glancing over at Sandra, Lavania asked, "Did Lee give you the grand tour?"

"Well, we got as far as this room." With that, Sandra turned towards the window as she felt her face flush.

Silently aware of Sandra's discomfort, Lavania remarked, "I guess he has the right to be proud of this room. Did you know that he made all of the furniture?"

Sandra, not surprised, shook her head no.

Continuing with genuine pride, Lavania boasted, "He made every single piece, sure did. Just meeting him, you wouldn't give him credit for having a hand in something like this. It still amazes me what a little whittling can produce."

Once again, Sandra found humor in the woman's choice of words. She wondered if the older woman realized that what she referred to as simply being "whittling" was actually high dollar art.

"Well, let's head on back down. Knowing Lee, he has probably already dug into dessert. I hope that you like chocolate.

Chapter Nine

Despite her protestations, Sandra found herself sampling a rather large piece of Lavania's rich pastry. Lee suggested that they all enjoy their dessert in the cozy sitting room that Sandra had admired earlier. As the now heavy rain pattered against the windowpanes, Alphonse peppered the conversation with colorful and entertaining stories of the bayou.

The warm hominess of the setting made it easy to lose track of time, and for Sandra to temporarily forget the "almost" kiss that took place moments earlier. It wasn't until a clock struck the one a.m. hour that she fully realized the lateness of the night.

"It can't be after midnight already," she cried as she set down her coffee cup.

"What happens after midnight?" Lee joked.

"I don't know, it's been a while since I've been out this late...it's just that..."

Lavania, taking a guess at Sandra's thoughts, interjected, "I bet she's thinking about those babies of hers."

With a frown, Lee suggested, "If it'll put your mind at ease, why don't you call and check on them?" He had not given any thought to the lateness of the hour or to Sandra's children.

"I'm sure they're fine, but I should be heading back."

Understanding her concern, Lavania asked, "Who's sitting for you, your mom?"

"Usually she does, but Fridays are her bridge nights.

So, tonight the kids' Uncle Jack is filling in as sitter, that's why I'm positive they're fine. Now Jack is another question. He is probably pacing the floor by now."

Alphonse, blunt as always, asked, "Who is this Jack?"

"Oh, he's a very dear friend of mine. He was my husband's best friend and partner. The kids love him, and I guess that over the years, he's become something of a fixture around the house. He's a real prince."

"You know what they say about princes don't you?" teased Al.

Before Sandra could answer, Lee quipped, "When you kiss them, they turn into frogs?"

Sandra, joking in return corrected, "Wait a minute. I thought that it was the other way around."

"Well, it depends on who's telling the story. You or me."

Sandra, breaking from his steady gaze, quickly turned to the older couple. "Mr. and Mrs. Fontenot, I can't put into words how much I've enjoyed meeting you. Dinner was wonderful and your home is simply beautiful."

As he accepted her compliment, Alphonse nodded and warmly spoke, "We're going to have to work on you calling us Al and Lavania."

"Al, leave the girl alone," Lavania admonished her playful husband. Taking hold of Sandra's hand, she gave it an affectionate squeeze. "Sandra, we've enjoyed your company, and you're always welcomed back." Lavania turned towards Lee and directed him to stay put for a few minutes longer. "I want to fix up some sweets for Sandra's babies."

"That's not...," Sandra started to protest.

Lavania, waving her aside, hurried out of the room. Within minutes, she returned with a decorative tin laden with homemade confections, as well as an aluminum pie plate wrapped in heavy foil. Sandra thanked the couple again and followed Lee out.

As Lee made his way back to the highway, he turned the radio to a station that played rhythm and blues oldies. The rain, which had slackened, picked up once again, as they turned onto the main interstate back towards New Orleans.

The combination of the rhythmic pattering of raindrops against the glass, the soulful strains of the music, mingled with the scent of leather and Lee's cologne, filled Sandra with a warm, but unexplainable melancholy.

Lost in the rich, resonant voice of Arthur Prysock crooning 'Unchained Melody', Sandra stared back at her reflection in the glass and listened to the lyrics of the song. She wondered if or when she could ever go to the open arms of someone waiting for her.

As they crossed back over Lake Pontchatrain, Lee gently took hold of her hand. "I really enjoyed our evening. You were a wonderful sport to put up with that whole scene at the art gallery, but I hope I've made it up to you."

"You did. The trip out to the Fontenots was wonderful. You couldn't have shown me a better time." Conscious of his warm hand on top of hers, she suddenly felt as if she was on pins and needles. Things were moving much too fast. They had gone out only once, and already they had come close to kissing. Sliding her hand from under his, she noisily searched through her purse for her house keys.

Observing her from out of the corner of his eyes, Lee joked, "Are you always so eager to get away from your dates?"

Thankful that the darkness hid her embarrassment, she shook her head. "No... it's just that it's late, and I don't want to wake Jack or the kids by ringing the bell."

"So I take it that Uncle Jack is spending the night."

Sandra, not quite knowing how to take Lee's comment, frowned. "He might...I hadn't really thought about it, but it is almost two in the morning. Besides, he did do me a favor by offering to baby-sit the kids at the last minute after my regular sitter canceled."

"You don't have to explain. I'm just a little curious about the relationship between the two of you, that's all."

"There's nothing to explain. Like I said before, Jack and I are just good friends. Half of the time, I forget that we're not related."

Sensing that Sandra was becoming upset, Lee attempted to smooth things over with a wry remark. "Well, let's hope that big brother doesn't try to beat me up for getting you home so late."

Sandra's mental picture of Jack defending her virtue allowed her to relax until they pulled into her driveway. As soon as she spotted Jack's sports sedan, she wished that her mother had sat with the kids. It wasn't that she was fearful he would create a scene, but she knew that he would be upset over the lateness of the hour. With any luck, he'll be fast asleep on the sofa.

No such luck. Even before she could turn the key in the lock, Jack abruptly pulled open the door.

With a note of disapproval tingeing his voice, he gave Lee a practiced once-over and bellowed, "I thought I heard you two out here!"

Somewhat thrown off guard, Sandra cleared her throat. "Jack, um...I thought that you would be asleep." I wish that you were asleep.

As if such a suggestion was both incredulous and impossible, he sharply answered, "Sleep? Do you know what time it is?"

Not in the mood to hear a lecture, she gave him a stony glare and chose to ignore the question. Instead, she turned her attention back to her date, "Lee, you remember Jack, don't you?"

Grinning unflappably, Lee gibed, "The prince...how can I forget?"

If she ever had any doubts, she was now certain each man had a distinct dislike for the other. "Uh...you wouldn't want to come in, would you?"

Lee, purposely, not making the situation any easier for her, smartly rejoined, "No, I wouldn't." Chuckling at Sandra's nonplused expression, he took both of her hands into his and quietly explained, "No, it is rather late. But, I would like for us to go out again. If you're not busy, maybe next Saturday."

Sandra, mindful that Jack was still present, took her time to answer. "I would love to..."

With a gesture of mock helpfulness, Jack interrupted. "Sandra, I don't know if Saturday is such a good day. You usually go into the shop for a while, and if I'm not mistaken, Jesse has a game at 5:00."

Both Sandra and Lee shot Jack a quizzical look before resuming their conversation.

"Listen," Lee sarcastically suggested, "Why don't you check your schedule with your secretary and I'll give you a call in the next couple of days. We can plan something then."

Nodding in agreement, she accepted a quick kiss on the cheek and thanked Lee for the evening. With Jack standing watch, any further conversation or exchange of affection was all but impossible.

Once inside the house, Jack remarked in a parental tone, "Out kinda late, weren't you?"

Sandra, who had made her way into the family room, started to offer an explanation, but stopped short. "Well Jack, didn't I know you were keeping time."

After momentarily studying her face, he thought better of his tactics and changed his tone. "It's not a matter of me 'keeping time', it's just that with the rain and all, I automatically thought the worst. You left your cell phone here at the house, so if you had gotten yourself into a...a predicament..."

Sandra, not wanting to hear anymore, cut him off by carrying on a mock conversation with herself, "How was your evening, Sandra? I had a nice time, thank you. Where did you wind up going?"

Crossing to where she stood, Jack humored her. "Ok, ok. You've made your point." He stooped to look directly into her face, and said with all the seriousness he could muster, "Sandra, how was your evening?"

"It was fine, thank you," she answered.

"No, no... you are supposed to say, 'I had a nice time'."

Despite all of her efforts, Sandra found the corners of her mouth twitching in a smile. Giving him a light punch to the shoulder, she let out an exasperated sigh and kissed him lightly on the cheek.

"So, where did Lee wind up taking you?" Jack feigned nonchalance as he carried his coffee mug over to the sink.

"To a showing of his work over at the Sol Galerie. It appears that his talent is quite well known."

Not impressed, Jack shrugged, "He looks like the type."

"And what type is that?'

"Oh, you know...," Jack walked over to the French doors, double checked the lock and switched on the outside flood lights that he had installed shortly after Robert's death, "...free-spirited, the 'artsy' type. He even wears the prescribed long hair, washed out jeans, and banged up leather boots."

"Jack you are such a snob. Anyway, he wasn't dressed like that tonight." Putting on a mischievous smile, she continued, "But we all know that looks can be deceiving, don't we?"

Momentarily pausing from his customary security

check, Jack stared at her blankly, "What is that supposed to mean?"

Teasing, she sauntered over to where he was standing and casually smoothed his collar. "Nothing really...I mean, once a person gets to know you, you're not that old stuffed shirt you appear to be."

Possessively taking hold of her hand as it strayed across his shoulder, he held her eyes. "I think that you would know that better than anyone, Sandra."

With the warmth of his hazel eyes drawing her closer, she fought a surprising urge to lay her head against his chest.

Even though he read her thoughts, he simply responded with an easy smile. It would have been easy to take her into his arms and kiss her. His instincts assured him that she would have responded. But now wasn't the time.

In the background, the hall clock struck the hour, and heeding the cue, he murmured, "Come here."

Without hesitation, Sandra obeyed. Bewildered by her desire to have him kiss her, she could feel her heart race. He then set her emotions further askew by gently folding her in his strong arms. Before releasing her all too soon from his secure embrace, he whispered in her ear, "Good night, Sandra, sweet dreams."

Closing the door gently behind him, she stood bemused as she listened to his sedan back down the drive. Once in bed, she reflected first on the evening, and then willed away tears as a flood of distant memories filled her thoughts. Memories that had been shelved years ago, along with the silver watch that lay in her bureau drawer.

Sweet dreams indeed!

Chapter Ten

The ringing phone broke into her thoughts. Just in case it was Lee, she allowed it to ring a little longer than normal. Foolish she knew, but it left her ego feeling a bit more intact.

Sandra, despite a quickening pulse, greeted in an indifferent tone. "Hello, Lavender and Hops." To her disappointment but not surprise, Maggie answered and immediately asked how she enjoyed the previous Friday's date with Lee. Sandra, well used to her friend's prying, obliged and told her of the dinner with the Fontenots.

"This is good!" Hearing the wheels turning in her friend's brain, Sandra had no trouble imagining Maggie's mind cooking up another scheme.

"Sandra, Lee taking you out to the house must mean that he thinks you're pretty special. He's picked up some good vibes from you."

"Vibes? Do you know how dated that makes you sound?" laughed Sandra.

"All right, karma then. Is that better, more with it?"

"More of something," Sandra dryly quipped. "Besides, I don't know about how 'special' I am. Mr. Fontenot mentioned Lee having taken Aileen..."

"Psst!" interrupted Maggie. "He only took her there to show her some of the furniture he designed. They may have dated for a few months, but it was never anything serious."

"Maggie, I really don't care. After all, we've gone out only once."

"I know that Lee thinks you're cute," Maggie chattered.

Despite knowing better, she was unable to resist commenting on Maggie's remark. As casually as possible, she asked, "Oh, is that what he said?"

"Yeah! You remember that night he picked me up at your place?"

"How could I forget!"

"Well he asked a zillion questions about you. He seemed pretty fascinated, if you ask me. When's the next time you two are going out?"

Smiling at her tenacious friend's exaggerated response, Sandra shrugged, "He mentioned something about this weekend. He hasn't called though."

"Don't worry, he will."

Now it was Sandra's turn to interrupt. "Who said that I'm worried? If he does, he does, and if he doesn't, I still had a nice time, no big deal." Desperate to change the subject, she asked, "Am I still going to see you on Tuesday?"

"Um...," Maggie hesitated, "sure, but instead of my usual time, let's make it about a half hour earlier."

"Maggie, do you have a usual time?"

Hating to turn the conversation back to anything remotely close to Lee, Sandra, seeing little choice, asked for the Fontenots' address. As she made the request, she explained that she wanted to acknowledge their hospitality with a gift from the store.

In typical 'Maggie style', she seized the opportunity to enumerate Lee's many fine traits and talents. With a laugh, Sandra asked, "Why the hard sell? I'm beginning to wonder if there's something wrong with him. Maybe he has a dark side I haven't yet seen."

"Sandra!" admonished Maggie, "You've met him.

Now you tell me."

"Maggie," chuckled Sandra, "I will see you tomorrow, 'bye."

After placing the contents for the thank you package out on the counter, she went to the rear storeroom in search of a proper size box and spied a decorative cardboard container several shelves up. Adjusting the stepladder, she climbed gingerly up the rungs. The box and its lid were still just out of reach. If she could just reach the ribbon that dangled from its lid, she could tumble the box down. So, she tiptoed on one foot and stretched upwards as far as she could. Just when she thought she had it within her grasp, she lost her balance.

As a pair of strong hands lifted her off the ladder, she struggled free. Managing to spin herself around to face her capturer, her scream was stifled by a pair of warm lips firmly upon hers.

"Hi beautiful," a male voice whispered.

"Lee!

Making no move to release her, Lee held her close and asked with mock innocence, "Did I catch you at bad time?"

"Did I catch you at a bad time—very funny!" She pulled herself away indignantly as she straightened her clothes.

"Why, it's a good thing I came in when I did. You could've had a nasty fall."

"A good thing? Since when is scaring me half out of my wits a good thing?"

"I didn't mean to scare you. It's just that kissing you seemed to be the natural thing to do with you in my arms. Besides, I thought that you would want to kiss me.

"Want to kiss you?

"Yeah, as a way of saying thanks. Ignoring her protestations, Lee continued unfazed, "What were you trying to get anyway?"

Sandra grimaced and pointed to the item in question. "That moiré box up there."

With considerable ease, Lee reached up and pulled the box down from its perch. Smiling, he tossed it her way.

After a tight "thanks," she brushed past him and headed back toward the counter area. To her irritation, she could hear him chortling softly as he followed her over to the counter. Not to give away her pleasure at seeing him, she focused all of her attention onto the Fontenots' gift.

Lee, fully aware that Sandra was doing her best to ignore him, poked through the assorted gift items. Smelling a miniature sachet, he took note each time she looked up and pleasured him with a coy little smile.

Totally unaware of just how enticing Lee was finding her coquettish manner, she played the role of flirt to the hilt.

Lee, whose observant dark eyes were now casually skimming their way across her low cut silk blouse and slim fitting pants, used all of his reserves to stay seated. At that moment, he would have given anything to slowly trail his fingers down her satiny, nutmeg neck. Instead, he inhaled deeply and contented himself with admiring the way the blouse's silk fabric wrapped itself invitingly around her softly curved form.

Veiling his amorous thoughts, he began to fiddle with the variety of ribbons she laid on the counter top.

"I gather you didn't hear me come in?"

Shaking her head no, she explained, "Way in the rear, I can't hear the door."

"With crime the way it is, maybe you ought to invest in a security system of some sort."

Placing the lid carefully on the box, she glanced over at Lee. "You're starting to sound a lot like Jack. He has what's getting to be an abnormal fixation on my safety."

With a raise of an eyebrow, Lee remarked, "Well, I have a feeling that concern for you is the only area that Jack and I have in common." Who's the gift for?"

"It's a little something for the Fontenots. I just wanted to let them know that I appreciated their hospitality and company the other night."

Feigning hurt feelings, he griped, "I took you out, and they get the gift."

"Well, I can remedy that," sassed Sandra, as she leaned far across the counter and offered him a sachet in one hand and a small fragrant pillow in the other. Her large chestnut brown eyes locked onto his steady gaze as she demurely asked, "It's your choice. Which would you like?"

With a sly smile, Lee wondered if she was aware that the revealing cut of her blouse, along with her forward position offered much more enticing choices than the items she held in her hand. "My choice—aren't you generous." Grazing the curves of her breasts with his eyes, he rested on her face and seductively commented, "I know what I would like, but I don't think you'll let me have it."

Understanding the nuance behind his comment, she discovered that she thoroughly enjoyed the flirtatious game they had going.

"Well, maybe if you ask." As each took in the suggestive twinkle of the other's eye, Sandra abandoned caution and lowered her eyes towards his well-defined rugged lips.

In response, Lee fingered the soft, ruffled neckline of her blouse. The silky thin fabric, enhanced the pleasure of touching the rounds of her full breasts. "Sandra," Lee's voice slightly thickened, "right now I would like to kiss..."

Ring! Ring! The telephone seemed to thunder as it broke the intimate moment. As the phone rang out the fourth time, she picked up the receiver and answered in a very short and clipped voice.

"Sandy?"

"Jack," she answered, making no great effort to hide her irritation. "What can I do for you?"

"You shouldn't sound so excited," Jack dryly remarked. "Did I catch you at a bad time?"

As she answered, she watched as Lee impatiently walked towards the other side of the store. "Um...Jack...Is this important? I'm sorta with a customer right now." She crossed her fingers at the half-truth. She hated to stretch the truth, but this was definitely not the time for small talk.

Jack, accepting her explanation without suspicion, quickly gave the reason for his call. "All right, I'll make it quick. I just wanted to remind you that I'm picking the kids up from school today. Your mom mentioned some sort of club meeting at church, so I volunteered."

Half-listening, she did her best to rush him off the phone, "Sure, Jack, that's fine. I'll see you at home around the usual time, all right? Bye..."

"Hey, not so fast," he interrupted. "Do you want me to get dinner started?"

"Um... that'll be great, thanks." As soon as he made the offer to help out with one of her least favorite chores, she unconsciously gave him a bit more of her attention. "Well, since you're volunteering, I did plan on cooking the chicken that's defrosting in the fridge. Just fix it the usual way."

"Easy enough. Sandy?"

"Yes?"

"Be careful, it looks like rain."

"I will," she promised. "I'll see you later."

As she hung up the phone, Lee walked over to the counter area and remarked with a trace of annoyance. "I don't mean to eavesdrop, but it sounds like ol' Jack makes himself pretty indispensable."

Not quite knowing how to take his comment, she shrugged her shoulders. "Like I've said before, he's a good friend. Over the years he's always been there for me and the kids."

"Sorta like a guardian angel," gibed Lee as he idly flipped through several sheets of scented paper that were displayed near the register.

His emphasis on the word guardian didn't pass unnoticed. She found herself becoming irritated. The tone he used when saying the word implied that he took Jack to be some sort of safety net. Piqued, she replied, "Jack is not my guardian angel. Like I said, he's a kind, wonderfully considerate..."

"...friend," Lee finished for her.

"I have a feeling that you don't approve of my friendship. It's as if you're passing some sort of judgment," she bit out through tight lips.

Unfazed by her anger, Lee chuckled as he picked up a container of potpourri, "Who am I to pass judgment? Even though I must admit that I do find your and Jack's relationship rather...how shall I put it, interesting."

"Interesting? What's so interesting about our relationship?" She was now definitely put out.

"As an outsider looking in, it appears that the two of you have some sort of quasi husband and wife thing going. Personally, I find it very confusing."

"It's my opinion that you're confused," colored Sandra. "Your comments are terribly unfounded. There is nothing wrong with a man and a woman having a friendship. Why, if anything, it's..."

She pursed her lips as she tapped her fingertips against the round of her hips. Ugh! Why am I explaining this to you anyway?"

Never was it Lee's intention to make her angry. But it was simply no fun dating a woman whose life was so enmeshed with that of another man. It was becoming increasingly obvious to him that Jack's involvement in her life went much deeper than simple friendship. So flabbergasted was she at his assertion, he was convinced that she had little inkling of what was so apparent to him.

Reaching out, he lightly touched her arm, "Sandra, listen," he conciliated, "you're right. You don't need to explain anything to me. What I expressed was strictly my opinion, and you know what they say about opinions."

As he pressed on to restore her good mood, he asked, "Now, am I back in your good graces, or are you still angry?"

"No I'm not angry," she reluctantly shrugged.

"Good." Lee leaned over the counter and planted a kiss on her forehead.

Despite her resolve, the gentle gesture, brought forth a smile.

"What was that for?"

Instead of answering, he deferred.

"What do you have planned for Friday evening?"

"Depends." Actually she had nothing planned, but she didn't want to appear eager, nor did she want to stroke his oversized ego."

"OK, Ms. Petain, so now you're doing that woman thing. This one time, I'll play along."

Interrupting, she quipped, "What? No pearls of wisdom on petulance?"

"No pearls of wisdom." Still in good humor, he cleared his throat. "Sandra, I would love it if you would accompany me to a play at the Desire Theater."

Even before he asked, she had made up her mind to say yes. But, now hearing his plans, she found herself unable to answer.

Lee, quickly tiring of what he assumed was a continuation of her 'hard to get' game frowned.

"Sandra, if you would rather that we did something else, that's fine. Or if you're simply no longer interested in going out with me, just tell me."

"No, no don't be silly," she responded a bit too quickly. "A play sounds good. *Fences* is being performed, right?"

Nodding, Lee sensed that she wasn't completely happy with the selection. Once again, he offered her an out. "If you've seen it before, tell me. There's always the movies or ..."

"I said that I want to go. What time do I need to be ready?"

"Well, how about 7:00?" supplied Lee, still puzzled at her unenthusiastic response.

"I'll be ready."

Stuck in evening traffic, Sandra fiddled with the radio. She felt so on edge emotionally that everything sounded like noise, she just switched it off. Ever since Lee's visit, she found herself feeling agitated, actually ever since Friday night. She didn't know if she was coming or going. On one hand, there was Lee—fun, debonair and suave, though quite probably an undercover lady's man, badgering her about Jack. Then there was Jack—her loving, stand up kinda guy, who made forgetting the past impossible and complicated, but oh so necessary. She hadn't felt this crazed since high school. One minute playing the tease with Lee, the next house with Jack. No wonder Lee thought that she was crazy. And what must Jack think about her? Lately she'd been taking far more than she'd been giving. Her friendship with him was fast turning into one of unhealthy dependence.

Even though Jack was an indisputably steadying element in both her life and the children's, realistically she knew that he would not be around forever. Frowning at the prospect, she realized that the idea of Jack not always being there had never entered her mind. When he had unexpectedly arrived back in town almost eleven years ago, she swore that God had decided to measure her out a portion of hell while still on earth. But gradually, she had been able to lock away the demons of their past, that is, until recently.

Driving along North Broad Avenue, she crossed Abundance Street, and then Treasure. The names of the two roadways prompted her to automatically think of Lee. Of all places he could have chosen to take her to see a play, it had to be the Desire Community Theater. It wasn't that she had anything against the neighborhood, but in her mind, it represented a sorrowful turning point in her life. The theater sat on the same block where Robert was killed three years earlier. She had only driven past there twice since that horrible night.

The first time was on the very night that he was shot. No one knew, not even her mother nor Jack, that late that night she paid a visit to the crime scene. After Jack and Robert's supervisor broke the news of her husband's death, she convinced her mother, whom Jack had notified, that she needed to lie down and rest. Waiting until her mom and children were asleep, she quietly left the house.

As tears spilt from her eyes, she remembered how she slipped the car down the driveway and drove to the address where the shooting had taken place. In order for her mind to grasp the horrible tragedy, she had to go to the crime scene. With a shudder, she recalled how she slowed the car as she approached the block. So as not to be recognized, she made sure to keep her distance and parked alongside a crowd of spectators.

It was all very surreal. From the crowd of people and their comments, to the yellow police tape flapping in the balmy breeze. In her mind, she could still see the scores of haphazardly parked police cars with their red and blue lights flashing garishly against the clear night sky. One of the thoughts that would always stay with her was how eerily invisible she felt. As if watching the events of someone else's life. The last thing she remembered clearly was seeing Jack stooped next to Robert's splattered pools of blood. How she got home that night, she had no idea.

The second and last time she drove past the theater was almost a year later. That time it was with Jack. She and the children underwent therapy to handle their grief, and as part of the treatment, the psychologist suggested that they visit the site, it would help to close the chapter on that part of their lives.

With a heavy sigh, she couldn't help thinking of all of the chapters that had unhappy endings. Maybe Friday's date with Lee would be the start of a new chapter, one hopefully with a happier ending.

Chapter Eleven

As she eased into the driveway, Sandra heard children's laughter and Jack's gregarious voice booming from the patio not far from the house. Before she had the chance to turn off the ignition, both Whitney and Jesse were at her door chattering full speed.

"Mommy, Mommy! Guess what? Uncle Jack's making us his all time favorite he-man cheese burgers." They laughed as they poked out their chests and flexed their biceps.

Flashing Jack a tired smile, Sandra made a face. "He-man burgers? Don't you mean cholesterol-loaded, fat-laced, and artery-blocking..."

"Hey!," interrupted Jack good-naturedly. "You don't grill the cook!"

With Whitney holding onto one hand and Jesse the other, the three made their way over to Jack. "I thought that we were having chicken?"

Jack explained as he flipped a burger with exaggerated flair, "We were, but it was such a beautiful day, I thought it would be fun to break out the grill. I have burgers going for the kids, and steaks are on for us."

Simply nodding, she watched as Jack with natural ease managed to keep an eye on the hot coals and joke with the kids. With her earlier concerns still weighing heavily on her mind, she unconsciously let out an audible sigh.

Out of the corner of her eye, Jack took in her fatigued expression. "You look a bit beat. Did you have a rough day?"

"No, not particularly. You know how Mondays are. I just have a lot on my mind."

If she thought it possible to fool him, she was mistaken. It was obvious to Jack that Sandra's weak smile was strictly for his benefit. Although he wanted to press her further, he quickly changed his mind. The children were eager to eat, and it was obvious that Sandra was not in a talkative mood. Whatever problem she was wrestling with, he was certain that he would have to pry it out. And from past experience, he knew that it would take not only time, but his full attention. So instead, he suggested, "Why don't you go in the house and take a shower. By the time you're out, dinner will be ready. You might feel a little better."

"I couldn't do that. I'm sure your day has been just as long as mine, if not longer."

"But you're the one tired, not me," reasoned Jack as he patted her shoulder. "It doesn't have to be a long shower. Just stay in until that pretty smile is back on your face."

Feeling her eyes tear over, she impulsively reached up and gave him a quick hug.

Now puzzled and extremely curious, he watched as she slowly made her way into the house. If it were not for the children playing nearby, he would have left the hot grill and insisted that she tell him what was troubling her. Smelling the food burn, he turned his attention away from the house and back to the food.

Despite the playfulness of the kids and Jack's usual good humor, the evening did little to lift Sandra's melancholy mood. Outwardly, she joked and played, but inwardly her emotions were still a muddled mess.

In Jack's typically helpful fashion, he assisted her with getting the children bathed and settled into bed. He even read them each a story.

When the children were finally asleep and the dishwasher loaded, Jack rolled down his sleeves, took Sandra by the hand and led her over to the sofa. "OK, Whitney and Jesse are finally off to dreamland, the food has been put away and the dishes are done. Now I want you to sit down and tell me what's worrying you."

"What makes you think that I'm worried?"

"Sandra, I've known you far too long. I can tell when there is something wrong."

Not yet prepared to share her jumbled feelings, she denied the charge.

Jack wisely decided not to push, but instead demonstrated well-practiced courtroom ease and changed tactics. "All right, I'll take your word for it and won't press the issue." Rising, he walked over to the kitchen island and poured two cups of coffee, instinctively preparing Sandra's to her liking. After he handed over her mug, he pulled up a chair directly across from her.

As he leaned forward and narrowed the space between them, he allowed his eyes to casually peruse her face. He couldn't help noticing how over the years, she had grown more beautiful. The remnants of her youthful spirit and enthusiasm remained, but added to it were serene sophistication and individual style. It all made for a combination he found both charming and exciting.

"A penny for your thoughts?" he quietly teased.

"Only a penny? I think my thoughts are worth far more."

Maybe you're right. I tell you what, I'll give you a whole nickel then."

"Raise it to fifty cents and I'll tell you," challenged

Sandra with a chuckle.

This carefree way of joking was one of the things that she enjoyed most about Jack. He had an easy way of relaxing her anxieties.

Satisfied that her reserves were beginning to melt, he very gently asked, "What is going on inside that pretty little head of yours?"

Well aware that he was attempting to dispel a bit of her somber mood, she drew her legs up to her chest and hugged her knees. "I see why you are such a successful attorney Mr. Thibodeaux. You have an uncanny knack of getting just about anyone to open up and spill their guts."

Allowing her the time to 'spill her guts', he kept quiet and settled back onto the sofa cushion.

"Do I...do you feel that I take advantage of you? And when you answer, don't spare my feelings. Be honest."

Jack, truly surprised by the question, set down his coffee and quietly echoed her question. "Do I feel that you take advantage of me?" Looking into her eyes, he doubted that she could handle the truth. If he were to do as she requested and answer the question honestly, he would have to let her know that it wasn't about being taken advantage of, but about love.

"Sandra, I don't think that you understand how..."

Not allowing him the opportunity to finish his declaration, assuming she knew what he was about to say, she interrupted. "Oh, you know how. Think about it. If I'm not asking you for favors, I'm allowing you to do far more than you should. Things like picking the kids up from school, taking them to soccer, cooking, handling problems that come up at the shop. I mean, since Robert's death, what haven't you done?"

As the question momentarily hung between them, he impulsively set aside his vow to take things slow. "It's been a long time since I've done this." Moving to sit next to her on the sofa, he leaned forward and kissed her gently but very passionately on the lips. Surprising both herself and him, she made no move to pull away, but instead, with her heart racing, placed a trembling hand on his shoulder.

"Mommy!" Whitney's cry interrupted their embrace. With a start, Sandra jumped up and fled the room, more than a little thankful for the plaintive intrusion. Jack's kiss, to say the least, had thrown her completely off guard. Rounding the staircase, she entered her daughter's room.

"Mommy...," the little girl whined. Walking over to the child's bed, she kneeled and touched Whitney's forehead. "Yes sweetie?"

With sleepy eyes, Whitney cried, "Mommy, I had a dream."

"Was it a bad dream or a good dream?"

"I don't know, I dreamt that I saw Daddy. He was happy. I couldn't see his face. It's funny, I don't remember what Daddy looked like, but in the dream I knew it was Daddy."

Giving the girl a comforting hug, Sandra smiled, "Oh, it's good to dream of Daddy." As she pulled the blanket around the child, Sandra took her daughter's hand, "Do you know that I still dream of Daddy too?"

"Mommy, I wish Daddy was still here."

"I know you do. But you know, he will always be in our hearts and our thoughts."

"And in our dreams," piped Whitney.

With a kiss to the forehead, she turned off the lights, and blew a final kiss. "Good night sweetie."

"Good night, Mommy."

Not yet ready to go back downstairs and face Jack, she stopped at Jesse's bedroom door and peeped in. Tiptoeing across the wooden floor, she straighten his blanket and planted a loving kiss on his forehead. As she did this, she noticed as she had so many times before, the striking resemblance between the young boy and his father.

She would have given anything to be tucked in bed and fast asleep. Now what? She had to go back down and face Jack. Deciding not to mention the kiss, to play it off as if it didn't quite happen, she slowly headed back down the stairs

While she was gone, Jack had taken his coffee over to the French doors. Not knowing quite what to say, Sandra walked over.

"Well," she began, sounding a bit too chirpy even to her own ears, "it looks like Whitney just had a dream about her dad."

Abruptly Jack turned, concern evident both in his face and voice, "Oh? I hope she's able to get back to sleep."

She nodded.

"Good, good. Um, look Sandy...about what just happened here. I hope..."

It was obvious to Sandra that Jack was uncomfortable. So, she interrupted, "We know one another too well Jack. You don't have to explain. I know how you meant the kiss."

Not realizing that Sandra was purposely misreading his true intentions, Jack'ssmile was broad as he pulled her into his arms.

"Jack, we're good friends, she continued, deliberately choosing her words. "Best friends, almost like brother and sister."

As her choice of words slowly sank in, Jack quickly released her. "So that's what I've become to you, a brother?"

Sandra, unable to honestly answer the question, desperately tried to reestablish their conversation's previous playful tone. "That's right. A much older brother," she chided.

With more disappointment than Sandra could ever know, Jack glanced down at his watch. "Well, it's getting late and you know the elderly, we need our sleep." Grateful for any task that would hide the state of his emotions, he quickly made his customary check of the door and window locks.

When they reached the front door, he paused and gave her his usual good-bye kiss on the cheek. He then took her chin gently in his palm, and looked her squarely in the face. With a quiet seriousness that was evident both in the tone of his voice and dark hazel eyes, he whispered, "Patience; accomplish thy labor; accomplish thy work of affection." Holding steady, he rested his eyes in the deep chestnut pools of Sandra's. "You remember that verse?"

As her heart caught, she nodded. "How could I ever forget that night?"

"I knew that you hadn't when I saw you wearing the watch."

In the bright light of the foyer, she noticed for the first time that evening, traces of fatigue. Gone was the familiar easygoing manner, the soft crinkles around his eyes. In their place was evidence of sadness and perhaps even disappointment.

"Jack..."

Before she could finish, he opened the door and left.

In her dreams that night, Sandra like Whitney, dreamed of Robert. While Whitney's dream of her dad was wonderful and pleasant, Sandra's was very disquieting.

The dream began with her paddling a small wooden boat through what appeared to be a mist-enshrouded swamp. Sitting across from her was an uncharacteristically placid Robert. The air, heavy with humidity, caused their clothes to cling hopelessly to their skin. Silently, they made their way through the meandering swamp, stopping at a point where marshy land slopped up from the still dark waters.

Looking up into the graceful canopy of trees, Sandra immediately caught sight of the wispy figure of a most unusual and strikingly beautiful woman. Without uttering a word, the raven-haired sylph coolly offered a disarming smile as she beckoned Sandra to join her.

As she prepared to join the enchantress, Robert reached over and gently kissed her on the lips. Taken by surprise, Sandra looked deeply into his eyes and was stunned to find that they no longer belonged to Robert, but to Jack. Instead of pulling away from his embrace, she burrowed herself deeper into his arms. As she took in the heat of his strong chest, she felt as light as a feather, as free as a bird. Resting in the warm, secure strength of his arms, she closed her eyes.

Sandra made several vain attempts at trying to fall back to sleep. Finally giving up, she stepped onto the cold wood floor, two hours earlier than her normal six a.m. hour. Shrugging into her robe, she sought out her slippers before walking over to the large bay window. Almost protectively, she pulled the folds of the robe across her chest. The melancholy of the previous night still weighed heavily on her soul. Usually, she relished the calm of the early morning quiet, but today, as she sat on the window seat looking out across the treetops and into the still twilight sky, she felt very unsettled.

Absently peering through the dew that splayed out like watery fingers across the glass, she sighed heavily and remembered her dream. It left her feeling uneasy. Glancing over at the rumpled bedclothes, her pulse quickened as she recalled the sweet intimacy of her midnight flight. Jack's blissful kiss and embrace seemed all too real. Shaking her head at the madness of it all, she thought of Jack's kiss from the night before, as well as his manner before he left.

She simply wouldn't...couldn't allow herself to consider the possibility of a romantic relationship with him. There was just too much between them, too many unexplained questions, too much at stake.

None of it made sense anyway. Up until a few weeks ago, Jack and she had a comfortable, uncomplicated friendship. It wasn't until Lee entered the picture that things became topsy-turvy.

Tiredly, she headed for the shower. She had been up for only a hour, and already there was too much to deal with.

Yoga was a routine Sandra tried to follow each morning. It not only left her shapely curves tight, but she often found that it aided her in sorting her thoughts as well as in focusing on the day ahead. This morning was the exception. Yoga failed her. Frustrated, she listened to the grandfather clock strike half past five, and picked up the phone. It was still too early to wake the kids, but she was confident that her mother would be awake. Since childhood, Mom's credo had been "the early bird gets the worm."

"Mom?"

"Sandra?" Maureen answered in a surprised tone, "Is everything all right?"

Reassuring her, Sandra answered. "Everything's fine. I just woke up early and couldn't get back to sleep."

Knowing her daughter, Maureen got straight to the point. "So what's worrying you?"

Truly unable to answer the question, Sandra moaned. "That's just it. I don't know!"

"Why don't I drop by the shop a little later. We'll get things sorted out. Let's say 9:00, and I'll bring muffins."

Since she had more time than usual, she decided to fix the kids a larger breakfast than their normal fare. The smell of the pancakes, scrambled eggs and sausage greeted the children as they came to the table. The kids were so content with eating, they kept their morning bickering down to a minimum. As an added bonus, their mom even allowed them to turn the television to one of their favorite cartoon shows.

As they ate, Sandra remembered her daughter's dream and glanced over at Whitney several times. Feeling certain that the young girl had forgotten about it, she decided not to bring it up. As if reading her mind, Whitney licking her sticky fingers turned to her brother, "Jesse, guess what?"

"What?" Jesse was still focused on the cartoon.

"I saw Daddy last night!" Whitney smugly supplied.

"You did not!" Jesse automatically retorted.

"Did too! Ask Mommy."

Jesse, thoroughly tired of his sister's interruptions, brushed her off with, "Daddy's dead, you dope!"

"Jesse, what did I tell you about calling your sister names," reprimanded Sandra.

"Mom, will you tell this dopey girl that Dad is..."

"If you had given her a chance, you'd know she's trying to tell you that she had a dream about Dad."

This time it was Whitney's turn to irritate her brother. "Yeah, a dream, you dope!"

"OK, you two, go wash your hands and get your jackets. Mrs. Rainey will be here any minute."

Watching the two run up the stairs fighting, she realized that Jesse and Whitney had successfully come to terms with their dad's death. For them, Robert had become a distant memory. Someone who only occasionally flitted across their thoughts and dreams.

By the time she arrived at Lavender and Hops, Maureen Phillips was already waiting. She was every bit as beautiful as her daughter, but her style was more understated. They both shared the same almond-shaped eyes, flawless nutmeg brown skin, and shapely frame. But whereas Sandra's hair was a mass of long curls, Maureen's was stylishly cropped and an elegant gray. After making a pot of tea, the two settled on stools up at the front counter.

After several minutes of chatting, Maureen, in her characteristic manner, charged forward. "OK, we made our small talk. You've complimented me on my blueberry muffins, and I've told you how beautiful the store looks. Let's cut to the chase. What's bothering you? You were almost in tears when you called this morning."

Well used to her mother's bluntness, Sandra took a sip of tea, set her cup down and muttered, "Oh Mom, where do I begin? Just when I thought I had all the pieces of my life finally back together, something, or in this case 'someone' scatters them again."

"Who is this someone?"

"Jack...Lee.."

Maureen patted her daughter's hand. "Well let's start with Jack. I know him. What did..."

Sandra clipped, "He kissed me last night."

The older woman chuckled, seemingly unsurprised. "Well, it is about time. I was wondering when he was going to get around to..."

"Mother!"

"Don't Mother me. You've had to be as blind as a bat not to see that one coming. It's no secret how Jack feels about you and the kids. You know that he never got over you marrying Robert."

"That's nonsense. Besides, that was another lifetime ago. There's no romance between the two of us now. He...we have purposely kept it that way. He's always been more of a friend, a brother."

" And I suppose that's what you told him."

"Yeah!"

Allowing several minutes to pass, Maureen sipped her tea and studied her daughter's face. Setting down her mug, she raised a simple question. "Then why the tears?"

With a shrug, Sandra futility tried to explain. "I don't know, Lee..."

"Lee?"

"Remember the fella I went out with last weekend?"

She vaguely recalled Sandra's remarks regarding him. "Isn't he some sort of artist type?"

"Now you sound like Jack. He's a folk artist, and quite an accomplished one from what I have seen."

"So I take it that Jack has met him?"

Nodding, Sandra added, "And he doesn't care for him very much."

"In light of his feelings, can you blame him?"

Twisting her mouth, Sandra tapped the counter top. "He can be so damn judgmental."

Aware of her daughter's agitation, Maureen said, "I think we all are a little guilty of that. But that isn't what is bothering you though, is it?"

"No, it's just that Lee said some things that got me thinking about my life. I thought I finally had all of the pieces in place, and then I realized that I really haven't.

Sliding off the stool, Maureen walked behind her daughter and lovingly rubbed her shoulders. "Oh, I don't know about that. You've opened the shop, own a thriving business, raise kids, you really have made a new life for yourself. If that doesn't sound like having all of the pieces together, you're pretty darn close.

"Mom, it all sounds good, and even looks good on the surface, but..."

"Look, you've become a stronger person since Robert's death, more confident, sure of yourself."

"But am I happier?"

Letting out an amused chuckle, she swung her daughter around to face her, "Happy. That's one of those words that sounds so simple; that is, until you try to define it. It describes a feeling that is never complete within itself, and it's always dependent upon someone or something else. You know how the line goes; I'll be happy if..., I'll know when I'm truly happy when..."

"When Prince Charming comes along and sweeps me off my feet," inserted Sandra.

Sagely shaking her head, Maureen differed. "I don't think that's what you're searching for, Sandra. Besides, you already had your Prince Charming, and if I recall correctly, you weren't so happy. No, I think you're wrestling with something else."

Feeling a bit uncomfortable, Sandra toyed with her cup and frowned.

Fully understanding her daughter's turmoil, Maureen put forth some motherly advice. "Sandra, perhaps you're unconsciously not allowing yourself to be happy, as a means of self protection. Maybe deep down, you're afraid of loving and losing again. And I don't just mean losing a loved one, but that chance of losing a part of yourself in the process. You know, after your dad died, I found myself in the same dilemma. There would be days when I felt the world was my oyster, and then several weeks would go by and I would feel so utterly alone."

Letting out a heavy sigh, Sandra responded. "So what do I do? There's a side of me that fights so hard to stay in control and maintain as much independence as possible. But deep down inside, I find that I like the idea of having that someone special to share my problems, dreams, or just the little things that the kids do day to day. Maybe that's why I lean on Jack so much."

Reaching out, Mary stroked Sandra's arm and softly asked, "Has Jack ever complained?"

Sandra slowly shook her head from side to side.

"Well, maybe Jack is that someone special."

"I don't think so, Mom. Our relationship is more of a friendship than one of romance. Besides, I wouldn't want to take the risk. Talk about being afraid of losing someone. If by some outside chance we did become romantically involved, what would happen if things didn't work out? I would lose a very dear friend, and this time forever."

Picking up on Sandra's last statement, Maureen intently surveyed her daughter. It was obvious that there was something going on much deeper than what she was expressing. She had a feeling that Sandra's and Jack's relationship was much more complex than one of simple friendship. Listening to maternal instincts though, she decided not to voice her suspicions but instead to passively listen.

After several minutes of silently sipping her tea, Sandra asked, "So what do I do?"

Maureen refrained from directly responding. "Sandra, I can't answer that. Everyone deals with the question of love, companionship, affairs of the heart differently. Take Charles and me for example."

At the mention of Charles' name, Sandra smiled. Up until this time, her mother had never acknowledged her male friend as being anything but one of her bridge club partners. For some time though, she'd had her suspicions. Mr. Charles, as she affectionately called him, and Maureen were often together. On one or two occasions, upon dropping in at her mother's early in the morning, she caught them "breakfasting" together.

Teasing, Sandra gave her mother a kiss, "Well this is the first time I've heard you mention Mr. Charles as being your someone special!"

"Sandra, for goodness sake, sometimes you carry on as if you're older than I am!" Looking up at the clock, she took her daughter's hands into her own.

"Listen dear, you're going to be swamped with customers soon. So, before you open up shop, I want you to promise me that you'll let go of your fears, trust your instincts and be patient. You'll find that all of your questions and concerns will work themselves out. They simply must. It is something that is forced by time."

Clearing the counter of their mugs, Maureen asked, "So when do you plan on seeing this Lee again?"

"This Friday."

Smiling, Maureen remarked, "Good, maybe going out will resolve some of your feelings, and if not, you had fun in the process."

Just then, the phone interrupted their conversation. "Hello?" Sandra answered. To her delight, Lee was on the other end.

"Sandra, how are you doing?" Despite the relative straightforwardness of the question, Sandra noted the way he flirtatiously caressed her name.

"I'm doing just fine...you're a pleasant surprise. I wasn't expecting to hear from you until the end of the week."

"Oh, and why is that?"

Very much aware of her mother, Sandra simply replied, "I don't know. What's up?"

"I'm going to be out of town for the rest of week, so I was checking to see if things are still on for Friday."

"Unless something unavoidable comes up, Friday is still fine."

"Good. I'll pick you up at your place around 7:00. I'm late for class, so I can't talk right now, but...," he softened his voice, "have a good week and I'll see you then."

"Have a safe trip." Slowly hanging up the phone, Sandra's face looked much brighter than it had earlier.

Taking in her daughter's happy smile, Maureen impulsively volunteered, "What do you say to me taking the children for the weekend? I don't have plans and I haven't done it in a while."

"How about your bridge club meeting?"

"Don't worry about it, just let me do this for you." Thoroughly happy that her daughter's morose mood seemed to have lifted, she continued with a twinkle in her eye, "In fact, since I'm feeling so generous, why don't I watch the store for a couple of hours while you go out and buy yourself a new outfit."

Sandra, with her eyes softly sparkling, hugged her mother.

Chapter Twelve

ncharacteristically the day dragged on. Not only was the stream of customers unusually slow, but much of her day had been taken up with troubleshooting problems. Only 45 more minutes, and then she could close. Dismayed, she watched a tour bus of shoppers converge on the quaint shop. Ordinarily, she would have taken the barrage in stride, even with a bit of glee, but today was different. In less than two hours, Lee would be picking her up, and home was a good 20 minutes away.

She had hoped to take a relaxing bubble bath, reset her hair, and work at looking all out gorgeous for Lee's arrival. But as each minute ticked away, it was obvious that her plan was growing increasingly improbable. Finally, after hurrying the last indecisive customer out of the door, she quickly locked up.

As she entered the house, she sent up a quick prayer of thanks for her mom's offer to keep the kids. Glancing over at the hall clock, she calculated that she could either reset her hair or take a 15-minute soak in the tub. Choosing the bath, she hurried up the stairs. Perhaps a calming soak would help her to get a grip on her nerves.

While the bath water ran, she placed an herbal gurnee—a small herb filled muslin sack—under the running water. Then she laid out her clothes—a sinfully soft silk blouse and slacks set and poured a glass of wine.

She found the perfumed bubbles, soft music and wine intoxicatingly relaxing. Resting her head on the bath pillow, she slowly closed her eyes and allowed her limbs and mind to float...

"Sandra, Sandra! Wake up." A familiar masculine voice gently aroused her. As she opened her eyes, she realized that she had fallen asleep and that the voice was Lee's. Instinctively, she slipped under the remaining bubles, not realizing that he had already gotten an eyeful.

"Hey, I thought we had a date tonight?" he teased.

Embarrassed beyond belief, she stammered, "What...what time is it, and how did you get in?"

"The answer to your first question is 7:15 and to the latter..." Reaching into his pants pocket, he held out her key ring. "You left your keys in the door. Not a very smart thing to do."

"I was in such a hurry to... " Growing more embarrassed by the second, she brusquely asked, "Do you think that you might leave so that I can dry off?"

Taking a towel from the wall rack, he obliged. "Do you need any help? Would like for me to lend you a hand?" he teased with mock innocence.

"No thank you!" she exclaimed.

With a hearty chuckle, he placed the towel on the small chair near the tub and left.

Believing neither the turn of the evening nor the audacity of Mr. Lee Chienier, she wanted nothing more than to hide under a rock and die. She could not believe her carelessness.

After quickly drying off, she wrapped the towel around her torso, carefully tucking the ends under her arms. Cautiously, she tiptoed out the bathroom into her adjoining bedroom. Her instincts told her that Lee could be trusted, but memory reminded her of the stepladder scene at the shop. So, just as a safeguard, she locked the door.

After she slipped into the periwinkle blouse and pants, she quickly applied makeup and twisted her hair into an elegant topknot. Upon assessing her image in the chifforobe mirror, she pulled out a few wisps of hair and added a delicate antique silver charm bracelet and a pair of matching hoop earrings. Hurrying down the stairs, she slipped into her heels, took a deep breath and feigned what she hoped was an air of nonchalance.

As she hit the bottom stair, Lee rounded the corner carrying two mugs of freshly brewed tea. "I hope you don't mind me helping myself. I thought maybe we could sit and talk while we rearrange our plans." Looking at his watch, he continued, "It looks like we're going to miss the first half of the play."

"I'm sorry. I only planned to take a quick bath. There's no excuse for falling asleep the way I did."

"Obviously you had to be pretty beat. I take it your day was especially stressful?"

As she accepted the mug, she shook her head, "No more than usual. I had a run in with a supplier over a shipment that was incorrectly billed. During lunch, I ran up to the kids' school for a committee meeting, and right before closing, a tour bus full of tourists pulled up at the door. And then there was the usual rush hour traffic."

"You know, you could've called and canceled."

"I know, but I've been looking forward to seeing you again," she sincerely explained.

Lee, in response, flashed his distinctive flirtatious grin.

After a moment or two of comfortable silence, he resumed the conversation. "I was thinking, why don't we just stay in tonight? Obviously, you're tired. I can cook something, or better yet, order Chinese. We can talk, watch a movie, play a board game. Just play it by ear. I gather your children are gone for the evening?"

"My mom has them for the whole weekend." She had to admit that Lee's suggestion sounded very appealing. "Sounds great to me, that is if you're sure that you don't mind missing the play?"

"The play has a four week run. We can catch it next week maybe." Rising, he pointed his finger and directed, "You stay put, and I'll order the food. I know of a great little place not too far from here that delivers."

While waiting for him to call in the order, she kicked off her shoes, folded her legs under her and with eyes closed, willed the night to progress wonderfully. While musing, it dawned on her that Lee might have more specific, more romantic plans for the evening's end. If that was the case, she hoped that her comment about her mom watching the kids for the weekend didn't sound like an open invitation.

"You're not going to sleep on me again, are you?"

"No, I was just thinking."

With a sly smile, he slouched back on the sofa next to her and played with a wisp of her hair, "About what?"

To avoid answering, she walked over to the cabinet where the board games were kept. "I'm thinking that you look the type that would enjoy a friendly game of Master Labyrinth." Without giving him an opportunity to beg off, she placed the board on the floor and began to set up the game in front of the fireplace.

Having set the tone, at least temporarily, the evening progressed leisurely. While stoking the fire, Lee turned and found her staring deep into the flickering flames. "Again, what has you so deep in thought?"

"Oh, I was just thinking. Sitting on the floor like this, talking, playing board games, reminded me of the early days of my marriage.

Lee, replaced the stoker and casually studied the framed photographs that lined the mantle. Picking up one of the silver laced frames, he remarked, "I can see that she resembles you. The same coloring and hair. Whitney right?"

"Yup, she's the baby of the family. The one next to her is Jesse. He has his dad's looks and temperament. The same type of easy charm."

With the mantle clock softly ticking, Lee studied the pictures. "Good reminders are nice to have." Taking in the rest of the photographs, he remarked, "The manner in which your husband died must have been pretty rough on the three of you."

Pointing to a photograph of a handsome man smiling broadly, he asked, "Is this him?"

Sandra, whose eyes took on a far off cast answered, "That was taken about a month before he was killed." Absently pulling at the fibers of the throw rug she was sitting on, she hesitated briefly. "Um, Jack killed one of them there at the scene...he and Robert were partners, and the other guy was caught a couple of days later. They found him hiding out at some friends, down in the 9th Ward, a couple of blocks from where the shooting took place, the corner of Abundance and Metropolitan."

Upon hearing the two street names, Lee remarked half aloud, "That's the Desire Theater." As the pieces fell into place, he let out an audible groan. "So, that's what the other afternoon was all about. Why didn't you say something when I mentioned the name of the theater? We could have easily planned to go somewhere else."

Shrugging her shoulders, she lied. "It was no big deal. I can't avoid the place forever."

"Well, it seems as if you have a handle on things." Replacing the fire screen, he rejoined her on the floor. As he made himself comfortable, he once again pulled at one of the tendrils that had fallen across her face. "Your hair catches the firelight rather beautifully. You make an attractive picture, Sandra.

As he spoke, he studied her face with the intensity of an artist trying to capture the spirit, as well as the beauty of his subject. "What lies behind that pretty face of yours, hmm?"

Feeling the mood fast becoming much too intense, she purposely steered the conversation back towards a more neutral topic. "Your life must be pretty carefree. Not only do you love your work, but you're heralded as a true artisan.   And you're paid substantially for your efforts. But, more importantly, you are incredibly comfortable with who you are."

"Carefree.   That's a relative term, Sandra. For instance, if I had a 'nine to five', I could look at your life and make the same observation. You're a successful businesswoman, have two beautiful children and not one, but two men. One who is exceptionally handsome, and the other who has dedicated his life to being at your beck and call."

"Beck and call!" Don't you think that you are exaggerating quite a bit?"

"On which count? One fella being particularly handsome or..."

"There is no or. There is no one at my beck and call, and the issue of one being more handsome...I think it's best that I leave that one alone," chuckled Sandra.

"Chicken!" teased Lee.

"I'm hardly a chicken."

"Maybe not, after all you do own your business. But you do strike me as being a bit cautious." Lee's teasing suddenly took on a double meaning.

Sensing the veiled implication behind his comment, she stiffened. "And what is that suppose to mean?"

Taking his time to answer, he ran a finger down the length of her arm. There was something very sensual, suggestive about his familiar gesture. Holding her gaze with the mesmeric web of his own, she felt transfixed, unable and unwilling to move.

"I have a feeling Sandra, that you usually go with what is safe, what's familiar. You know, the unknown can be quite exciting, just as fulfilling, and maybe even better."

Leaning forward, he pulled her towards him and gently caressed her lips. As his tongue captured hers, Sandra, so tired of thinking, tried to do what he suggested and throw caution to the wind. With her heart rapidly beating, she felt her lower being betray the common sense of her head. Lee's warm, strong hands masterfully caressed the skin under her blouse, willing her body towards his. Despite the desire to give in and venture down the unknown road that he had alluded to earlier, her head warned her otherwise. The emotions that she was feeling were not wrought out of shared love, not even a mutually spoken romance, but out of sheer physical lust.

What sent up the warning flags, she wasn't sure. It could have been the familiar ticking of the mantle clock, coupled with the glimpse of one of Whitney's mislaid toys lying in the corner. It didn't much matter. What did matter though, was her desperate foothold on reality.

Feeling her body tense against his own, Lee sensed that her sudden stillness was not in response to impending delight, but to trepidation. Frustrating as it was, would never he knowingly force her down a path she was unwilling to follow. Holding her close to his chest, he could literally feel the racing beat of her heart, measure by measure. Its syncopation matched that of his own.

Despite his outward control, his desire was just as great as Sandra's. His loins ached with anticipation. Relaxing his arm, he gently freed her hair from its topknot. Slowly running his fingers through a mass of curls, he seductively murmured, "Sit back and let me massage your shoulders."

Giving in to the pleasing pressure of his fingertips, she found herself sighing.

"You like the way that feels, don't you? Just give me a few minutes and I'll have your whole body feeling just as good."

Despite her body responding to the suggestion of his manipulative fingers, she let out an uncontrolled giggle.

Puzzled, he queried, "What's so funny?"

Dissolving into outright laughter, she fell back onto the floor, "Oh Lee...honey...I'm sorry, but just how many women have you used this...this move on?"

Feigning mock chagrin, he sat back and sheepishly grinned, "Move? I'm simply trying to be a gentleman. Trying to make my lady fair more comfortable."

"Lady fair? This is getting funnier by the minute. Come on, Lee, get real. You're trying to seduce me." She playfully charged as she swatted him with a pillow.

Throwing up both hands in defeat he chuckled, "Guilty as charged. But you know it's not my fault."

"Really? Then whose fault is it?

Yours. You're so damn beautiful."

"This chivalrous manner of yours is flattering, but somehow I don't think that it is very genuine."

Cupping a handful of her hair, he smiled. "I meant the compliment sincerely. But you're right, chivalrous is not how I would describe myself."

Realizing that whatever there was of a romantic mood had hopelessly evaporated, he stood. "Well, it looks like the only 'dessert' I'm going to get tonight is a piece of that chocolate cake over there on the counter. Why don't you find an old 'black and white' for us to watch while I slice it up."

As Sandra sorted through her collection of video-tapes, her mind flew back to the events that had just transpired. She realized that the evening could have easily charted an entirely different course. Glancing over at the spot where they had embraced minutes earlier, a scene of passionate lovemaking filled her mind.

Humorously shaking her head, she listened to Lee's whistle wafting in from the kitchen. Immediately recognizing the song as an old blues classic, "It's a Lover's Question," she realized that he chose it to tug at her heartstrings. Every so often, he would ham it up and sing the lyrics just loud enough for her to hear.

Posing the song's dilemma to her own heart, she wondered in terms of love, what was really real. When Lee crooned the question asking if she felt what he felt, she shook her head at his audacity. He was definitely a lady's man. One minute he was intriguingly arrogant and cavalier in manner, the next, tender and thoughtful. It was difficult to discern if he was truly a charming paragon of contradictions, or if his actions and words were all a well-calculated effort. As with all things, time would tell.

Lee was well aware that if he hadn't overplayed his hand and was less of a gentleman, he could have quite easily taken advantage of the evening. Heaven knows, it took all of his resolve to stop when he did. As he searched through the drawer for a cake knife, he found himself recalling how Sandra's nipples hardened as he ran his hand under her silk shirt. He had a feeling that from this point on, the touch of silk would recreate some very sensual memories.

For the remainder of the evening, both Lee and Sandra purposely kept the conversation light, and neither made mention of the evening's earlier events. Halfway through the old Bogey movie, both of them fell asleep on the sofa. It was well past 3:00 a.m. when she stirred and found herself lying in the fold of his strong arms. Quietly reaching for the remote, she turned off the television. Through his denim shirt, she could still smell his after-shave.

Resisting the urge to snuggle against his chest, she

recalled how close they had come to becoming intimate earlier in the evening. So, she noiselessly slipped from under his arms, walked to the foyer closet, and pulled out a plaid throw. After gentle laying it over the sleeping man, she quietly turned off the nearby table lamp and crept up the stairs.

When she finally arose, it was well into mid morning, a quarter past ten. As she collected her senses, she thought of Lee lying downstairs on the sofa and wondered if he was still asleep. Quickly she went into the bathroom, washed up and ran a comb through her hair. On the way out, she grabbed her voluminous terry bathrobe.

She half expected to find Lee still asleep. From the quiet of the house, she was convinced that her suspicions would be confirmed. Entering the den, she immediately noticed an empty sofa with the cotton throw she had taken out earlier folded neatly on its cushions.

Frowning, she called out. "Lee?" No answer. As she made her way into the kitchen, there sitting on the table was a half-filled glass of orange juice and a hastily scrawled note:

Good morning. You looked so peaceful, I didn't have the heart to wake you. I woke up with a wonderful idea for a design and am anxious to get started, you understand. If you have the time, why don't you run on out to the workshop. The weather is perfect for a drive. Here's a map...

Quickly glancing over the hastily drawn map, she noted that it would be at least an hour to an hour and half trip one-way. Not quite sure what to make of Lee's departure and somewhat impersonal invitation, she hurriedly finished reading the note. At the bottom of the page was a postscript:

*Oh by the way, good ol' Jack dropped by around
8:30. He said something about surprising the kids with a
bike outing. I told him that they were at your mother's.*

Lee

Placing the paper back on the table, she reached for
the phone to call Jack. Just as she began to punch in the
numbers, she was startled by sharp knocking coming
from the direction of the French doors.

As she unlocked the doors, she joked, "You must
have ESP. I was just about to call you."

"Oh?" Jack dryly remarked as he scanned the room.

Oblivious to his dour mood, she continued chatting.
"Sit down while I make us some coffee. As you can tell,
I'm getting a late start this morning." As she ran the tap
to fill up the coffee carafe, he picked up the note.
Frowning, he commented, "I understand Lee spent the
night."

She faced him with a pleasant smile, still unaware of
his less than friendly demeanor. "Yeah, we both fell
asleep last night, so..."

"Spare me the details," Jack flashed.

Picking up on his insinuation, it was now Sandra's
turn to interrupt. "Details? Jack, what has gotten into
you?"

With an uncharacteristic scowl, the usually self-pos-
sessed man raised his voice. "Into me? I should be asking you that question. You just met this Lee character,
and already you're...you're..."

"I'm what?," demanded Sandra.

Tapping the top of the table, Jack visibly forced himself to calm down and momentarily refrained from directly answering the question. With derision he usually
saved for the courtroom, he finally answered. "Well, put
it this way. Are the kids calling him Uncle Lee now, or

does he just sleep over when they're not at home?"

Sandra, upset and angered by his incredible audacity and presumptive line of questioning, retorted in a voice equally cold. "Jack, I don't mean to be rude, but did you come over to give me the third degree, or do you have a specific reason?"

Rising, he stuffed his hands into his pockets and in a controlled voice commented, "Do I have a reason? Now that's sweet. Let's see, is taking the kids biking specific enough? Or coming over to cut the grass? How about fixing the leaky faucet you mentioned the other night. I can go on if that's not specific enough for you. Or, maybe this is the answer you're looking for..." With a roughness born of anger, unrequited love, and penned up frustration, he cleared the space between them in one stride and grabbed her shoulders. Pinning her against the counter, he captured her lips with his own. For a very brief second, she felt a rush of excitement course through her blood, and then anger once again claimed her emotions.

Tearing herself away, she lashed out with a stinging slap across the face. In disbelief, she raised her trembling hands to her own face. Jack, equally stunned, raked his eyes over her now tear streaked face, across her quivering lips and rested upon her expressive eyes. As their eyes locked, he felt as if time had purposely stood still in order to render an absolute punishment. For what he saw in her eyes was not anger, but raw pain and broken trust.

At a complete loss for words, he silently watched as she hastily retied the robe that had fallen off her shoulders. As she shrugged the wrap across her arms, he couldn't help noticing the faint bruises starting to appear on her upper arms. Realizing that he had held her much too tightly, he whispered, "Sandra, I'm sorry," and quickly brushed passed her, through the French doors and on out of the house.

As she caught the door before it slammed, she followed him only as far as the porch.

Listening to his car engine fade off in the distance, she sat motionless on the porch swing, heart pounding so hard she could feel the pressure of it in her ears. Slowly she touched her lips, still sore from Jack's merciless kiss. Protectively pulling the notched collar of her robe aross her chest, her emotions ran the gamut of anger, hurt, disappointment and mistrust. What now? Call Jack on the phone and leave an angry message on his machine. Keep her distance and warn him to stay out of her life and away from the children?

The raucous merrymaking of the blackbirds broke into her thoughts; with paranoia she felt that they were mocking her. Their carefree noise making and jocular play left her with the overwhelming temptation to stand and scream in retort.

Feeling close to suffocation, she ran into the house and up the stairs. Hastily throwing on a pair of jeans and a denim shirt, she grabbed her purse and keys as she ran out the door. Where she was going, she had no idea. One thing she knew for sure: If she didn't get away to sort things out, she was going to lose her mind.

Chapter Thirteen

Sort things out—in Jack's mind, things couldn't be clearer. It was fast becoming apparent that Sandra was bent on simply classifying him as 'trusted family friend' and after this morning, he seriously doubted that she would even give him that consideration. He lost count of the number of times he ran Sandra's stricken face across his mind. During the drive back to his condo, he could think of nothing else. Several times he had been tempted to turn around and drive back to the house. Once he even went as far as to turn off the main thoroughfare he was traveling and pull into a gasoline station driveway to make a U-turn. Intuition and, if he was to be honest, pride stopped him short.

True, he had no right to question her involvement with Lee Chienier, and certainly not to kiss her the way he had, but he wasn't a saint, or some kind of damn eunuch. Still, rarely did he lose control the way he had earlier. Even when he had arrested the vilest criminal, he had maintained constraint. This was different though, very different. At least with a criminal there was some hope of justice being served in the end. But there was no vindication in loving someone who could, or as in the case of Sandra, would probably never return the affection.

As he approached the beautiful, restored riverside building that housed his condominium, his mind wandered back to the afternoon the real estate agent first showed him the apartment. He had just graduated with top honors from Tulane University Law School and had been asked to join a small but prestigious law firm.

A year before graduation, to his surprise, he was courted by several area firms. It seemed that he had become a local hero, a celebrity of sorts, for fatally shooting the man that gunned down his partner. *The Times-Picayune* ran the shooting as their lead story, complete with an enlarged photograph of him kneeling in a pool of blood, cradling a dead Robert in his arms. From the moment the story ran the next morning, he was beset with phone calls and letters. Most of the correspondence offered simple words of sympathy, but some included business offers as well.

Immediately following the shoot out, all desire to remain in law enforcement soured. His initial idyllic desire to protect society remained, but he felt very ineffectual. Since his youth, he had always wanted to be a part of the legal justice system. It was while being interviewed for a newspaper article that it was suggested he run for political office. At the time, he laughed it off as being pretty far fetched, but after giving it some thought, the idea began to appeal to him. But before embarking on a political crusade, he wanted to be properly prepared. Quitting his job and using a portion of his pension money, he fulfilled a long-standing dream and entered law school. When word got around, several benefactors offered words of encouragement and promises of partnerships. One firm even established a scholarship fund solely for law enforcement officers interested in entering the field of law. He was its first recipient.

Still reminiscing, he remembered how he had taken Sandra, as on previous occasions, with him to house hunt. He valued her opinion and sense of style, and thought that she would be useful in helping him choose new digs. Not only did he want a larger place suitable for entertaining, but he also wanted to be closer to both the firm, and Sandra and the kids. They looked at homes, duplexes and apartments before they stumbled across this elegant former hotel. It was located in an area that had gone through the usual urban transformation. Once a posh district that hosted some of New Orleans' more colorful politicians and crooks, it had given way to trendier areas uptown. But as is often the case, the area metamorphosed and came back full circle, catering to the growing "yuppie" population.

His building sat in a beautiful neighborhood, one that Jack thought went unappreciated by those who sought the automatic refuge of the suburbs. The hotel itself sat across from a beautiful slip of a park that abutted the Mississippi River. He was fortunate to be able to buy an apartment that offered a beautiful view of the waterway. Some evenings, he caught himself spending hours staring out at the water, wondering what secrets it held and taking solace from its vastness, strength and maturity. The mighty Mississippi, with a mind of its own, had a way of putting problems into perspective.

As he entered the lobby, he nodded to the cleanng crew vacuuming the lush, forest green carpet that blanketed all nine floors of the ornate apartment building. Glancing over at the bank of ivory iron mailboxes, he noticed several envelopes poking through the elaborate filigree. First pressing the button to signal the notoriously slow elevator, he walked over to the mailbox and retrieved his mail. Looking over at an oversized gilded mirror that graced the beautifully papered walls, he saw that the elevator had arrived. He had to give the developers of the building credit; they had faithfully restored and replicated everything down to the smallest detail, from the set of heavily ornate skeleton keys each tenant received, to the ivory iron-gated elevator door.

As the elevator made its way upward to the seventh

floor, he absently poked through the bundle, noticing most of it was junk mail, save for one credit card bill and a bright yellow envelope decorated with youthful crayon drawn pictures. Smiling, Jack looked at the handwriting and immediately recognized that it was sent by Whitney, probably one day last week.

As he entered his apartment, he tossed his keys and the mail, save for Whitney's letter, on a small glass console that sat in the foyer.

His particular condo, unlike the public areas of the building, was not carpeted, but was floored in a richly shined parquet wood tile over which were placed softly patterned blue-gray Berber area rugs. In the immense main room, the rugs visually separated the space into two areas, a living room and a dining room. Unlike the restored lobby of the building, the developers, accommodating the tastes of the prospective tenants, updated the apartments so that they were an appealing combination of both old and new. Jack's apartment beautifully reflected that effort.

The wall facing the river front had originally been plastered over, save for four small French doors that opened out to balconies They had been replaced with one long wall of glass that ran the length of the room from floor to ceiling. This revision, especially when the midnight blue jacquard drapes were pulled back, offered a fantastic view of the river and the harbor, as well as providing a breathtaking backdrop for the furnishings.

He had found decorating this wonderful find especially daunting. He knew the look he was after, but had no idea how to achieve it. So once again, he solicited Sandra's help, giving her a budget and free reign, aside from the insistence of no florals. She intuitively knew exactly what he wanted and in four months, had the apartment completely furnished.

Usually coming home was something he looked forward to, but today was different. The sight of the lazy Mississippi filled with barges and sailboats immediately turned his already melancholy mood to outright depression.

Staring down at Whitney's yellow envelope, he immediately remembered the children's reaction when they saw the apartment for the first time. "Wow, Uncle Jack," was all Jesse said as he surveyed the room. He remembered hugging Sandra and commenting with the same expression. She had turned empty quarters into a sophisticated home.

She had created a dramatic masterpiece with the color scheme of smoke and midnight blue, cream and pale amethyst. The walls were painted a rich smoky blue, while the ceiling was a creamy white. The same shade was picked up in the supple midnight blue suede sofa. Across from the other sofa, were two white on white striped upholstered armless chairs, with a side table placed in between. Off to one side was an amethyst armchair. And against one wall was a small desk with a cane backed armchair with a seat done up in a muted amethyst, blue and cream plaid. The one thing that tied the furnishings together was a handsome black grand piano that sat behind the sofa and directly in front of the window . It had been in his family for at least 75 years, and was one of the few items saved from his previous apartment.

Flopping down on the soft sofa, Jack found himself again replaying the morning's events, and the anger he felt when Lee opened Sandra's door. Anger from not only seeing Lee, but by being struck head-on with the realization that the two of them, in a matter of a few weeks, had perhaps shared a level of intimacy that he and Sandra had never fully explored. The revelation was far worse than a slap to the face. It represented a breach of trust. With what appeared to be little deliberation, she had allowed a relative stranger to intrude into their relationship. Mentally he was aware that what he felt defied common sense. But on an emotional level it still hurt.

As he wondered what his next move should be, he absently opened Whitney's letter. Inside the envelope was a colorful drawing of four smiling figures, holding hands. The background was filled with flowers, butterflies and hearts. Jack immediately noticed that the child had placed him and Sandra in the center of the picture, at least he presumed it was him. Underneath in a child's scrawl was a narrative that explained they were going on a picnic.

After momentarily studying the drawing, he placed it on the coffee table. With an exasperated sigh, he rose and started towards the study. Maybe work would take his mind off Sandra. Changing his mind, he reached over and grabbed the phone from off the sofa table and quickly punched in her phone number. He listened to the ringing phone as he mulled over an appropriate apology, words that would convey sincerity, but still leave his pride intact. As the phone continued to ring, he realized that she either wasn't answering or had left. "Damn!" He considered dialing the shop, but feeling like some lovesick schoolboy, muttered another oath and threw the receiver back on its hook, unbuttoned his shirt, and headed for the bedroom.

Sure, he owed her an apology for kissing her the way he had, he had no problem with that. But he'd be damned if he was going to chase her down. He had more than made his feelings clear. Now the ball was in her court. Perhaps at one time he would have tolerated, and maybe even played the usual courtship 'mind games' that women seemed to thrive on. Hell, not now. Not only was he a bit too old for this schoolhouse nonsense, but as far as he was concerned, Sandra knew his feelings quite well, always had. Not only that, his love for both her and the kids had been tested and proved. It should be unquestioned.

While changing into his running wear, it struck him that perhaps in the past he had been too available, always there, ready to pitch in and help. No wonder she viewed him as good ol' Jack, like an 'older brother'. Remembering Whitney's drawing, he finished lacing his running shoes and searched for it and the rest of the mail, under a pile of clothing that he had hastily gathered from the living room and tossed on his bed. When he found it, he smoothed it out and stuck it into the wooden frame of the mirror that hung over the dresser. It'd be one thing to distance himself from Sandra, but quite another to do it from the kids. Not only wouldn't they understand, but personally it would be very difficult, if not impossible. Whatever happened between him and Sandra must never affect the children's well being or happiness. It wouldn't be fair.

As he quietly closed the door to the condo and made his way to the elevator, he realized that he was no longer angry, but disappointed. Disappointed in Sandra's refusal to look at him as being anything but some gen-der-neutered friend. Realizing the paradox of the situation, he grimly smiled and noted that after the morning's kiss there should be little doubt in Sandra's mind that he was as warm-blooded as the next man.

Chapter Fourteen

Sandra had no real idea where she was headed. She was behind the steering wheel driving aimlessly towards nowhere, an absolute paradigm of her present emotional state.

She compared herself to an angst-filled motorcyclist headed down the highway of life towards some idealistic truth. Except here she was, a 32-year-old woman, driving a minivan headed down the highway of what? Love? Naw, that sounded too cliché even for her maudlin frame of mind. Besides, were her jumbled emotions even about love or just hurt feelings? Considering the emotional roller coaster that both Jack and Lee had taken her on over the last twenty four hours, there was no telling. From Lee's passionate kisses the night before, coupled with his emotionally detached note, to Jack's unfounded accusations and...

As the tears well up in her eyes, she quickly wiped them away. Clutching the steering wheel, she angrily growled, "Men!" Somehow they had a knack for taking a perfectly pleasant life and...well, she'd be damned if she allowed herself to become further fodder for either one of their oversized male egos.

If she was going to have a relationship with a man, whether Jack or Lee, or somebody else, it would have to be on her own terms. She was an older and a far different sort of woman than the woman who married Robert. This time around, things would have to be different. She had learned how to appreciate her talents, strengths, and even weaknesses. She had prove to herself that she could stand and make it on her own. Yes, she was ready for a serious relationship, perhaps even a permanent commitment. But she was no longer willing to allow a man to overshadow her life.

Driving along, she debated and discarded various destinations. She considered going over to the shop, and even headed in that direction. But given her state of mind, the thought of listening to the prattling of carefree tourists would be just as annoying as staying home and listening to the jabbering birds in her yard. Ironically, in the past she would have sought the wise insight of Jack. But now the mere thought of him brought unexpected tears to her eyes.

Highly emotive, her mind returned to the memory of the warmth of his chest and the strength of his hands as he roughly pulled her to him. God, he had smelled good. Unlike Lee's kisses of the night before, Jack's were filled with a storm of passion. No matter how hard she tried to forget the memories that haunted both of them, she and Jack would always be connected.

As she forced her mind away from Jack, she found herself thinking of Lee and his stupid note. For crying out loud, how long would it have taken to personally invite her along, let alone call once he had reached his beloved workshop? Obviously, their evening together meant very little. With a sick feeling and a shudder, she offered up a quick word of thanks that their lovemaking had gone no further.

At a stop light, she glanced up at the rear view mirror and caught sight of the historic St. Charles Trolley lumbering up alongside the van. Looking at the green streetcar filled with both tourists and locals, she was immediately reminded of the trolley ride she took about a month after Robert's funeral. The day before, she had finally sorted and boxed most of his belongings. As she sealed the last box and studied the half-emptied closet and drawers, the finality of his death suddenly hit. That afternoon, like today, she had had to get away from the house, to sort her feelings and plan on how to move ahead.

Remembering that breezy afternoon three and a half years ago, she recalled how she had boarded the St. Charles purely on impulse and rode it to the end of the line and back. She was able to "get lost" and put her life into perspective.

If it worked once, why not again. So she pulled ver and parked at a city operated lot bordering the French Quarter. Within minutes, she found herself stepping on the trolley she had spied blocks earlier.

As the street car made its way up St. Charles Avenue, away from the "Central Business District", she observed the passengers boarding and exiting, and found herself reflecting on the passing buildings and faces. The cityscape changed with each streetcar stop, from the commercial and high rise office buildings of the 'Central Business District', to Lafayette Square with its bronze of Henry Clay and the beautiful Greek Revival architecture of Gallier Hall. Squinting at the sun's reflection off the beautiful white marble portico of Gallier, she noticed a bedraggled man pulling a wobbling cart laden with clothing, paper and other miscellaneous items across the grassy square. She found herself sinking deeper into her melancholy mood.

Onward the streetcar progressed along St. Charles Avenue, through the historic working class Irish Channel community and then through the stately bastion of antebellum 'riche', the 'Garden District'. And any hope of the ride lifting her spirits dwindled.

The next hour and half did little to dispel her teariness. In fact, the rows of wrought iron fences and the well-ordered and resplendent 'Garden District' mansions, if anything, made a mockery of her entangled emotions. Usually she appreciated the elegance of the beveled lead glass windows and stunning porticoes that graced the likes of the wonderfully replicated 'Tara' or the Georgian Colonial Revival 'Wedding Cake House'.

As the trolley neared the end of the line, most of the passengers disembarked and headed towards the Audubon Park and Zoo, except for Sandra and a young couple. Deciding to continue the ride to the end of the line and return, she rode on to Riverbend, an area not far from the Mississippi River, filled with restaurants and shops. As she exited, the conductor explained that it would be a few minutes before the trolley could be turned around to face the opposite direction for the return trip.

Not in any hurry to get home, she glanced at her watch and debated on whether to walk over to one of the restaurants for a leisurely, but lonesome lunch. She could catch another streetcar back to the van, or wait the few minutes and head back down to the French Quarter and perhaps take in one of the park service's walking tours. Deciding on the latter, she settled on a bench across from the same young couple, who by this time were lost in an ardent session of kissing.

By the time the streetcar neared the stop where she had to transfer to the Elysian Field bus, she was anxious to see the trip come to an end. As she looked out the bus window, she perused the lacy iron balconies that graced the elegantly-aged buildings of the Vieux Carre, the narrow walks and well-worn cobbled alleys were filled with tourists. She was now more resolute than ever to shake her mood. She wanted to embrace life, much in the way determined by New Orleans generations ago, and enjoy it on her own terms.

As the bus pulled up to its stop near Jackson Square, the heart of the French Quarter, she gathered up her shoulder bag and queued up with the rest and made her way off the rear of the bus.

Just as she neared the bottom step, the vehicle unexpectedly lurched forward, causing her to stumble. Reaching out, she braced herself against the ramrod back of the older gentleman exiting ahead of her. Abruptly the man turned and bared a face that momentarily startled her. Upon recognition, the elderly man's vinegary glare transformed into a friendly smile. Offering his arm, he assisted her to the sidewalk.

"Mr. Fontenot!" she beamed.

"Why Sandra! Fancy seeing you. You know, we were just talking about you the other night here."

"Only good things I hope" she chuckled.

"Wouldn't be anything else but. When is Lee going to get you back out to the house?"

Quickly turning the conversation away from Lee, she remarked, "I didn't see you board the bus."

Her move to change the subject did not go unnoticed by the older man. Perceptively smiling he explained, "Oh, I got on with a bunch of tourists back on Magazine. I promised an old friend of mine that I'd drop by his antique shop. Why he calls it an antique shop though, I'll never know. Looks like a bunch of second-hand junk to me."

"Well, you know what they say. One man's junk is another's treasure."

Chuckling, Alphonse's topaz eyes twinkled. "So what treasures are you out to find today? I gather you were uptown to do some shopping? Since I don't see any bags, you must not have found anything to your liking."

Hesitating briefly, she put on a good face and shook her head. "No, fortunately for my wallet, I wasn't in the mood to shop today. Mom has the kids, so I thought I'd take advantage of my spare time and this gorgeous day by enjoying some of New Orleans' charms." Looking across the square up at the spires of the late 18th century St. Louis Cathedral, she continued, "In fact, I was thinking of signing up for one of the Park Ranger's tours. I haven't taken one in a while. I thought it might be fun."

Al, eyes sparkling, suggested, "Hey, I've got an idea. Why don't you let me be your tour guide. I know the Vieux Carré as well as I know the Teche. That is, if you're up to it?"

Sandra needed little convincing. "Are you sure you don't mind? You must have other things planned for your Saturday."

"Sh! I have the time. I come in every Saturday. I like to ride the streetcar, visit some old friends who still keep shops over at the market. Besides, Lavania tires of looking at this sour old face all day."

Looking up at the elderly blue jean clad man, Sandra smiled at his humorous though accurate description of himself. "Well, I'm game if you are. Where should we begin?"

"First, what kind of shoes you've got on your feet?"

"These shoes are made for walkin'," Sandra sang as she held out a sneaker adorned foot.

With a faint smile, he adjusted his weathered hat. "Let's head towards the French Market. I can show you off to some of my old friends, make them think I done and got myself a gal. And...," looking down at Sandra's bare head, "buy you a hat. It's gonna be a hot one."

As the odd pair made their way over to the market, she soon forgot her troubles. Al's colorful conversation filled her thoughts and enlivened the bustling antiquated streets and buildings of the Vieux Carré with the spirited shadows of New Orleans' past.

As they walked along, he began to reminisce. "In our courting days, Lavania and I used to do a lot of strolling up and down these streets. Come early evening, the banquettes would be filled with young couples.

Sometimes, we would catch a streetcar and head uptown, over to one of the clubs like the Dew Drop Inn. It was the granddaddy of them all. Man, talk about the Dew Drop. I can remember it like yesterday. We'd listen to the likes of "Gatemouth" Brown, Tommy Ridgley, Earl King. Yup, the banquettes were hopping."

"Banquette...," Sandra chuckled. "As soon as I moved down here from Dallas. I fell in love with this colorful old town. Now I couldn't imagine living anywhere else. Is there any other place in the U.S. of A. where they call a sidewalk a banquette, or a porch a gallery? Not to mention the thoroughly unique food. When I first met my husband, Robert, I must have just about driven him mad with my questions. For our first Valentine, he gave me a little glossary of New Orleans' terms and culinary delights.

"Robert...you met him in college?"

"Um, hum. We were both students over at Dillard. I had great plans to head for either New York or Chicago with degree in hand and land a high-powered position at an ad agency. But instead, I fell in love.

"I bet your parents were none too pleased about that," quipped Al.

Laughing, she agreed. "Not hardly. My dad threw a holy fit, and after he met Robert, it only got worse."

"He didn't like your young fella, eh?"

Thinking back to what seemed like ages ago, her voice became thoughtful. "That's putting it mildly. If the truth be told, he kept trying to push Jack on me."

"Jack, the young man you were telling us about at the house?"

"Yes, Jack and Robert were roommates in college. They were best of friends even back then. When Robert would drive me home for the holidays, Jack would come along to keep him company on the trip back. The three of us would have so much fun talking and just acting outright silly. My little boy, Jesse, reminds me a lot of his dad. He's quite the charmer, so full of spirit. He has that same disarming way of making you laugh. There was very little in life that Robert took seriously. Jack on the other hand was," Sandra gave a sharp chuckle, "still is, I should say, the total opposite. He has a dry sense of humor that at times can come across as being condescending, and he takes responsibility, and life very seriously. He's always weighing the pros and cons, very deliberate."

"More of the level-headed type," supplied Al.

"Exactly. Robert would sometimes tease him when he saw Jack out and about. He'd call out, "Here comes the rain." Jack always managed to take it good-naturedly though.

As they entered into bustling French Market alley, Alphonse took hold of Sandra's elbow in a somewhat quaint, but endearing fashion.

"From a father's point of view, I can see why your daddy preferred Jack. Love is a very complicated emotion. Decisions of the heart take thoughtful deliberation. In the end, you're always forced to consider what you have to gain, against what you may lose." Pointing to a bronze life-sized sculpture, the elderly man continued. "Take ol' Martha here for example."

Smiling, Sandra stopped in front of the forlorn bronze of a young woman sitting on a wrought iron bench holding a basket of produce on her lap.

Alphonse leaned towards Sandra and with his characteristic intensity began to speak. "Here sits a girl who is torn between the love of her life and the wishes of her family," explained the old man as he condensed the 'Legend of Martha'. "Does she have the courage to entrust herself to the man who wants to share his life or will she defy love and play it safe?"

Momentarily holding Alphonse's gaze, Sandra

uneasily looked at the sad beauty of the sculpture. Al, once again taking her elbow, guided her through the open market square towards a produce stall owned by one of his friends.

The day was fast becoming quite enjoyable, and Alphonse was living up to his self-proclaimed reputation as a wonderful, if not unusual tour guide. After leaving the Market, they continued touring the Quarter and its outer reaches. In his dour manner, Al filled their conversation with obscure references to apparitions and ghostly voices that are said to haunt the Vieux Carré, some were documented, others simply passed word-of-mouth over the years.

So effective was his presentation that as they walked along Esplanade Avenue, the Creoles' grand promenade of days long ago, the hair rose on Sandra's arms. As the tangible presence of these denizens past brushed by, she closed her eyes and heard their voices waft from the beautiful old brick and plastered buildings that once were their residences.

When they approached a block along Bourbon Street, an area known for its voodoo queens and doctors, Alphonse joked about the men and women who still came seeking 'spiritual' advice and to have various gris-gris prescribed for their businesses and affairs of the heart.

As they continued walking down Bourbon towards St. Ann, Sandra raised a brow as she wondered what gris-gris Alphonse would suggest for what was troubling her now.

"Don't think that the belief in potions and charms was strictly reserved to the poor and illiterate," Al reminded her. "The wealthy and privileged also called upon the powers of Marie Laveau. Her abilities at spell casting, healing and fixing broken hearts were held in the highest of regard.

Stopping, Al placed one leathery hand on his lean hip and pointed across the street with the other. "Many of the voodoo rites were practiced by slaves and free persons of color across the way there, in Armstrong Park. Back then it was known as Congo Square."

Studying the area he was pointing to, she followed the older man as they crossed the street. With great interest, she listened to Alphonse talk of the voodoo rituals practiced by voodoo queens such as Marie Laveau. Despite the warmth of the sunshine, she felt momentarily chilled as she imagined the spiritual gatherings amongst the dancing shadows and rustling quietness of the massive oak trees.

"Where to next?" she asked, fondly enjoying their time together.

Mischievously smiling, Al answered, the 'City of the Dead', of course!"

After an afternoon full of talk about apparitions, voodoo and assorted gris-gris, Alphonse's response was not a total surprise. "Of course, where else?" laughed Sandra as the pair walked on up the block towards St. Louis Cemetery #1.

Immediately upon entering the gates of the St. Louis, it was easy to understand why New Orleanians fondly referred to its oldest graveyard as the 'City of the Dead'. The cemetery was strikingly void of any signs of life. Save for an occasional tree or shrub, everything was absolutely still.

As she and Al carefully picked their way through the impossible labyrinth of closely packed above ground tombs and shoulder high monuments, she was once again chilled. The heat of the sun's setting rays dazzling off the white stone did little to warm her. Carved ethereal angels and other assorted fetishes of grief and sorrow lent a definite coldness and unsettling feeling of finality throughout the yard.

Alphonse, seemingly oblivious to the cemetery's stillness, took pleasure in telling macabre story after story of
ghost sightings and unexplained apparitions. He told of
taxi cab drivers that picked up and dropped off phantom
passengers at the cemetery's gates, as well as apparitions who not only showed themselves, but left behind
talismans for loved ones.

Stopping in front of a half sunken tomb, he recount-
ed one particularly morbid tale of a father so grief strick-
en over the death of his daughter that he crawled into her
crypt, lay next to her casket and killed himself.

As he spoke, her eyes were drawn to a tomb everal
graves over. Mesmerized by the sad eyes and heavy-
laden shoulders of the sculpted marble woman placed to
stand watch over the crumbling tomb, she immediately
thought of the French Market's bronze figure, Martha.
But unlike Martha, these eyes, along with the deceptively bewitching smile, slowly began to take on an eerie cold
cast. What at first appeared to be an expression of for-
lornness, suddenly seemed horribly wicked.

Chiseled across the stone was...

A Superscription

Look in my face; my name is Might-have-been;
I am also call No-more, Too-late, Farewell;
Unto thine ear I hold the dead-sea-shell
Cast up thy Life's foam-fretted feet between;
Unto thine eyes the glass where that is seen
Which had Life's form and Love's, but by my spell
Is now a shaken shadow intolerable,
Of ultimate things unuttered the frail screen.
Mark me, how still I am! But should there dart
One moment through thy soul the soft surprise
Of that winged Peace which lulls the breath of sighs,-
Then shalt thou see me smile, and turn apart
Thy visage to mine ambush at thy heart

Sleepless with cold commemorative eyes.
                                        Dante G. Rossetti

Inscribed under the poem was the epitaph...

Lost love, and in turn happiness to
the surreptitious sylph, "Might-Have-Been."
Do not make the same mistake...
Sacred to the memory of
Darlene Frasier
Born June 12, 1840
Died August 10, 1875

After reading the inscription, she looked back into the figure's wicked eyes and felt as if she was being silently warned of some impending heartbreak. Unable to look away, she felt her heart quicken. As if on cue, Alphonse gently took her arm and whispered, "Who but the dead know better of that fateful missed window of opportunity, yes?"

Turning her face towards his, she caught a ragged breath as she met his intense gaze. For a fleeting moment, she sensed that he knew much more about her than he let on. "Mr. Fontenot, you know about Jack and...?" As if reading her mind, he gently answered, "Just call it serendipity, Sandra." With a kind smile, the old man slowly searched her face, glanced back up at the marble woman and walked back towards the cemetery gate.

Before following, Sandra too gave the tomb one last perusal.

Chapter Fifteen

Juggling an oversized handbag and briefcase, Sandra unlocked the door of Lavender and Hops. As she entered the shop, she felt as though it had been months instead of two days since she had last walked through its doors. With a relieved sigh, she laid her bags on the old wooden counter top and allowed herself to momentarily bask in the fragrance of the botanicals. With the sunlight dancing in through the crisp lace curtains, the mulled scent of the dried rose petals, lemon verbena, honeysuckle and tansy was simply heaven as it wrapped her in its familiar cloak of comforting warmth and stillness. Within minutes, this wonderful respite lifted her dark mood and she was humming off to make her usual pot of coffee.

As she donned her cotton apron, she found it wonderful not to have her mind filled with thoughts of the egomaniacal Lee Chienier or the reproving Jack Thibodeaux. As she reached for her favorite mug, she instructed herself to keep her mind focused on matters pertaining to the shop, and with any luck, she could get through the day without troubling reminders of the previous weekend.

Shortly before lunch, a delivery woman trolleyed in several crates. After quickly signing the manifest, she carefully began opening the smaller of the boxes, saving the larger, oversized parcel marked fragile for last. The first two boxes contained the usual orders of botanicals and assorted gift items. Frowning as she prepared to open the remaining larger box, Sandra tried to remember what had been ordered that was large and heavy. The shipping label offered no clue, only the name of an unfamiliar company, 'Lamentation Furniture'.

She was able to lift away the crate's lid after pulling out several nails. Pushing aside several layers of packing material, she could see that whatever was inside was made of willow. Now more puzzled than ever, she hadn't a clue as to what it could be. Since the box was almost as tall as she was, using a pair of pliers, she began to open two of the box's side seams. With that task completed, she proceeded to remove the shredded newspaper that served as protective packing. Finally, a delicate willow twig rocker was revealed.

Gasping in total surprise, she immediately recognized the chair as being one of Lee's featured pieces at the 'Sol Galerie'. Gingerly pulling the chair away from the box and out of the mass of packing, she stepped back to admire Lee's craftsmanship. It was then that she noticed, tucked in between the graceful curves of twisted branch, an elegant ivory-colored note card.

Lee's bold hurried scrawl read:

Sandra,
Don't look upon this as a gift, but as an artist's effort to protect a portion of his soul.

Lee

Rereading the message, she couldn't help noticing that there was no evidence of affection, neither a mention of Friday night nor his silent departure the day after. Sandra, you're being down right petty. Just look at the beautiful chair. It was no use, try as she might, she just could not forget or ignore the events of the weekend and focus on the thoughtful gift.

Just as she was in the midst of taking the chair to the rear workroom, the front door clapper bell announced a customer.

"Hel-lo." Maggie's mellifluent voice pleasantly broke the quiet.

"Maggie!" Sandra greeted her good friend as the woman offered her a warm sisterly hug.

"Oh Sandra! So, you finally agreed to accept Lee's gift. I'm glad. I know how much he wanted you to have it."

"Now wait a minute, I didn't exactly accept his gift. Actually, I had little choice, he sent it over by..."

Maggie sat in the rocker and caressed the silky mooth wood. She sighed appreciatively. "It's even more beautiful than I remembered. Why don't you want it?"

"Maggie, it's not that I don't want it, I love it. But, don't you think that it's a rather extravagant gift? It would be one thing if we were..."

"Involved? Psst!" Maggie waved aside Sandra's concern. "This is about as involved as I've seen big brother get in a very long time." Shrugging her shoulders as she slowly rocked back and forth, she advised, "If it'll make you feel better, don't think of it as a gift. Look at the rocker as being a sign that you're on his mind."

Suddenly rising from the chair, Maggie pulled Sandra towards the rocker and made her sit. "However you choose to analyze it, just enjoy it."

Sandra fingered the card she had placed in her apron pocket and shrugged, "Maybe you're right."

"I know that I'm right. Knowing my brother and that creative mind of his." Maggie's face took on an overly dramatic expression as she caricatured Lee's eccentricy. "I bet ya, in some peculiar way, he looks at it as giving you a piece of himself. And believe me, he doesn't do that too often. I doubt if he's ever given Miss Aileen anything more than a piece of broken twig." Imitating the woman's affected carriage and attitude, Maggie mimicked, "And she's his greatest admirer."

Despite laughing at her friend's catty, though accurate interpretation of the agent, Sandra purposely changed the subject as she rose from the chair. "Maggie, I'm used to your last minute schedule changes, but aren't you a bit early for your facial? You're not due in for at least another three hours."

"I know, I had a dentist's appointment and it took less time than I thought. So, I was hoping that I could persuade you to close shop for a hour or so and join me for lunch."

Before she made a decision, Sandra wondered if the lunch hour would be filled with conversation regarding Lee. "Maggie, I just can't close up shop..."

"When was the last time you treated yourself to a nice, leisurely lunch?"

"Well, it is Monday, and things are a bit slow." A proposition to enjoy the wonderful weather was hard to ignore.

"C'mon Sandra, live a little, take a walk on the ild side and..."

"All right, all right! You have convinced me." She laughed as her hands went up in mock surrender. "Where did you have in mind?"

"Well, let's see, it's so pretty out, why not Emanuel's? We could get a table out in the courtyard and dine alfresco."

Opting to take full advantage of the late spring sunshine, the two women walked to the corner to catch the streetcar. Feeling the light warm breeze against her skin, Sandra was pleasantly reminded of the afternoon she spent with Alphonse. When she mentioned the outing to Maggie, she was surprised as her companion nodded upon hearing the story.

"David and I were out there this weekend. You

should have seen Miss Lavania's face when he told her that he had spent his day with a young, beautiful woman that he had met on the streetcar. On and on he went. You could tell that whoever this woman was, he was quite smitten. Miss Lavania went out of her way to pretend that she wasn't the least bit bothered, but she didn't have any of us fooled. Finally, after having his fun, Mr. Al let on that the "pretty young thing" was you."

As she chuckled, Maggie continued, "If you could have seen her face. Lee and I hadn't laughed so hard in a long time."

Trying not to sound too interested, Sandra smiled and casually commented, "So Lee was there?"

"Um hmm, he walked in right after me. Ms. Lavania promised to cook him up his favorite dish, seafood gumbo, if he shelled the shrimp. So, he came on in from out of that dreary workshop of his. Sometimes he's in there for so long, I wonder how his skin keeps color."

With the confirmed knowledge that Lee had a few spare moments over the weekend, but had chosen not to call, Sandra felt her mood darkening.

Unaware of Sandra's thought, Maggie tugged at her sleeve. "Well, here's where we get off."

As the two woman followed the maitre d' across the bricked courtyard adorned with lush green plants, colorful hanging baskets, and an intricately tiled fountain, Sandra heard a warm familiar chuckle.

Turning in the direction of the laughter, she caught a glimpse of Jack seated across the table from a beautiful woman. Jack, unaware of Sandra's arrival, continued laughing and making carefree conversation. The woman, from what Sandra could briefly assess, was quite a bit taller than she, for her long legs seemed to extend endlessly from under an elegant and short black knit dress. Her beautiful coriander brown complexion was flawless, as was her makeup. The woman's reddish brown hair was expertly highlighted with flecks of gold, and was cut close in a stylish cap.

Much to Sandra's chagrin, the maitre d' seated them at a table that offered a perfect view of the carefree couple. Despite all of her efforts to listen and keep track of Maggie's prattling, Sandra soon found herself glancing across the yard towards Jack's table more than once. She couldn't help noticing how the woman from time to time would casually, if not suggestively, brush Jack's charcoal gray trouser leg with the tip of her red calfskin pump, and how her perfectly manicured hands sensually caressed the coffee cup each time she brought it to her pouty scarlet-painted lips.

Curious as to how Jack was responding to his date's very obvious flirtations, Sandra took some pleasure in noticing that several times he unconsciously smoothed down his tie. Knowing Jack as well as she did, she knew that this was a subtle telltale sign that he was well aware that his companion was being much more than just a bit coquettish. Once again, he smoothed down his tie, and this time she noticed that the silk paisley was one that she had helped the kids to pick out as a birthday present several months before.

"Earth to Sandra...Sandra?"

"Mm...what?" she replied.

"What's so interesting over there?"

"Nothing," she answered just a bit too quickly.

"Nothing? Well, nothing is definitely not the term I would use to describe HIM." Maggie's tone made it quite clear that she found Jack very attractive. "Now that woman that's with him is quite another story. Look at her. God, have you sever een anyone more obvious."

"Maggie!" Sandra reprimanded her friend. Though she couldn't help feeling a little happy that her companion found the woman's mannerisms to be equally calculating. "That's not nice, you don't even know her."

"Oh, I know little "Miss Thing" over there. Her name is Darlene Lafleur."

Sandra couldn't help asking the obvious. "Where do you know her from?"

"She moved around the house the year before Lee left for art school. Lee's 'little shadow' is what Miss Lavania used to call her. He couldn't make a move without Darlene showing up. Let's just say that they were very close." Maggie dramatically shuddered. "Even then I knew that there was something phony and wicked about that woman."

Studying Jack's companion, Sandra wanted to ask her friend just how close was close, but thought it best that she didn't know. Watching as Jack poured her a glass of red wine, she wondered just how close Ms. Lafleur was to Jack.

As they spoke, the target of their disparaging comments rose and walked in the direction of the ladies' room. She was even more gorgeous standing than seated.

"You have to give it to her though, she does have a drop dead body," Maggie ruefully acknowledged. Again, Maggie glanced over in Jack's direction, "But where have I seen him before?"

"What makes you think that you've seen him anywhere?"

"His is a face you don't easily forget." Taking a sip of water from her goblet, Maggie's eyes lit up. "Now I know. I've seen him at the shop."

Carefully choosing her words, Sandra looked down at her menu and answered with all of the casualness she could muster, "Probably, so, what are you going to order?"

Surveying her friend suspiciously, Maggie twisted her mouth and raised a brow. "Changing the subject, now that's a sure sign."

Sandra, not sure herself as to why she was making such a big deal out of Jack's presence, drummed her nails against the table and piquedly asked, "A sure sign of what?"

"That there's some reason you don't want to talk about..."

"Ugh!" Sandra sighed in exasperation. "All right! His name is Jack Thibodeaux, satisfied?"

Slowly repeating the name, Maggie narrowed her eyes and studied Jack's profile.

"Thibodeaux...Thibodeaux, it seems like I've heard you mention his name before." After several seconds passed, she exclaimed, "Now I know. He's YOUR Jack!"

No longer making an effort to hide her annoyance, Sandra hissed, "He's not MY anything!"

Thrown by her friend's agitated state, Maggie teased, "Hey what's gotten your underwear in a pinch?"

Finding little humor in Maggie's behavior, Sandra ignored her friend's question. "Here comes the waiter. I bet you haven't even looked at your menu yet."

After giving their order to the waiter, any hope Sandra had that their topic of conversation would take a different course was soon dashed.

"So why don't you go over and say hello," Maggie persisted.

"Maggie, I swear, you have a one track mind."

"There, he's looking this way." With a warm smile, Maggie raised her hand and waved.

To Sandra's dismay, Jack was not only looking their way, but had risen and was walking over to their table. Once again noticing his dress, she gathered that today he must be "in court." Jack's easy-going manner was often reflected in his style of dress. Usually he opted for a look that was stylishly comfortable, but today he was impeccably dressed. She noticed the gold eyelet pin that held the collar of his freshly starched white shirt in place.

His warm golden skin complemented the brightness of the shirt almost seductively. The fitted cut of his shirt's line accentuated his strong, broad-shouldered physique, as well as the sharply creased flannel trousers that seemed to lengthen his frame and offset his burgundy harnesses perfectly.

"Hello Sandra," came Jack's familiar, deep-timbered voice.

Silently quelling her rapidly beating heart, she did her best to sound equally casual. Offering a small smile, she returned his greeting and glanced towards Maggie. "Hi, Jack. Um...I don't know if you remember Margaret Doucet."

"It's been a while, but of course I do. It's a pleasure seeing you again Margaret." Jack warmly cupped Maggie's offered hand as he flashed a boyish grin.

It was easy to see why Maggie found him so attractive. When smiling, his face was instantly friendly. Faint crinkles softened his chiseled good looks and complemented what she could only describe as being 'gentle' eyes.

Maggie gushing like a love struck schoolgirl, returned his smile. "Please, call me Maggie."

"All right, Maggie it is." As he said her name, a look of realization crossed his face. "You wouldn't be Lee Chienier's sister, would you?"

Maggie was now the one surprised. "Why yes, I am. Are you a friend of Lee's?"

In what Sandra often humorously thought of as being the 'lawyer's stance', Jack's face though friendly, instantly became unreadable. Choosing his words carefully, he placed his hands in his trouser pockets. "I wouldn't call us friends, but we've run into one another several times." Half-turning towards Sandra he added, "Most recently this weekend, didn't we, Sandra?"

As a response, Sandra noisily stirred her iced tea.

Oblivious to the creeping tension between the two, Maggie commented. "You know, this is a small world."

Still remaining in his deceptively relaxed stance, hands in pockets, Jack refocused on Maggie, "Hmm...how so?"

"Well, I was just telling Sandra that your lunch date is one of Lee's lost loves from his youth. In fact, he took Darlene to her senior prom."

At this comment, Sandra with smiling blankness, stared across the table at Maggie. "Great, you ninny, just what he wants to hear!"

If Jack was surprised or vexed by this bit of newfound information, Sandra couldn't tell, for he continued smiling. "Well, what do you know. I'm going to have to let Darlene know that you're here. Here she comes now."

As the woman made her way across the courtyard with cat like grace, heads of many of the men turned in her direction. Maggie leaned over towards her friend and murmured through clenched teeth, "I would give anything to see those spiked little heels of hers catch hold to one of those bricks." Squeezing her friend's arm, Sandra nudged her to hush.

"Darlin', I didn't know that you knew Maggie," the woman purred as she looped what Sandra humorously thought of as a "branch of an arm" through Jack's.

With a teasing wink in Maggie's direction, he smiled. "It's been years since we've last seen one another. I almost didn't recognize her."

Feigning an air of friendliness, Darlene remarked in a saccharin voice, "Maggie, I'm surprised to see you out. I thought that most of your time these days was spent home with hubby and the kids."

Maggie, with obvious disdain, followed the woman's lead. "You know, Darlene, David does allow me time away for good behavior. But I'm the one surprised. I thought you only came out at night."

With a look of amusement, Jack interrupted the two women. "Darlene, I would like to introduce a...a friend of mine, Sandra."

As she possessively caressed Jack's arm, Darlene brushed Sandra off with a cursory smile and asked Jack if he was ready to leave.

Maintaining the same blank expression, Sandra murmured sarcastically, "It was nice meeting you also."

With a reproving raise of the brow, Jack silently warned Sandra that he didn't approve of the comment or her attitude. Patting his date's hand, he suggested that she wait by the bar while he had a "word" with Sandra. Turning to leave, Darlene flashed Sandra an extraordinarily wicked smile.

Before giving Jack a chance to speak, Sandra commented. "Really Jack, she hardly seems your type."

Searching her face, Jack, with controlled quietness asked, "And exactly who is my type, Sandra?"

As their eyes locked, she discerned a bit of weariness in the depths of his warm, gentle eyes. His question, demanded an answer that she was not yet ready to give.

As if reading her mind, Jack's aloof demeanor returned. "Sandra, I was meaning to call this morning, but something important came up. I..."

As he spoke, she, anticipating an apology of some sort, couldn't help noticing his choice of words. With scorn very apparent in her voice, she interrupted. "I wonder who that something was."

Offering little more than a grimace, Jack continued. "...I wanted to remind you that I promised Jesse that I'd take him to softball practice after school."

After receiving no further comment from Sandra, he continued in a tone that suggested that she'd not only forgotten, but that somehow was derelict in her duties as a mother.

"You do know that Jesse has practice at four p.m. don't you?"

With apparent irritation, Sandra retorted, "I remember the children's schedule just as well as you." As she looked into his darkened eyes, she momentarily caught her breath. Gone was his usual gentleness, and its place was an emotion that she took for disdain.

"Then I'll pick up the children as usual." Jack's tone brooked no room for argument. "Maggie, I hope that I have the pleasure of seeing you again soon."

"Don't worry, you will," Maggie promised. Just as he was about to leave, she caught his arm. "Say Jack, you wouldn't have a business card would you?" With a sly wink, she continued, "An honest attorney is hard to come by, especially one who is as attractive as you."

Jack, with his FBI training, missed very little. He understood Maggie's intentions and casually handed her a card. "Why Margaret, if I didn't know better, I would say that you are trying to pick me up," he teased. "Don't hesitate to give me a call, both my office and cell number are on the card."

"Thanks, I'll be sure to keep your number handy. In fact, I may even have a connection that you may find to be useful."

He knew that the "useful connection" wasn't about business, but something much more personal in nature. "Well Maggie, thank you, I look forward to your call."

Feeling very much spurned, Sandra focused her attention on the luke warm glass of tea. Sure that it would taste as flat as she now felt, she pushed the glass away.

Maggie, eager to learn the details that led up to the non-too friendly tête-à-tête between Sandra and Jack, asked a question whose answer she was certain she already possessed. "So, what's going on between you and Jack?"

With a shrug, Sandra murmured, "You'll have to ask

him."

"How could I have forgotten how handsome Jack was? All this time, I've sort of pictured him as this bespectacled pudgy little homebody sort."

"I don't know, I guess I can ask myself the same question. Over the years, I've just gotten use to thinking of him as simply being 'Jack'." Feeling very close to tears, she fiddled with her napkin. "Is it okay if we change the subject?"

"Sure," Maggie smiled mischievously. "In fact, I want to ask you if you think that you could get your mom to baby-sit the kids over a weekend sometime during the next few weeks."

"Probably...why?"

"Well, my birthday is coming up soon and I thought that it might be fun to celebrate out at the house. You're a hit with Ms. Lavania and Alphonse, and Lee. Plus I thought it would be nice to have a relaxing 'adult week-end'. We're leaving our kids with David's folks."

Although happy that her friend had moved on to a different topic, Sandra was far from being in the mood to discuss any future plans involving Lee. "It sounds like fun, but before I say yes, you have to promise that you're not trying to play Little Miss Matchmaker again."

"Promise? I don't have to. You seem to be doing just fine on your own."

"Meaning?"

"Oh, nothing." Maggie smiled as she glanced in the direction that Jack had just left.

Chapter Sixteen

Well, so much for luck," Sandra ruefully thought as she drove towards her house. Gripping the steering wheel, she shook her head as she recalled how she started the day naively promising herself not to dwell on either Lee or Jack.

As she approached the foot of her driveway, she spotted Jack's car and prepared herself for his cool aloofness. After their disastrous meeting at lunch, it was obvious that he no longer had feelings for her, romantically or otherwise. It would now be impossible for them to return to the same easy relationship that they once shared. In fact, common sense told her that it would only be a matter of time before he started breaking ties with the kids.

Promising herself that she would not get emotional and let Jack see her cry, she pulled up alongside his sedan and took a few moments to pull herself together.

Jesse and Whitney, running up to exuberantly greet her, gave her a much-needed hug. Whitney, holding on to her mother's arm begged, "Mommy, Mommy did you bring me anything?"

Not giving his mother a chance to answer, Jesse urgently interrupted, "Hey Mom, guess what, I made three runs."

"All right you two," she chuckled as she listened to her son give a play by play of his softball practice, "give me a chance to get in the house." Smiling at the children's gibbering, she prayed that Jack's mood would be just as pleasant.

Standing at the screen door, Jack waited. Not smiling, nor speaking, he simply stood holding the door open as he had done so often in the past. As she walked up the steps, she noticed for the first time how comforting it felt to see him standing there. His presence seemed so natural.

"See you made it home," Jack flatly commented.

As she brushed past him, she felt an incredible urge to lay her head on his chest and feel the strength of his protective arms about her. As she looked up into his darkened eyes, she felt her heart self-consciously race. "Jack...thank you. You know...I'm sure the kids appreciate all that you..."

Patting Whitney's head, Jack warmly looked down at the beaming child and winked, "Oh, I know they appreciate me. There's never been any doubt." He reached down, gave the young girl a kiss goodbye, and called out to Jesse that he was leaving.

"Uncle Jack, you're not staying for dinner?" Jesse, surprised, looked over at his mom. Without giving him a chance to reply, Sandra looked directly into her dear friend's face, and in a voice tinged with sadness, answered the child's question. "Your uncle's a busy man. He has a life outside of us, you know."

Jack, perused her eyes as, he allowed the wall o rise further between them.

Oblivious of the pair's pain, Jesse shrugged with childlike acceptance, and moved on to another topic. "Hey Mom, Uncle Jack said that he'll take us to the zoo on Saturday, that is, if it's all right with you. So can he?"

Whitney jumped up and down and pleaded, "So can he? Please Mommy, Mommy please?"

Still looking into Jack's face, she tentatively answered, "Um...we'll see, we may already have other plans. But we'll talk about it a little later." Looking down at the children, she gave them a quick kiss on the forehead, "Now run along. I'll be up in a minute."

As the kids headed off to their rooms, she nervously began picking up several mislaid toys, "Jack, it's probably best that you don't make plans with the kids until you first clear them with me. Besides, I would hate to see them disappointed."

Angered by her insinuation that he would callously hurt the kids, he narrowed his eyes as he shoved his hands in his pockets. In a very level but deceptively calm tone, he took exception to her request.

"Let's get our facts together here. A: I didn't make plans with the children. We drove past a billboard and they asked me to take them to the zoo. I in turn reminded them that they had to clear it with you first. And B: I had assumed that you would be adult enough to keep the kids out of whatever crap that might be going on between us. Now, if you're not capable of doing that, then I am extremely disappointed in you, Sandra."

Feeling ashamed for even thinking that Jack would hurt the kids, she was prepared to offer an apology. But as he continued, she felt her temper flare. She could not believe that he dared to speak to her in such a fashion. With all of the emotions that were raging inside, she responded with incredulity. "Disappointed in me? Ha! Look at who's calling the kettle black."

Holding her gaze, Jack with great restraint remarked, "I take it that you're looking for some sort of apology from me for the other morning?"

Sandra, arms folded protectively against her chest, stood wordlessly as he continued. In a very flat and insincere tone, he offered the words that she had so hoped would set everything right.

"Well, I apologize for any hurt that I may have caused you, Sandra." After a pregnant pause he quietly demanded, "But just who are you angry with? Me, for reminding you how I feel, or are you angry with yourself for once again falling for the smooth, fast-talker? I would have thought that after Robert, you would have learned your lesson. I just don't get you. What's so difficult about giving yourself to someone who sincerely loves you?"

In a voice hushed by the knowledge that the children were right upstairs, Sandra turned her back and hissed, "How dare you. I gave myself to you once...remember? And look what good it did me." Unable to continue without the well of tears spilling over, and still determined not to let him see her cry, she squared her shoulders. "I simply refuse to talk about this. Now would you please leave?"

Walking around to face her, Jack, his weariness obvious, looked deep into her large brown eyes, and noticed the tears that threatened to fall. After running his fingers slowly through the waves of her loose dark curls, he allowed his hand to rest on her shoulder. In a dull and troubled voice, he murmured, "Sandra, you know how to reach me when you're ready to talk. I'll pick up the kids Saturday afternoon around two."

With her head in her hands, she stood silent and listened to the door softly close.

"Damn that woman," Jack muttered as he walked across the kitchen to the refrigerator. Pulling the door open, he reached in and grabbed a cold bottle of spring water and headed for the spare bedroom that he had set up as an exercise room.

Hoping that an hour of intense physical activity would clear his head, he began his warm up routine with a series of stretches. In between reps of sit-ups and the stationary bike, he could think of little else but Sandra and the day's events.

Of all the days to run into Darlene, why today? What had started out to be a quick lunch after a morning in court, had turned into an afternoon fiasco. It was as if Fate herself were sitting and vigilantly waiting for the perfect opportunity to squash any chance that he had to resurrect his relationship with Sandra.

As he left the Orleans Parish Court Building, he had run into Darlene Lafleur, a former client. She just happened to be in the building taking care of a parking ticket when she spied him. In fact, it was her suggestion that the two of them go out to lunch. As he recalled their chance meeting, he had to admit that it took little prodding to accept her invitation. In fact, if he were to be totally honest, his male ego was immensely flattered by her attentions. On second thought, maybe their chance meeting was a good thing. Perhaps now Sandra realized that he was not just sitting around pining away.

Off the bike, he wiped his brow with a towel and draped it behind his neck. As he slowly drank from the water bottle, he replayed their last conversation. Common sense told him that he had long blown any chances of marrying her. She seemed hardly fazed by the fact that he was dining out with a beautiful woman. If anything, she appeared annoyed that he interrupted her conversation with Lee's sister, Maggie. Heading out of the room to shower, he admonished himself to move on, as Sandra had, and turn his attention elsewhere. He had hung around in the shadows far too long.

As he walked into the master bedroom towards the bath, he passed the mirror where he had placed Whitney's drawing. Stopping short, he let out an oath and grabbed the phone from the nightstand. With vengeance, he punched in several numbers.

"Hi beautiful, Jack..."

Immediately recognizing the voice, the woman let out

a friendly chuckle as she interrupted, "...Jack! You don't need to tell me who you are, I would know that sexy voice of yours anywhere. What can I do for you?"

"Meet me for lunch tomorrow."

"Tell me the time and place."

"Great, let's see...Adelaide's at 11:30."

"I'll be there," and with a warm good-bye she rang off.

Jack looked into the dancing eyes of the elegantly dressed woman seated across from him. Remembering Adelaide's as being one of her favorite haunts, he had purposely chosen the grand old tearoom. As he listened to her witty critique of a book that she had recently read, he couldn't help appreciating how beautifully she complemented the restaurant's 19th century continental decor.

Maureen, wearing a stylish lilac silk dress, fitted in elegantly with the tearoom's rose brocade walls, muted lighting, crisply starched table linens, and sparkling Austrian crystal. After the waiter served their meal of grilled shrimp and tasso pasta, his date set her wine glass to one side and softly commented, "Jack, I know you didn't invite me to lunch just so you could listen to a literary review. You could've picked up a copy of the *Picayune*." Raising a knowing brow, she quipped, "I'm going to save us some time here, and take a mad stab in the dark...you're madly in love with my daughter and need my help."

Letting out a hearty laugh, he leaned back, "Maureen, you always did know how to get right to the point."

"Jack, I've known you for a very long time. Besides, I don't need to be a rocket scientist to figure out that you care deeply for my daughter. You love her...and my two grandbabies."

As Maureen spoke, Jack became instantly subdued. Picking imaginary lint off the table, he cast his glance downwards as he searched for the right words to express his feelings. When he looked up, gone was his easy smile, and in its stead was sober seriousness. "Maureen, you're right. I am in love with your daughter, and your two grandbabies. I have been in love with Sandra ever since..."

"...Ever since well before she married Robert," finished Maureen.

Jack, thrown by her remark, was at a lost for words.

Flashing an unabashed smile, the woman continued, "Oh, I know all about you, Jack Thibodeaux."

Not quite sure what she meant, he became very still as he wondered if she was referring to the run-in that he had with Sandra the previous weekend. As he looked across at the woman, her smile, though friendly, now seemed a bit reserved. Quickly searching his memory, he wondered if Sandra had confided anything else.

Maureen chose her words deliberately. Searched his face and finally met his eyes. "You are a very kind and gentle man, Jack Thibodeaux. These days, there aren't very many..." After interrupting her own words with a short chuckle, the older woman corrected herself. "What am I talking about? There never were very many kind and gentle men. I guess it has never been a popular notion. That's why, simply because of the nature of people, especially women, the gentle ones often get overlooked."

After taking a sip from her wine glass, she continued, "Jack, I'm telling you this because I want you to hang on in there with Sandra. You possess many of the qualities that make for a fine husband. You're honorable, responsible, dependable, and you've been taught how to love."

Surprised and somewhat embarrassed by the

woman's words, Jack attempted to lighten the mood. "Well Maureen, if I'm so perfect, then why am I having such a hard time with your daughter?"

"Remember, I only said that I knew all about you! Only Sandra knows the real answer as to what is holding her back." Momentarily pausing, she gave Jack a wink. "Anyway, who says you're perfect?"

With a look of mock hurt, he responded, "Definitely not Sandra."

"So how can I help?"

Pushing his plate to one side, Jack placed both elbows on the table, leaned forward as he cupped the palms of his hands together. "First, listen to my idea. I don't want to get you caught in the middle of anything, so if you don't agree with what I am about to ask, simply tell me."

"Fair enough, shoot."

"I want some time to 'court' Sandra, away from the kids, without pressure. It has been ten years since I've had a chance to formally take her out on a date. So, I was hoping you could take Whitney and Jesse on a sort of vacation for a couple of weeks, my treat of course. Their summer break begins in two weeks, and ..." He stopped searching for the right words, "...it'll keep them from out of the midst of things. Then if Sandra and I don't get together, my relationship with them won't be jeopardized."

Maureen with a mischievous glint, sat back in he chair and asked, "So where did you have in mind, and for how long?"

Flashing a conspiratorial smile, he offered, "Well, it's up to you of course, but I thought perhaps Disney World. You could spend a whole week there easily, and I understand that you have a sister who lives in the Orlando area. And I know that Robert's mother has been bugging Sandra to send the kids down "

After a few moments of thoughtful silence, Maureen reworked a portion of Jack's plan aloud. "I'll tell you what. I usually spend a month every summer with my sister. And I have mentioned to Sandra that I wanted to take the kids along this year. I'm pretty sure that I can get her to agree. She'll jump at the chance not to have to visit Dorthea. Every summer, Sandra's in such a quandary as to what to do with the kids. We could still visit Disney World, but we could do it in several small jaunts from Helen's house. That way I won't feel as if I'm totally deceiving Sandra, and she won't be able to accuse you of sneaking behind her back."

As he listened to Maureen's idea, Jack nodded. "Great, the more honest we can be about this, the better. In fact, why don't you casually mention to Sandra that you confided in me your hopes of taking the kids to Florida this summer. And, that as a gift to the kids, I convinced you to allow me to pay for the air fare and the tickets to Disney World."

With a laugh, Maureen reached across the table and took Jack's hand and gave it a firm squeeze. "I think that it'll work. Now Jack, you have to promise me that you'll relax, not push too hard, and just let nature take its course. Everything will work out as it should."

Returning her smile, he sighed, "I hope so. If things don't work out this time around, they never will."

Chapter Seventeen

"Mother, you did what?" Sandra demanded incredulously. "I don't need Jack to pay for the kids' plane tickets. Besides, aren't we getting a little ahead of ourselves? You only mentioned taking the kids with you to Florida a little while ago. I didn't know that we had agreed on anything...no, no, I don't mind them being with you...yes, I know that we juggle the kids' schedule every summer...yes, I know that Disney World is expensive..., you're right, it was very thoughtful of Jack...but, a month!"

Just as she was about to offer another objection, the overhead bell clapped. "Listen Mom, I have a customer. Yes, we'll talk about it later...Bye."

"Hey beautiful!"

"Lee! Despite her resolve to play it nonchalant where he was concerned, her face broke out in an uncontrollable smile.

In response, he rounded the counter and gave her a very friendly kiss hello.

Truly offended by his familiarity, Sandra pulled away. "Aren't you being presumptuous? Where do you get the gall?"

Nonplussed, he raised his hands in surrender and backed off. "Forgive me. I misread things, it's just that you seemed happy to see me."

"What you saw was a look surprise. You were the last person that I expected to see today."

"Oh, why is that?" After it was clear that Sandra wasn't going to answer, he glanced around the empty shop and purposely made a remark that he was sure would elicit a response. "Business seems slow."

"Business is doing quite well, thank you."

Amused by the success of his strategy, Lee watched as she moved about the shop. "It's amazing, even when you're ticked off, you're beautiful. "

Well familiar with his cavalier 'game', she snapped. "I guess that this is where I'm suppose to say thank you and not what I'm really thinking." Like go away.

As if reading her mind, he remained unflappable and grinned. "I'm not going to go away, you know." After several more attempts to draw her into a conversation, he leaned against the wrap stand, folded his arms and with a quirk of his brow, began a humorous soliloquy. "Am I up to a game of 21 questions? Sure I am. I love games. Besides, what else do I have to do with my time?

Question #1: Is she angry with me because I dropped in without calling first? Naw, I've done this before and she's never seemed to mind. Question #2: Is she angry with me because I sent her the rocker? Nope, that can't be it either. After all, she sent me a pretty little thank you note, complete with a gold seal and everything. Question #3..."

Interrupting with her hands on her hips, eyebrows nettled and mouth twisted, Sandra finally turned and gibed, "Well, a note was the least I could do."

"Ah, I am sensing that she's given me a clue." Furrowing his brow, he walked over to where she was working and playfully motioned his hands as if picking up on some sort of mystical aura. "A note was the least I could do...I've got it. Could it be that you are angry about my leaving a note on last Saturday?"

Despite all of her attempts at maintaining a surly front, she found herself smiling.

"It seems to get back in your good graces, I owe you some sort of explanation, and perhaps an apology."

"It would be nice."

"Ok, here goes. In my sleep, you came to me as a beautiful angel offering a truly God-inspired idea for a piece that's been giving me problems. Anxious to do you proud, I left without waking you." Offering his hand, he humbly lowered his head and appealed for her under-standing, "So what do you say, are we still friends?"

Fully aware that she was being suckered hook, line and sinker by his creatively manufactured lie, she accepted his hand. "Considering how I am a beautiful angel, do I have any other choice?"

Leaning over with the hopes of planting a kiss on her sexy lips, he chuckled as she purposely turned her back and continued with her work.

"Lee, just why are you here?"

Finding great amusement in her prim response, he playfully took her in his arms and gently spun her around. "I don't know, maybe to catch a glimpse of that lovely smile of yours, maybe for a kiss, maybe to ask you out to dinner."

For a split heart-stopping second, she could have sworn that Robert was standing before her. Feeling an uneasy chill, she once again moved away, but this time she lengthened the distance between them. "You know, you're all charm."

In a very self-deprecating manner, he said, "You think that I'm very self-centered, don't you?"

As she took in his form in the darkening shadows of the late afternoon, she answered, "No, not self-centered, but self-absorbed. It sounds a bit kinder."

Not the least offended, he filled the store with laugh-ter. "Mrs. Petain, you know me pretty well, don't you? Not only are you beautiful, but as I said the other night, you are very discerning." Walking over to where she stood, he once again extended his dinner invitation, but this time with a note of genuine sincerity.

Despite not wanting to come across as playing "hard to get," she shook her head. "I wish I could say yes, but I have the kids to consider..."

"If you can't ditch them, bring them; really, it's not a problem," he suggested. "They have a delight for a mom, so I'm sure that they can't be too bad," he added with a sincere twinkle.

"It's not that simple. After I pick them up from my mom's, I need to drop Whitney off at the rec center for her gymnastics class and run Jesse over to the library to pick up a book for a class project. Then there's that little question of checking homework and baths. Besides, I don't usually introduce the kids to my...dates."

Lee, amazed at her schedule, raised his brow, stepped back and eloquently responded with a respectful, "Oh!"

Not wanting him to feel rebuffed, she clarified her reasoning. "The children are still young, and I'm just afraid that it could be very confusing for them to see me about with assorted men." Allowing a meaningful pause to fall, she continued, "Besides, I don't think that it is wise for them to get attached to someone who might not...um...stay around."

"I tell you, skip out on a woman, and she holds it against you for life."

"Lee!"

"Sandra, I am only teasing. I do understand. In fact, I respect your reasoning. Everything that you have said makes perfect sense. But I've picked up that things still aren't quite settled between us regarding Saturday morning. So, let me make amends and prove that there was no slight intended."

"Slight?"

That was not the word that she would have chosen to describe his actions. She would have used 'insensitive' perhaps, but not 'slight'. Plus his apology, if she could call his words an apology, made no mention as to why he hadn't called."

Undeterred by her raised brow, he continued, "That's right, for lack of a better word, slight. I know that it is customary for a man to stick around the next morning after he's spent the night with a beautiful, and yes, special woman. I have no excuse except to say that I was self-absorbed."

Encouraged by the evidence of a smile, he hurriedly continued, "Since you can't make it this evening, how about dinner tomorrow, or should we be daring and try a Friday evening again?"

As she thought over his request, she reminded herself that he did come all the way over to the shop when he could've just as easily called. Besides, for what it was worth, he did seem sincere. Before giving herself the opportunity to change her mind, she accepted his invitation.

Friday night found Sandra sitting in the resplendently magical setting of the very elegant and internationally renowned "Sazerac." Looking across the grand dining room, she caught sight of her reflection in one of the many oversized mirrors. Grateful that she had wisely listened to her intuition and worn one of her favorites, a simple sophisticated sleeveless black crepe cocktail dress, she nervously checked the clasp of one of the diamond drop earrings that she had borrowed from her mother.

Lee casually draped an arm around the back of her

chair. Leaning in close, he caressed her shoulders as he whispered a compliment, "With you in that dress, I'm going to have to keep you close this evening. You look very nice." And indeed she did. The little black dress, with its deep V-cut back and fitted form, was an alluring departure from her usual habit. Its above-the- knee length showed off her shapely legs to their full advantage.

Feeling very flattered, she settled back against his arm.

While he ordered the meal, she took in the restaurant's gilded embellishments, luminous lighting, and fine lace. On dove-gray striped walls hung oil portraits of Louisiana's societe. Taking a sip of her cocktail, she tried to hide a grimace. Lee had urged her to try the bar's namesake, the Sazerac, a concoction of bourbon, bitters and ersatz absinthe, when she displayed curiosity in the drink. She should have stuck with her simple glass of white wine and passed on the suggestion.

"I gather that you don't like your drink," her dinner date teased.

Twitching her nose as she softly laughed, Sandra looked up into his face. "Is it that obvious?"

Without a word, Lee, with urbane suaveness, motioned to the sommelier. Promptly the gentleman walked over and Lee, with smooth practice, ordered a bottle of Kistler Chardonnay 1992.

Once again free to return his attention to his date, he asked, "What are you thinking about?"

"You"

"Me?," Lee softly chuckled as he continued to visually caress his companion's face. "Are they good thoughts or bad?"

"Neither...I was just noticing how comfortably you fit into all of this...this...," searching for the right phrase, she slowly perused her surroundings, "...this rather lavish scheme."

With a good-natured smirk, he responded, "Well, once again I ask, is that good or bad?"

Coyly, she shrugged her shoulders as she continued to search his face, "I haven't decided yet." And in truth, she hadn't. Lee was quite easily most women's dream. He was charming, wealthy, and when he wanted to be, very attentive. Tonight, dressed in a custom-made navy suit, he looked as handsome as ever.

After enjoying their dinner and a bit of light conversation, she found herself being whisked over to Poydras Street and the river—the jazz club home of the Dixieland maestro, Pete Fountain. The very posh and plush late night hangout was not only packed, but a line of fans hoping to get in had formed outside the club. Lee, recognized by the maitre d', was promptly admitted. As the couple was shown to their table, Sandra noticed how he casually patted several backs and was familiarly greeted by quite a few friends. It was obvious that this man whom she had initially been led to believe was a simple unconventional artist and college professor, was quite popular with New Orleans' haut monde.

The evening fast became quite intoxicating. Within minutes of being seated, Lee, after very charmingly introducing her to a small group of 'friends', several of whom she recognized from the *Picayune*'s society column, was hailed by Mr. Pete Fountain.

Immediately after greeting the famed musician, Lee wrapped his arm around Sandra's waist and introduced her as his very 'special friend'. Extending a sincere smile, the man graciously accepted her compliment that she looked forward to hearing his set. As he spoke to Lee, she found herself thinking how great it would be to get his autograph for Jack's jazz collection. Wondering how to make her request without sounding too gauche, she heard herself blurt, "Mr. Fountain, uh...do you think that perhaps I could get your autograph?" With a friendly smile, the musician reached for a cocktail napkin and quickly signed his name. "How could I turn down a beautiful lady?" Taking her hand into his, he said his good-byes and wished them a lovely evening.

When she glanced over in Lee's direction, she noticed a humorous grin, "Are you laughing at me?"

"No, no. You're just so refreshing to be around," Lee sincerely complimented as he beckoned to a harried waitress.

Raising her voice above the din, she teased, "Now it's my turn. Is that good or bad?"

As a response, he gave her an unexpected kiss on the lips, "That's good." And with a squeeze of the arm, he turned and said hellos to another passing group of acquaintances.

And so the evening went. Sandra soon realized that most of the club's patrons were not jazz aficionados, but guests who either wished to be seen or to people watch. After several hours, she found herself occasionally glancing at her watch and wondered when Lee would tire and suggest that they leave.

Not that she wasn't enjoying herself, but she was ready for a bit of intimate conversation. Even though he had gone out of his way to introduce her to his startling array of friends, she felt somewhat disappointed that they had not spent more time together, alone. She would have much preferred dinner at a quiet little bistro, a walk along the riverfront or a romantic ride across the Mississippi on the ferry, maybe ending with coffee and dessert at an intimate river cafe.

As if on cue, he turned in her direction and asked, "Are you enjoying yourself?"

Evading his question, she slowly replied with a smile, "You must be on the "A" list for many a party."

"The "A" list?" He threw his head back and laughed.

"You work the room quite well, you know. I've never seen anything quite like it. They come to you! This evening has been a wonderful study of human nature."

"A study of human nature?"

"Well, this room is filled with many people who I am sure are just as witty, talented and good looking as you, but they literally flock over here to be seen with the master artisan and college professor, Lee Chienier. Why is that?" Answering her own question, she continued, "Because you act as though you could care less if you're recognized or noticed. But I think that you do. Why else would we be here?"

"And we couldn't be here because I want to show you a good time?"

"No, you have no idea whether I like jazz or not."

Before Lee could respond, she inwardly flinched at the sound of an approaching familiar voice. "Lee...Lee darling, Carling said that you were here. We missed you last week at the Pitre's. Darling, you've met Frank haven't you?"

After rising to give Aileen a hug and quick kiss, Lee shook the man's hand. In her rather affected style, Aileen continued talking without missing a beat, "...but I'm not sure if you know Walker. " Once again, Lee shook hands.

As Sandra expected, Aileen ignored her throughout the round of introductions. Lee, quickly realizing the glaring oversight, introduced Sandra to his agent's somewhat bohemian coterie.

While the group stood and conversed, Aileen summarily turned her back on Sandra, who was still seated, thereby shutting her out of the group's conversation. Possessively grabbing hold of Lee's arm, Aileen gushed, "Lee, I'm having a little gathering over at my place after Pete's last set. Why don't you drop by?"

Patting her hand, he politely declined, "Thank you dear, but Sandra and I have..."

Before he could finish, Aileen turned in Sandra's direction and flashed a less than sincere smile. "Why little Sandra is invited as well, or better yet, drop by after you've taken her home."

As if Sandra had a fatal condition, the spiteful woman reached over and patted her hand. "Dear, I know you can't stay out too late. Lee mentioned that you have two children."

Lee, well aware of the tension between the two women, gave Aileen a brotherly embrace and graciously agreed to keep her invitation in mind.

Soon after the group's departure, Sandra suggested that they too leave. "Listen, I don't mean to be a wet blanket, but it is well after midnight and after you drop me off at the house, I still need to run out to mother's to pick up the kids."

"Well...it's only 12:30," he frowned.

"Exactly my point!"

If she had hoped that the ride home would provide an opportunity for her to get to know her dinner date a bit better, she was disappointed. Watching him fiddle with the radio, she realized that he was still on the high that the club had brought about and raring to get over to the other party, while she could only think of getting to sleep so that she could deal with the shop and the children's Saturday activities.

When they reached her driveway, Lee walked her to the van. As she turned to thank him for a lovely evening, he gathered her in his arms and held her chin gently in the palm of his hand. Momentarily their eyes locked, then he lowered his eyes and kissed her slow and thoroughly.

His lips coaxed hers open as she gripped his arm. It would have been so easy to give in to his passion, but with an abrupt sigh, she pulled away. Still holding tightly to his sleeve, she whispered, "Lee...I..."

Placing a finger to her lips, he silenced her with a

light kiss on the forehead and released her from his embrace. "Sandra, there is no need to explain. I know that you weren't too pleased with our conversation on our ride back over here. It's just that my week gets long and I use the weekend to relax." Searching her face once again, he kissed her lightly on the forehead. "I hope that you had a nice time?"

Quickly acknowledging that she had, she nodded. "Oh, the evening was wonderful. Thank you for dinner...and the show afterwards. Tonight was my first visit to Fountain's."

Smiling, he relaxed against the van. "Well, I'm glad that I was the one to take you. Where are you going to put your autograph?"

She had completely forgotten about the cocktail napkin and quickly opened her purse when he mentioned it. Spying the napkin carefully tucked into an inside pocket, she quietly smiled. "Oh, the autograph isn't for me. Jack is a real lover of jazz, and I thought that he might get a kick out of having Pete Fountain's autograph."

With a raised brow, he fingered the keys in his jacket pocket, "Once again, I take you out and Jack gets the reward."

Not quite knowing how to respond to his statement, she felt her face grow hot. "Lee...I..."

Patting her shoulders, he interrupted with a short laugh. "Serves me right. Listen, it is getting late and we both have a drive ahead of us. I'll give you a call in a day or two." And with a quick kiss, he was gone.

On the drive over to her mother's, she decided that it was far too late to bundle the kids back home. Besides, the thought of returning to an empty house was not very appealing, so she decided to spend the night. When she arrived at the condo, she started to ring the bell, but thought better of the idea in fear of waking the kids. Instead, she took out her key ring and opened the lock with the spare she carried in her purse.

"Mommy!" Whitney greeted with a squeal as Sandra entered the living room.

Returning her daughter's excited greeting, she bent down and gave her a loving hug and kiss. "Hey baby cakes, you're still up? Where are Grandma and Jesse?"

"They're in the back. Grandma made him take a bath, then he fell asleep. Guess what we did tonight?" Not waiting for her mother to respond, Whitney chattered on. "Uncle Jack came by and took us on a ride down to Lafourche Parish. He took us for a walk along the swamp and he killed a snake. And guess what else? We saw a dead alligator and everything."

"A dead alligator?" Not knowing what to make of her daughter's tale, she listened as the young girl continued.

"Yeah, Uncle Jack's cousin showed us one that he killed just this morning. And guess what else? His cousin's wife, I think her name was Gla...Gl...Gladiolus or something, well she gave us a giant hunk of chocolate cake." With her eyes widening, Whitney spread her arms out wide to emphasize the size.

"Why would Jack take you out to Lafourche Parish? That's over a hour away?" Although she would trust Jack with her life, she was more than just a little curious.

Giggling, Whitney explained, "He told Grandma that he had to drop off some legal papers. We got to stay up as late as you, Mommy."

"Sandra! I didn't hear you come in."

"Hi Mom."

Whitney was just telling me about you all's little outing," Sandra commented with obvious disapproval. "Whitney said that it had something to do with Jack's cousin and some papers?"

Dumbfounded by her daughter's reaction, Maureen explained, "It was a perfect evening for a drive, and I didn't see any harm. Actually, I thought that it was quite nice of him to include us in his plans. He called over here looking for you, and when he found out that I was baby-sitting, he suggested that we ride out with him to his cousin's. What's the big deal?"

"Mother...," Sandra interrupted with more than just a hint of exasperation. Casting a glance at Whitney's observant little face, she cleared her throat and gave her mom a meaningful nod.

"I just made up her bed. I told the children that the three of you would probably be spending the night.

Biting her lips, Sandra stood silent.

As Maureen took her granddaughter's hand, she noted Sandra's agitated expression. "Whitney, tell your mommy good night." After the two exchanged kisses and hugs, the little girl followed her grandmother into the bed-room.

Still angry, Sandra dropped onto the overstuffed sofa, kicked off her shoes and propped her feet on the coffee table. Looking around her mother's stylishly decorated condo, it struck her that her mom had made a complete-ly new life for herself since her dad's death. Gone were the homey furnishings that she had grown up with. In their place were bold colors, pickled furniture and abstract art.

What a night. Too fatigued to think, she closed her eyes and laid her head back on one the numerous multi-colored pillows that dressed the sofa. Almost on the brink of falling asleep, she was entirely oblivious to the silent figure that had entered the room.

"Sandy?" Jack whispered as he stared down at her still form. Taking in her beautiful face, he found himself remembering the first time they had...

Startled, Sandra called his name. "Jack!" For a moment, she thought that she was lost in one of her dreams that had become all too frequent.

As he spoke, his previously loving expression

became unreadable, "I came over earlier..."

"Yes, Whitney told me." Rising, she ran a tired hand through her mass of curls. With unmistaken edginess she continued, "Jack, I thought that we agreed that you would clear all plans with me first?"

Steadily holding her gaze, he restrained his anger and answered the accusation. "I would have if you were home. In fact, I had rather hoped that all of us could take the drive. Besides, why should the kids be punished just because their mother is off...off...painting the town red."

"For your information, I wasn't painting the town red," Sandra retaliated. "But whether I was or not, that still didn't give you permission to abscond with my children."

With an abrupt laugh, he retorted, "Abscond? Well, I suppose that I absconded with your mother as well?"

Overhearing the argument taking place in her living room, Maureen entered with a chuckle, "No dear, I went on my own free will."

"Mother! Don't encourage him," snapped Sandra. "Jack knows perfectly well that what he did was wrong."

"Sandra, please! After all, he did have my permission. And since the children were left in my charge, and I did go along..." Maureen shrugged as she sweetly smiled at Sandra.

"Mother! You aren't helping matters."

With a shrug, Maureen purposely chose to sit in the club chair opposite Sandra, leaving the sofa as the only natural place for Jack to sit.

More than a little miffed at her mother's defense of Jack, Sandra childishly rose just as Jack sat next to her. "Mother, I should be leaving. It's late and we've kept you up far too long."

"Don't be silly! Jesse has taken his bath and is in the bed sleep, Whitney's tucked in...it just wouldn't make sense to leave," reasoned Maureen.

"Besides, it's too late for you to be out anyway. It

seems to me that Lee would've insisted on dropping you off," added Jack.

Ignoring Jack's two-cent dig, Sandra knew that her mother's point was valid.

"I suppose you're right. The kids have already been kept up way past their bedtime." Angrily turning towards Jack as she finished the last sentence, she made it clear that she placed blame squarely on his shoulders.

"Good, now that that's settled, come over here and sit down," coaxed Maureen. "We need to talk about our summer plans."

With her arms crossed, Sandra, fatigue apparent, sighed, "Do we have to talk about this right now?"

In a voice far too chipper for two in the morning, Maureen remarked, "Why not? We're all here. Besides, if I'm going to get halfway decent airline rates, I'm going to have to make reservations in the next day or two."

Unable to deny the truth in her mother's statement, Sandra grudgingly turned towards Jack. "Mom told me of your generous offer to buy the tickets for the kids. Thanks, but..."

"But I would like to do it," quietly finished Jack. "If it makes you feel better about accepting the tickets, don't look at it as a gift to you, but as something that I would like to do for Whitney and Jesse, as well as for your mother."

Looking in his face, she was convinced of the sincerity of his offer, and knew that it was presented with genuine love.

Maureen in a very motherly tone nudged, "Sandra, I think that his offer is very sweet and generous...and very practical. Just think about it. This way you will be able to fly in for a few days, maybe take in Disney World with the kids. I know every summer you feel guilty about not spending more time with them."

Maureen wisely spoke no more of Jack's offer, and

instead announced that she was going to bed. After giving them each a kiss, she said her good nights and affectionately patted Jack's shoulder as she left the room.

After making sure that her mother was no longer in hearing range, Sandra turned towards Jack. "So how long have you and mother been planning this?"

With total innocence, he queried, "Planning what?" Continuing his innocent act, he explained, "It just came up in passing. You look pretty."

Feeling far from pretty, Sandra gave him a tired smile and murmured thanks. Aware of the temporary truce between them, she reached for her purse and dug out the cocktail napkin. In a very thin voice, she offered the autographed souvenir as she explained, "Um...I thought that you might like this..."

As Jack unfolded the napkin, she continued, "After dinner, Lee took me to Pete Fountain's. I know how much you enjoy his music, so I...I..."

"Thank you."

As silence cloaked the room, Sandra felt very aware of Jack's presence. As she sat, trying to remain calm in spite of her pounding heart, she wanted so much to feel his arms around her. Just when she thought that her longings would go unfulfilled, Jack, to her wonderful relief, reached over and pulled her into his arms. His first kiss was very gentle, almost caressing in nature. Then as she pressed her breasts against his strong warm chest, his kisses turned ardently sensual. His hands slid along the thin material of her dress, stopping finally at her hips. This time, there was no hesitancy in her response. Her whole body felt on fire as she savored his touch. It was exactly as she had remembered; the years had changed nothing.

Releasing her gently, Jack's voice, thick with emotion, whispered in her ear his familiar adieu. "Have sweet dreams, Sandy."

With tears rolling down her face, she listened to his receding footsteps.

That night, her sleep was anything but restful. She dreamed not of Robert nor of Lee, but once again of Jack.

They were lying in a bed of lilac orchids beneath a canopy of towering cypress. The trees' feathery fingers were laced with whispery webs of Spanish moss. With the song of the warbler echoing from above, Jack, body glistening under the soft rays of the moon, sensuously unlaced the loose ties of her diaphanous nightgown.

As the delicate garment slowly fell away, he took her into his arms and kissed her with passion so ardent, it left her quivering in his embrace. With the intoxicating scent of the wild azalea and orchids filling the air, her soft body responded with a wave of erotic passion as Jack's strong fingers gently tantalized the hardening dark nipples of her breasts. In response to his hands slowly sliding down her stomach to the inviting warmth of soft hair, she instinctively arched toward him. Pulling him closer with each sensual movement of her hips and gentle massage to the hollow dip of his strong rippling back, she yielded every part of her soul.

Just as their bodies began to move in exquisite harmony, a chilling wind began to blow, sending the moss fluttering and silencing her moan of pleasure. As the cold began to seep through her being, she realized that the man of her dreams had left with the wind.

Sandra awoke early the next morning-tears still fresh on her lashes, pillow wet.

Chapter Eighteen

The following two weeks were a flurry of activity. After closing shop, she and the children did last minute shopping for their upcoming trip. Wanting to take full advantage of the remainding days, she kept in touch with Lee only through phone conversations. Jack was still very much a presence in their lives, but he made no reference to their Friday night kiss. Relieved, she simply enjoyed his visits and hoped that their relationship was slowly returning to its former easy manner.

The evening before Whitney and Jesse's plane trip, she felt especially blue, and wondered if every summer would find her alone. Summer used to be such a wonderful and carefree time for her and the kids, but since Robert's death, the season had begun to represent a harried time both at the shop and at home.

Whitney and Jesse, oblivious to their mother's feelings, were preoccupied with thoughts of Disney World, drives to the beach, and playing with favorite cousins. As Whitney watched her mother pack the final outfit, she impulsively ran up and gave her a tight hug.

"Mommy, I'm going to miss you," she cried as she wrapped her little arms around her mom's neck.

She pulled the little girl into her arms and sniffed her

hair with the hopes of capturing the memory forever in her mind. "My little baby girl, I'm going to miss you too. But, I'll come out and visit in a couple of weeks, and before you know it, you'll be back home." Rocking her daughter to the silent melody of maternal music, she thought of a way to ease her daughter's apprehensions.

Impulsively reaching for her silver locket, Sandra unfastened the clasp. "Baby cakes, why don't you wear Mommy's locket? We can place a picture of me inside, and whenever you start missing me, you can just look at the picture." As she fastened the chain, Whitney's face broke into a bright smile.

Jesse, who had entered his sister's room, slipped under his mother's arms and nestled himself in her embrace as well. "Mommy, I love you," he murmured in a voice so low that only she could hear. Kissing the top of his head, she whispered back, "I love you too."

During the drive to the airport, Whitney and Jesse were chatting away excitedly. Any qualms they might have had were long gone. As she parked, Maureen wondered if Jack had arrived. He had suggested that they drive out together, but she thought it better for him to meet them at the gate since she had to head back to the shop after she said her good-byes.

Checked in and ready to go, the children bounced around full of "hyper" energy and excitement. Already waiting at the gate was Jack with a friendly smile and brightly colored gift bag.

"Uncle Jack, Uncle Jack," Whitney yelled as she ran across the terminal into his arms. Jesse, running close behind, soon overtook her little steps. Grabbing his knees, they begged that he tell them what was in the bag. Good naturedly, he bent down and gave them each a kiss.

"What's in the bag, Uncle Jack?" Jesse asked for a second time.

Both Maureen and Sandra admonished Jack for spoiling the pair.

Whitney, who had shrugged off her backpack, jumped for the bag. Uncle Jack, what is it, what is it?"

Continuing to hold the bag high out of their reach, he handed the parcel over to Maureen, "Your grandmother will give it to you on the plane, so be patient."

Temporarily satisfied with his promise, Jesse and Whitney ran over to the huge window to watch the activity on the tarmac, with Sandra following close behind.

Maureen and Jack picked up the boarding passes and found a spot to wait for the call to board. "I bought each of the children a Walkman and a couple of tapes to help keep them occupied on the plane." With a loving squeeze to her hand, Jack whispered, "And there's a box of Godiva's for you."

"Jack, this really wasn't necessary, paying for the trip has been more than enough."

Over the loud speaker, the final boarding announcement was made. "Ok you two," Maureen called as she beckoned towards the children. "It's time to go."

Before walking them over to the waiting flight attendant, Sandra knelt and hugged the kids, and whispered last minute words of love. Determined not to let them see her cry, she affectionately tickled their tummies and reminded them that she would soon visit them in Florida.

As her mother handed over their boarding passes, she kissed the children one last time. "Mind your grandmother and give Aunt Helen my love." Sandra then turned her attention to Maureen and gave her a kiss. "Mom, give me a call as soon as you reach Aunt Helen's, I love you."

After the final round of good-byes, the children cheerfully waved, and the three headed down the ramp towards the plane.

As the plane began to pull away from the terminal,

previously checked tears began to fall. Jack, quietly standing behind her, laid a reassuring hand on her shoulder and she in turn, buried her head in his jacket, "I know I'm being silly, but I miss them already."

"No, you're not being silly. Good-byes are always hard." He comforted as he ran a soothing hand through her hair. "Remember you just told Whitney and Jesse that you'll see them in a few weeks. The time will fly by, you'll see."

Knowing that he was right, she pressed her head against his chest and nodded.

When the plane had finally taxied out of sight, Jack, who was still holding her close in his arms, made a suggestion. "Listen, I don't have to go right back to the office, so how about breakfast?"

Just as quickly as her face broke into a smile at the suggestion, it gloomed over, "Jack, I would like to but..."

"But...?"

In a tense rush, she finished, "But I've made plans with Lee. With the kids leaving, I canceled our last date. So, I promised him an early lunch, but maybe we could..."

Sententiously cutting her off with a distant, "I see," Jack released her from his embrace.

Sandra, desperate to hold on to the small progress that their relationship had made over the last few weeks, made one more attempt at trying to explain, "Jack, I ..."

With a face devoid of all expression, he stared down. "Listen, you don't owe me any explanations. We can get together later on in the week. I have a hearing this afternoon, so I'm going to head on back to the office. Do you want me to walk you out to the van?"

"No, you go on. I have to make a stop at the ladies' room."

Without his usual kiss good-bye, he headed for the terminal exit.

Feeling the tears threatening to return, she quickly turned back towards the window and stared out at the empty tarmac.

"Oh, Sandra...," Lee softly called.

"Lee, I'm sorry. My mind has been in a million and one places all morning." Indeed it had been. Usually she looked forward to the soulful home style cooking and ambiance of Dooky Chase's. From its menu of Creole dishes, some more than a hundred years old, she had many favorites. "You were asking about the children?"

"There's no need to explain. It's perfectly under-standable that you're a little distracted. I was just saying that I hope that the kids got off all right," he inquired as he dug into the muffaletta he ordered for lunch.

Sandra, half-interested, picked at her Creole gumbo as she glanced over at what remained of Lee's sand-wich. To use the word sandwich to describe what he had just eaten was a vast understatement. His meal had con-sisted of a hearty round loaf of bread stuffed with ham, salami, cheese, all dressed with a well-seasoned olive salad. Smiling at what he had just devoured, she replied, "Yes, they did. Mom promised to call as soon as they get over to my aunt's."

"You don't seem very hungry. You've barely eaten a thing. There isn't anything wrong with your meal is there?"

Staring down at the generous portion of the aromatic reddish brown roux of okra, seafood, vegetables and spices served over steamed rice, she quickly shook her head. "No, the gumbo's fine, in fact, it's usually one of my favorites. You couldn't have chosen a better place for lunch. It's just that I have a lot of things on my mind."

"Anything that I can help with?"

"Sure," she laughed, "you can make me a twin so that she can stay here and run the shop while I hightail it on over to Florida."

"Why don't you give them a call when you get back to the store? They should have landed by then."

"I'm just feeling sorry for myself. What I need to do is to stay as busy as possible."

After taking a sip of her iced tea, she added, "Staying busy shouldn't be too difficult. Outside of Mardi Gras week, the summer with all of its tourists, is usually the store's busiest time."

As he wholeheartedly began to dig into the rather large slice of sweet potato pie that the waiter had just placed before him, Sandra giggled. Shamefaced, she put a hand up to her mouth and apologized. "Lee, I'm sorry. It's just that after watching you eat that enormous muffaletta, I can't believe you have room for pie."

Sheepishly, he looked down at his plate and laughed. "I guess I am over indulging a bit. But I promise to do an extra set of push-ups this evening, so let me eat guilt free!"

"I'm glad that it'll only take you an extra set. My body firmly believes in that old adage, a moment on the lips, a lifetime on the hips. It would take me a whole week of dieting, plus five extra miles a day on the bike."

Mid forkful, he flirted with an appreciative wink as his low Louisianan drawl flattered, "I don't know, Sandra, your hips look mighty fine to me."

Blushing, she changed the subject by voicing her admiration for the local African-American artwork that dressed the restaurant's walls. Lee listened as she offered her interpretation of one particularly unusual piece. He found her somewhat modest reaction to his compliment charming and appealing. With his artist's eye, he took in the rather attractive picture she created. More than once, he found his eyes peeking through her loosely crocheted sweater to the low cut tank dress she wore below. He couldn't help wondering if her demureness was just as much of an illusion as her sweater.

Unaware of his thoughts, she turned and offered a particularly beautiful smile that made her already lovely face even more enchanting. As he finished the last of his pie, he returned the smile and asked, "I hope with all of the comings and goings of your camera-carrying gapeseeds, you won't be too busy for a weekend getaway."

Caught off guard, she fingered her spoon, and fought for a polite way to turn down his invitation. "Lee, um...I don't think that I'm ready for anything quite like what you're suggesting. Going away for a weekend is well...somewhat premature at this point. I mean, we've only been dating for a short while..."

"My sweet demure Sandra, where is your mind? I was referring to Maggie's birthday bash this weekend. She said that she spoke to you about coming out to help her celebrate."

Twisting her mouth as he explained, she chastised, "Lee, get that silly grin off your face. You purposely worded that question the way that you did just to see what I would say. And I'm pretty certain that you wouldn't have turned me down if I'd agreed to go off with you somewhere. You see, I'm not as naive as you like to think that I am."

With a beguiling smile that brought forth a mischievous twinkle in his dark eyes, he remarked, "No one said that you were naive. It's just that being the carnal man that I am, I had to ask. Besides, can you really fault a guy for trying?"

"Ask yourself that question when I don't return any of your phone calls."

"Sorry," he laughed as he threw up his hands in mock defeat. "No more comes ons, promise."

"Promise! Ha! Forgive me if I don't believe you," she

smirked..

Raising his left hand in a pledge, he vowed, "Well, I promise to try, scout's honor." Offering his most sincere smile, he mischievously crossed his fingers.

"That's your wrong hand you ninny, besides, you just crossed your fingers! How can I believe anything that you tell me?"

"Sandra, you take life way too seriously. Me, I just go with the flow."

"Go with the flow? Life isn't always so simple, Lee."

"For me it is. For instance, I'm sitting here, talking to a beautiful woman. Wanting her so bad that it hurts. But in the back of my mind, I know that this thing between us probably won't develop into the type of relationship that either she or I want right now. Besides, she's hung up on another man. Do I sit back in despair? No, I make the best of the situation, enjoy her company, hopefully bring a little happiness, and if I'm lucky, form a lifelong friend-ship."

Genuinely touched by his words, she reached for his hands. "Lee, I'm the lucky one."

Chapter Nineteen

By the time Friday rolled around, she was genuinely looking forward to spending the weekend away. Leaving last minute instructions with Millie, she felt confident about Lavender and Hops being left in her assistant's capable hands for a few days. Business was booming and tourists were everywhere, but she was positive that the woman could handle just about any problem that could possibly arise. Just to be absolutely sure, she hired Millie's sister to assist part-time. Leaving the shop in their care was also a run through for when she planned on visiting the children.

With Whitney and Jesse gone, the evenings had become miserably quiet. In fact, if it had not been for Lee, it would have been downright lonely. Several nights after closing shop, he would stop by and they would either take in a movie or go somewhere for dinner. To his credit, he was always the perfect gentleman, never pressing for anything more than a brotherly good night kiss.

Though she genuinely enjoyed Lee's attentiveness, she still found herself longing for Jack's company. So certain was she that he was going to telephone the evening of the children's departure, she made a point of staying home. Disappointed when he hadn't called, she went to bed on the verge of tears, comforted only by the memory of the feel of his jacket and the calming warmth beneath it when he pulled her into his arms at the airport. It appeared that all of her hopes of rekindling their friendship were immensely unrealistic.

Setting her weekend travel bag down by the front door, she quickly glanced up at the hall clock and calculated that she had several more minutes before Lee was due to pick her up. A large part of her wanted to call Jack to let him know that she was going out of town. Even though she had left the Fontenots'phone number with both Millie and her mother, she rationalized calling Jack by telling herself that some other unforeseen emergency could arise.

Walking over to the kitchen phone, she talked herself out of calling, and then changed her mind once again. After punching in his number, she impatiently listened as the phone rang. When the answering machine clicked on, she hung up the receiver. There really wasn't any point in leaving a message. The reason she had called to begin with was to hear his voice and hope that he would say something to ensure her that she was still close to his heart. Feeling totally foolish, she made a silent promise to keep Jack out of her mind, at least for the weekend.

On the drive out to the Fontenots', Lee glanced up at the overcast sky and commented that rain was in the forecast, but advised that they shouldn't let it keep them from enjoying the bayou. Besides, he explained, the bayou had a mind of its own; showers could suddenly fall from what appeared to be a beautiful cloudless sky, only to stop in minutes. As he fondly described the swampland that surrounded his favorite stumping ground, her mind drifted back to her college days. Quietly smiling to herself, she remembered the English lit class she had shared with Jack. One of their assignments was to partner up and study a poem of Henry W. Longfellow. She and Jack had decided on Longfellow's Cajun inspired beautiful pastoral, *Evangeline*.

"Why the smile?" Lee asked. "I know that I can get carried away when I start talking about the bayou. Most people could care less."

"No, no, quite the contrary." With a dreamy cast to her eyes, she continued, "Your description just reminded me of Longfellow's *Evangeline*...

This is the forest primeval. The murmuring pines and the hemlocks,
Bearded with moss, and in garments green, indistinct in the twilight,
Stand like Druids of eld, with voices sad and prophetic,
Stand like harpers hoar, with beards that rest on their bosoms...

Enjoying her recitation, Lee took in her far off expression as she spoke,

...Loud from its rocky caverns, the deep-voiced neighboring ocean
Speaks, and in accents disconsolate answers the wails of the forest...

"Wow, I actually remembered it. That poem brings back a whole lot of memories," she whispered sadly.

It was pretty obvious to Lee that she was remembering more than just the poem. Attempting to lighten the mood, he commented on the thick ghostly colored gray-green Spanish moss that draped moodily from a stand of bald cypress. The brooding moss languidly trailed into the still swampy water that bordered the meandering blacktop highway.

Pointing out the window, he let out an appreciative sigh. "It's beautiful, isn't it? When the French and

Spanish explored these parts, they each had their own name for the moss. The French scornfully called it barbe espagnole—Spanish beards. And the Spanish, not to be outdone, named it-peluca francesa, or Frenchman's wig. Needless to say, the French won out. Now, my favorite story is one that I heard as a boy. According to Indian legend, a beautiful girl in the midst of her wedding ceremony was killed by an enemy tribe. Her family, stricken with grief, cut off her hair and lovingly spread it across the branches of the oak tree under which she was buried. Over time, the hair turned gray as the wind blew it from tree to tree. Its serene beauty is a lasting tribute to those who are fated not to live out their love."

The maudlin Indian fable prompted Sandra to immediately recall the poem of forlorn love she stumbled upon during her afternoon outing with Alphonse.

After several minutes of silence, Lee looked her way and noticed that the expression on his companion's face matched the gloom of the Spanish moss. Puzzled, he commented with concern, "Hey, my story was supposed to entertain, not make you unhappy."

Half-heartedly responding with a smile, she said, "Oh, don't mind me. I'm just feeling a bit weepy." Changing the subject, she glanced out the window and asked, "Do you collect the willow and cypress that you use for your furniture from out of these swamps?"

"Sure do, though I let old Mother Nature do most of the work for me. I wait until she unleashes a storm or sends a lightening strike, and then I go pick up the aftermath."

Chuckling, he added, "I try to pay no mind to some of the old folks around here who have warned me that if a woodworker builds his home from any part of a tree that has been struck by lightning, his house will burn. Obviously, I'm not very superstitious, for I could never bring myself to cut down any of these beautiful trees. You only have to spend a day in these mysterious waters to fully appreciate and understand their charm." As an idea brightened his face, Lee touched her arm. "Say, why don't you let me take you out exploring tomorrow morning? We can go out in one of Al's pirogues."

In a voice that echoed her trepidation, she asked, "I would love to, but...are you sure it's safe?" Feeling somewhat foolish as Lee let out a hearty laugh, she explained, "Well, haven't you seen the movie, *Southern Comfort*? When I think of the bayou, I imagine alligators, poisonous snakes, quicksand and ..."

"Crazed woods people who haven't seen the light of day since heaven knows when," supplied Lee with mirthful sarcasm.

Sandra, feathers ruffled, interrupted, "Lee! Stop putting words in my mouth. I've never thought any such thing. Besides, you can't very well expect me to feel the same as you towards a place I've never lived."

Lee, taking one hand away from the steering wheel, reached over and gave her hand a light squeeze. "Sandra, I promise you that after tomorrow, you will see the bayou in a whole new light."

As they drove along, she settled into the lulling hum of the tires grazing the road. The quiet that enveloped the Range Rover was as restful as the still landscape that lay before them. Looking out at the dense swampland through the open window, she gradually realized the lure of the bayou. The shadowy trees laden with moss and the idle waters seemed to gently beckon. Mesmerized, she began to imagine herself lifting the heavy gray drape of moss and discovering a world only second to Eden.

Lee, glancing her way, broke the silence, and in a hushed tone observed, "I see that the trees are beginning to cast their spell. They're inviting you to get lost in the bog's misty veil. Mark my words; before you leave here, these bayous will become a touchstone. Once it's in your system, it's impossible to shake."

In a voice husky with emotion, he once again squeezed her hand. "Sandra, I have found such solace in this place. Right after my parents were killed, I would come out here and just stare out at the trees. Or, I'd take out the pirogue and skim along the water. It's pretty peaceful, the crepey duckweed that sits on top looked like floating green carpet." Smiling as he fondly painted the picture of the scene that was so vivid in his mind's eye, he continued. "Birds literally filled the sky and trees. The warblers, blue herons, red-winged blackbirds, indigo and painted buntings...it was like drifting through an aviary."

Sighing, he reminisced, "I remember going out fishing with my old man one morning. We were just drifting along and Pops was teaching me how to distinguish one tree from another, which for anyone else, would have been a relatively simple task. But he had an uncanny way of taking a simple experience and turning it into a life lesson."

"Instructing me to close my eyes, he had me listen to the rustlings of the trees while he explained that each one whispered a different message. The white oaks with their papery thin leaves splayed out like small open hands, whispered differently from the dark green leaves of the magnolia when laden with beautiful full white blossoms. Whenever I start on a new piece, I go out and listen. When I listen to their murmurings, I'm inspired and soothed at the same time. It is like balm to my soul."

His words helped her to fully understand the extent to which his art was a part of his being. Without disappointment, she also became acutely aware that his work was the true love of his life. With this new perspective, she asked with fresh insight, "With all of the hundreds of trees that grow in the area, why do you choose the cypress and willow for so much of your work?"

"Do you realize that in all of these years, you're the only person to ask me that question?" Giving an appreciative laugh, he added, "And to be honest, if anyone else other than you had asked, I don't know if I would give them the true reason."

Accepting his statement as a compliment, she responded with a warm smile. Without explanation, he pulled off the main highway and drove onto what looked to be little more than a dirt path. As they stopped, she took note of the swampland that stood moodily alongside the narrow 'road'. Catching her breath at the surreal view, she unconsciously laid a hand on Lee's sleeve as her eyes darted across the still water that was thick with green delicate duckweed interspersed with foot long lotus pads. Growing along its banks stood huge moss-laced cypress and serene willow trees.

Breaking the silence, Lee leaned past her and pointed to what looked to be groupings of large round gnarled stumps that poked several feet above the murky waters. "Sandra, do you know what those are?"

Shaking her head, she guessed, "Well, they sorta look like dead tree stumps."

Chuckling, he explained, "Nice try, but they're quite the contrary. They are cypress knees."

Now it was Sandra's turn to let out a giggle. "Cypress knees?"

"I know the term doesn't sound very scientific, but they are the actual outgrowths of the cypress' submerged roots. Some believe that they increase the tree's intake of oxygen, while others seem to think that they simply help the cypress to stand strong and firm. Whatever the reason, the cypress is virtually indestructible."

"So, in your art, the cypress symbolizes strength?"

"You're half correct." In his persona of fine arts professor, he patiently explained, "The ancient Greeks and

Romans used the cypress to symbolize death and mourning. In part because of its dark mournful beauty, but also because if cut down, it'll never grow again. As a young boy out with my father in the pirogue, I vowed never to forget the essence of this place, its people, wildlife, and beauty. And, when my parents passed on, I was more determined to keep that vow by capturing their spirit in each piece of furniture that I craft. The sorrowful beauty of the cypress symbolizes that effort as well as enduring strength. A cutting of cypress from a fallen tree represents their loss. Maggie and I are outgrowths of the union of our parents, we are rooted in their spirit."

Moved by his reasoning, she supplied, "...likened to the cypress knees."

"You have earned an 'A'."

Gently laughing, she corrected, "But not without a whole lot of tutoring from the professor. Now tell me. The beautiful rocker you gave me is done in willow. What is the symbolism behind that?"

"If you noticed, all of the willow pieces that were exhibited at the Sol Galerie were designed to function as sources of comfort. Take the rocker, for example. What do you feel when you see it or sit in it?"

"Well, I feel a sense of calm. As I rest against its back and rock, my mind relaxes and I find myself using the time to daydream, reflect...pray..."

"Perfect. Now keep that in mind. When I create with willow, I draw from a lament in Psalm 137. The passage is set during the time of the Jews' captivity by the Babylonians. The lament's mournful words describe how they sat down by the rivers and wept, hanging their "harps upon the willows."

"Wow," she whispered. Genuinely overwhelmed, she allowed herself a few moments to absorb his words. "You know, the rocking chair was already special, simply because by giving it to me, you have entrusted me with a part of your soul. But now it is even more precious because I understand its symbolism. I will treasure that chair always."

As she turned to face him, Lee impulsively caressed her cheek with the palm of his hand. In a voice softened by her ingenuous pledge, he studied her face. "I think that our relationship is perfect the way that it is, friends, somehow wonderfully connected. Why mess it up, right?"

"Right." Sandra warmly agreeing sank back into her seat and smiled.

With a glint of mischief flashing in his eyes, he lightened the mood by teasing, "Now that I have your total and complete trust, and have proven that I am a sensitive kinda guy, do you want to fool around?"

Momentarily at a loss for words, she let out a reproving gasp, "Lee Chienier! After all that sentimental talk about us just being friends, how dare you!"

Tossing back his head, he filled the vehicle with his hearty laughter. "Sandra, sweet heart, come on, lighten up. I am only kidding. God, why are you always so serious?"

Fighting back her own laughter, she tickled his side until he pleaded for mercy.

As several heavy raindrops hit the windshield, they broke out in playful laughter. Putting the vehicle in gear, he spoke in a voice filled with humor, "Well, I guess that's our cue to leave. These roads flood with less than a moment's notice." Expertly backing the Range Rover onto the main highway, the two headed deeper into the bayou towards the Fontenots'.

The remainder of the trip consisted of light teasing and general conversation. They chatted about an upcoming series of lectures at the university, and about Sandra's plans for the shop. And as Lee predicted, the rain soon stopped, leaving the skies gray, but clear.

Within the hour, they reached their destination. As

they pulled up into the wide dusty clamshell drive, Sandra recognized Maggie's car. Parked alongside it, to her surprise, was Jack's sedan. Immediately her heart jumped into her mouth and without hesitation, she leapt out of the Rover before Lee had a chance to bring it to a complete stop. Frantically assuming that Jack was there to relay bad news regarding the children or her mother, she ran to the porch.

"Sandra?" Lee called after her in a concerned tone.

Not hearing him, she ran up the steps, stopping short only when she saw Jack stepping out from behind the screen door. Following close were Maggie and Alphonse. Quickly, her mind assessed the fact that Jack did not appear upset, in fact quite the opposite. It was obvious that he was sharing a joke with the two.

Noticing her upset face, his smile quickly faded as he reached out to steady her. "Sandy, what's wrong? You are shaking like a leaf, and your hands are ice cold."

Choking back the tears that threatened to fall, she sobbed, "I saw your car and just assumed that you were out here to tell me something had happened to the kids..."

Immediately, he recognized the scare. He had seen the same look on her face when she opened the door the night he came to break the news of Robert's death. Quickly pulling her into his arms, he reassured her that everything was fine. As he calmed her fears, the screen door creaked open. Out walked Lavania accompanied by Maggie's husband, David and Darlene, Jack's beautiful lunch date from several weeks earlier.

Quickly pulling away, she felt suddenly foolish and began to self-consciously smooth down her hair. Maggie, empathizing with her dear friend, placed a protective hand on her shoulder and cast Lee a furtive glance, appealing to him to help break the tension.

Responding to his sister's silent entreaty, he gave

Darlene an affectionate hug and teased, "Hey p'tit zo-zo, I see that you made it. It's been a long time."

Maggie, rolling her eyes upward upon hearing Lee's pet name for his high school sweetheart, leaned towards Sandra and murmured under her breath, "P'tit zo-zo, give me a break. I never did like that nickname. Besides, Darlene is hardly anyone's little bird."

Desperate not to laugh, Sandra bit down on her lower lip.

In a sugary sweet voice, Darlene responded, "Lee, it has been ages since you've call me that." Looping a willowy arm proprietarily through Jack's, she explained their presence. "Jack and I thought that it would be fun to get away for a little R & R. Heaven knows we both need it." Pointedly looking in Sandra's direction, she continued, "Some of his responsibilities have finally lightened up, so I thought that it might be fun to drive on down. The Fontenots have been after me to visit for the longest. Besides, I wouldn't miss Maggie's little birthday soiree for anything in the world."

Darlene smiled brightly as she turned towards Maggie. "At first, I thought it best that we not impose this weekend, but Mr. Al assured me that you wouldn't mind us being here."

At the mention of the conversation, Lavania smiled to herself, as Alphonse, Maggie and Jack exchanged mischievous glances.

"So Jack, you knew that Maggie was planning a party?" a very curious Sandra asked.

"When I heard that they were thinking about driving down. I called to invite him," piped Maggie. "You're always chatting on about him, and after we all ran into him at the restaurant, I thought that it might be kinda fun for all of us to hang out together."

Maggie, not missing an opportunity to throw a barb Darlene's way, walked over to Jack and guided him into the house. In a voice that replicated the attractive woman's sugary tone, Maggie smiled up at Jack and batted her lashes as she teasingly flirted, "Just what type of R & R did you have in mind, Jack?"

Shooing her into the house, Lavania playfully swatted Maggie on the rear. "Don't pay her any mind, Darlene. I warned you that this weekend would be like old home week. As you can see, Maggie hasn't changed one bit."

Chapter Twenty

As the group made their way into the charming Victorian parlor, Sandra quickly found a seat. "So, Sandra and Jack, it seems as if you two already know everyone here," observed David.

Alphonse, who had been uncharacteristically quiet, turned towards Sandra and added, "You won't believe this, but right before you and Lee pulled up, we figured out that ol' Jack here is the same little boy who used to come around these parts with his pa, Paulie Thibodeaux, a ways back. Can you beat that for a crazy kind of serendipity?"

Slowly shaking his head as if he still couldn't quite believe his eyes, Alphonse continued staring. "I knew he looked familiar, but I couldn't place him until I asked him his pa's name."

Still gazing at Jack, Al's topaz eyes twinkled as he fingered his pipe. "I remember Paulie all right...a damn good fishing guide. He could handle a pirogue like nobody's business." Still staring with his piercing eyes, he reminisced, "I can still see you sitting there beside him, always so serious."

Pointing at Maggie and Lee with his pipe, the older man continued, "You all probably don't remember too much about Jack. Paulie never would let him play too much. In fact, I remembered suggesting once to his pa that maybe he could let the boy stay here at the house and play while he took his group out." Fondly remembering Jack's father's response, Al continued, "Naw." He would say, "That boy didn't have time to play. He was there to work. He said that Jack had to get used to idea of work if he was going to make it in the world."

Rising to head towards the kitchen, Al momentarily stopped at Jack's chair and fondly patted him on the shoulder. "Well, son, I reckon that your pa knew what he was talking about. Just from talking to Sandra, I know that he taught you well."

Before leaving the room, Alphonse with his knowing eyes glanced over at Sandra and mischievously winked. At the mention of her name, Jack turned and thoughtfully measured her face, wondering exactly what she had discussed with the man. As their eyes met, she found herself blushing and quickly turned away.

"Here, let me help you with that," offered Lee as he jumped up to assist Lavania, who had just entered the room carrying a large silver tray.

"Don't be silly, I have it. Go on and sit back down," she shooed. "I thought you all might like some refreshments after that long drive." Placing the coffee service on a mahogany cart already laden with an appetizing assortment of tarts and cookies, she stood and admonished the group. "I'm going to go and get the iced tea. When I get back, I want to see everyone eating. And no crazy talk about diets, not this weekend."

As they sat and made small talk over their coffee, Sandra quietly took note of the seating arrangement. Lee and Darlene were catching up over on the sofa. Maggie and David were sitting on the window seat, and she and Jack were each seated in chairs opposite Darlene and Lee. Observing how everyone had paired up, she couldn't help but wonder how the bedroom assignments were going to shake out. Sneaking a glance over at Jack, she desperately hoped that he and Darlene weren't going to share rooms. She rationalized that even though the

Fontenots ran their home as a 'bed and breakfast' they probably would not approve of the two sleeping together. Deciding to ask, she turned towards Lavania who had just entered with Al.

"Miss Lavania, have you and Maggie figured out who is sleeping where?"

The older woman before answering sat down on the sofa forcing Darlene to scoot over close to Lee. Maggie, not allowing Lavania to answer, interjected, "Well, we know where Darlene won't be sleeping."

Immediately both Al and Lee broke out in uproarious laughter. Lavania, obviously trying her best to contain her amusement, scolded the men to hush.

Darlene, flashing Maggie a scornful glint, tightly grimaced, "That's all right, Miss Lavania, let them laugh. It's obvious that Maggie's sense of humor hasn't matured much over the years."

In a feeble attempt to lighten the woman's mood, Lee squeezed her hand and teased, "C'mon honey, you know that Maggie's only trying to get you riled up. Besides, you have to admit that the whole thing was pretty damn funny."

Alphonse, noticing the quizzical expressions of Jack, Sandra and David, humorously explained. "You see, when Darlene was in...oh, I guess it had to be about the tenth or eleventh grade, Maggie called herself confiding in Darlene that when Lee got home from school, he had this habit of going up to one of the third floor bedrooms to write in his journal. Somehow, she convinced Darlene here, to sneak on up to the room and hide. The plan was that Darlene was to wait until Lee got settled down at the desk, and then she would jump out of the chifforobe and give him a good scare. She even went as far as to lock the door from the outside, under the pretense that she didn't want Lee to find anything out of the ordinary."

Interrupting with a deep chuckle, Lee continued with

the story. "Well, needless to say, Maggie's little practical joke got way out of hand. It just so happened that Miss Lavania and Mr. Al took Maggie and me into N'Awlins to visit friends that evening. I guess we were gone until close to midnight. The whole time we were away, Darlene was locked up in that room screaming her pretty little head off."

Darlene, still very much upset, gave a scornful retort. "You would've been screaming too. I couldn't see a damn thing in that dreary old dark room."

Laughing, Sandra innocently asked, "Why didn't you turn on a light?"

Maggie, grinning from ear to ear like a Cheshire cat, boastfully supplied, "Because I took the light bulbs from out of the lamps. I even nailed the windows shut."

"My devious little wife," David chuckled. "From now on, I'm going to think twice before I cross you."

Jack, making a great effort not to laugh, asked, "So how long were you up there?"

Throwing Maggie a glower too wicked for words, Darlene in a slow measured tone replied, "All night! And soon after dark, it started to storm!" Then in theatrical fashion she looked piteously into Jack's eyes, "I finally cried myself to sleep. Fortunately, my parents had the good sense to summon the authorities and a house-to-house search was made. If it hadn't been for the sheriff knocking at the door, I don't know what I would've done."

Lavania, shaking her head as she remembered the night, remarked, "As I recall, your poor parents were beside themselves with worry. Your mother, because of the storm, was convinced that you had drowned out there in one of the bayous. They tried to reach us, hoping that Lee or Maggie knew where you were, but of course, we weren't home. Finally, about 3:00 in the morning, the sheriff woke Al and me. He went and got Maggie and Lee up...and that's when Maggie told us of her little practical joke."

Sandra, not believing that her dear friend could be so devious exclaimed, "Maggie, that was simply horrible! Oh how could you have been so scheming?"

Jack, shaking his head with laughter, glanced over at Maggie and winked, "It's obvious that she is quite the expert."

Patting Darlene's hand with maternal affection, Lavania advised, "Honey, it is long over and done with. But, just to make sure that you're not haunted by any past demons, you'll stay in the room next to mine and Al's."

Maggie, still grinning, quickly divvied up the remainder of the rooms. "Well, me and sweetie pie will stay in my old room, and Lee has his usual spot. That leaves Jack and Sandra in the room at the end of the hall..." Maggie's voice trailed off as she noticed Sandra's frown.

Interrupting her friend, Sandra sharply commented, "That will hardly be necessary Maggie. I can sleep in one of the bedrooms up on the third floor."

"No, no, you stay on the second floor with everyone else. I don't mind sleeping upstairs," Jack offered.

"Jack, it is no big deal, really. Before I close the door tonight, I'll make sure that all of the light bulbs are screwed in and working."

Chuckling at her comment, Lavania suggested, "Jack, now that I think about it, both of you might be more comfortable in the rooms up on the third floor. There are two rooms that adjoin a sitting area, and both are larger than the one on the second floor. In fact, one of them even has a king-size bed. Besides, it'll save us from having to work out a shower schedule."

Turning towards Sandra, Jack's eyes hinted of an old familiar twinkle, "Sounds perfect. Sandra, you don't mind do you?"

Sandra, heart beating rapidly, hid her pleasure as

she kept her voice quietly modulated, "No, I don't mind."

"Good," pronounced Lavania. "If you're ready, we can go on up now. I've aired out both of the rooms earlier this week, so everything should pretty much be in order."

As the three made their way up the staircase, Sandra glanced over the banister down at Darlene, catching the woman sinisterly staring up at her. Temporarily unable to draw her eyes away, she inwardly shivered and felt a momentary sense of foreboding. Gripping the wooden rail, she forced herself to smile down at the woman and flippantly promised, "I'll send Jack back down to you as soon as we finish unpacking."

In response, Darlene's eyes angrily flashed one more dagger before she turned around and suggestively asked Lee to keep her company while she unpacked.

Upon opening the first of the two rooms, Lavania explained that the bedrooms were actually a part of one large suite that was carved out of attic space that once served as servant's quarters. In between the two bedrooms was a sitting room and a rather large bath. As their eyes adjusted to the unexpected brightness that flooded in from the window and reflected off the polished wooden floor, Lavania walked over to one of the two dormers and drew closed its delicate lace curtain. Going from window to window, she adjusted the lace that flowed from behind each set of the burgundy velvet drapes.

"Sandra, I thought that you might enjoy this room, it's one of my favorites."

Nodding her head in agreement, she appreciatively caressed the beautifully crocheted ivory linen that dressed the mahogany Napoleonic sleigh bed. "Miss Lavania, this room is just wonderful. It reminds me of your sitting room. They both have the same warm, cozy feel."

Noticing similar handiwork on the scarf that adorned a rose moiré skirted dressing table over in the alcove, Sandra turned to Jack and with much admiration explained how the woman had crafted most of the linens in the house. "Not only does she do beautiful crocheted work, but she does embroidery as well. Just look at the pillows on the window seat and bed."

"Ms. Lavania, don't be surprised if I'm not downstairs too much. I have a feeling that I am going to be spending most of my time up here."

Jack, after placing Sandra's overnight bag on the bed, paused and affectionately watched as she handled the small heavy silver picture frames, various bibelots, and colored antique perfume bottles. Letting out an appreciative sigh, she sniffed the freshly cut grass-pink orchids that filled a crystal bud vase. Glancing into the small table mirror that stood in between a set of miniature candlestick lamps, she blushed as she realized that the two had been watching her. "You must think that I am nuts. I know Jack already has a definite opinion on the subject."

"Nonsense, it's a compliment to both my home and to yourself that you appreciate and derive so much joy from the simple things in life. I'm sure that Jack finds you as endearing as I do."

Shyly glancing in the mirror at Jack, her heart quickened at his smiling reflection.

"Jack, are you ready to see your room?" Lavania asked. Picking up his leather bag, he followed the women across the sitting room into the other bedroom. To Sandra's delight, this second room was equally as charming as the first. Whereas her room was papered in a rose pattern, Jack's was done up in a much more masculine fashion. The walls, covered in a rich black lacquered windowpane paneling, contrasted elegantly with the pristine white Battenburgs that peeked out from behind green, red and gold tartan plaid drapes. Directly across from the gleaming white wood and red brick fireplace was the focal point of the room, a magnificent four-poster bed.

Sandra stopped alongside the bed and rested one foot on an ornately carved stool. She giggled as Jack mouthed an appreciative wow! "Where ever did you find this wonderful bed?" she asked.

"Oh, it has been in Alphonse's family for years. It is so huge, that over time it has gotten moved form one bedroom to the next, until finally Al, Lee and some neighbors hauled it on up here."

As he walked around the high-riser, Jack asked, "Just how big is this?"

"Oh, it takes a king size sheet, but it's an extra long. I have had to sew the linens for it myself," she supplied with pride.

Sandra admired the woman's use of colors, from the curtains to the stunning quilted duvet done up in the same tartan plaid. "Lavania, you have such a wonderful eye for color and design."

"Well, most of it is a little imagination and a whole lot of trial and error."

Taking in the room's carved wooden lamps, the rich hues of the velvet gold tasseled pillows, as well as the handsomely crafted secretary and chifforobe, Sandra knew that the woman was only being modest.

Jack, who had walked into the bathroom, called out to Sandra. Curious, she joined him. To their joy, the bath was a wonderful eclectic mix of modern, old and whimsical. Its wooden floor was stained in the same beautiful hue as the remainder of the home, but high over the ivory porcelain sink was a breathtaking stained glass window. In great detail, the glass depicted an intricate scene of a storm's aftermath washed in the golden rays of sun and rainbow.

As the afternoon sunlight filtered in through the lead glass, it danced on the celestial shaped beveled prisms that hung from the high-pitched ceiling. The overall affect of color and light left them both speechless.

"This is...is...beautiful," gasped Sandra. "Now Miss Lavania, this room took more than just a little imagination and luck. Did you and Mr. Al have the window commissioned?"

Shaking her head, the woman smiled as she looked up at the window. "It is beautiful, isn't it? Believe it or not, there are two of them, one in each turret. We didn't even realize that this was here until we updated the plumbing about 25 years ago. The room that we're standing in used to be a storage closet. It seems that when Alphonse's parents built the house, his mother's brother, Al's uncle, made his living designing stained glass windows and lamps. The glass lamps, turret windows, and the pane in the front door are all his handiwork."

"This house is an absolute treasure," complimented Jack. "With you all being so close to New Orleans, I'm surprised that you don't stay booked."

"We like things just the way that they are. Not too busy, never too slow. We only open our home to those whose company we are sure to enjoy. Most of our guests have been people who have found out about us through friends of ours. And our friends are very selective about who they invite out or they might not be welcomed back.

"Do you hear that, Sandra? We better be on our best behavior," Jack teased.

Letting out a friendly laugh, Lavania patted him on the back. "I better let you two get unpacked. Now, there is no need to rush back downstairs. I'm sure that the others are still getting settled in. Just take your time and holler if you need anything."

Halfway out of the door, she turned and pointed to a wardrobe that stood across from the turn-of-the-century ball and claw tub. "There's plenty of linens and soap over in the chifforobe. You should be able to find just about everything that you need."

As the woman's footsteps receded down the stair-case, Sandra opened the cabinet door, and a floral fra-grance enveloped the room. "Mm....mm, I bet you I can guess what's hidden in here," she sighed.

Enjoying the way in which the tinted light danced in her hair, Jack walked over and teased, "You should, it smells like your shop."

Sandra inhaled his woodsy masculine scent and the gentle sweet bouquet of the potpourri. "I can't tell which smells better, you or the chifforobe." Finding the ensuing balm sensually intoxicating, she felt her pulse quicken. Looking up into his soft, twinkling eyes, she swallowed hard. "Um...Jack...we better finish unpacking."

As he moved in a bit closer, he placed a finger gen-tly to her lips and wordlessly quieted her voice." Just as he lowered his mouth to hers, they both heard footsteps ascending the staircase.

"Jack? Sandra?" came a low, cunningly sweet voice.

Darlene's voice was a cold reminder of exactly why Jack was visiting. It was mere coincidence that they were sharing a suite of rooms, not serendipity as Mr. Al allud-ed to earlier. Jack and Darlene were the 'couple'; Darlene should be the object of his attentions. Looking directly into his eyes with controlled evenness, Sandra distanced herself and dryly she dryly remarked, "Someone's calling you."

As she turned to walk away, he reached out and grabbed her arm, "Sandy...wait..."

"I don't know what little game you're playing, but you're not playing me for a fool again, Jack Thibodeaux."

Leaving him in the bathroom, she brushed past Darlene who was just rounding the last stair.

The serpentine woman, taking in Sandra's angry

expression, stepped in front, and suspiciously narrowed her feline eyes. "Where's Jack?"

Sandra had had her fill of both Jack and Darlene for one afternoon. She was in no mood for the woman's intimidating tactics. With hackles raised, she shot back, "Check his bedroom, I'm sure that's where you're headed anyway."

Darlene, with eyes still narrowed, watched as Sandra walked past her into the bedroom and slammed the door.

Chapter Twenty-One

After angrily emptying the contents of her overnight bag into the chifforobe, Sandra opened one of the dormers and curled up on the window seat. As she looked out across the backyard to the surrounding bayou, she felt her emotions slowly quiet. Watching the early evening sky gradually darken from a soft rose-tinged gold to a burnished iridescent amber, she found God's beauty gently restoring some of the peace that had eluded her over the past weeks. As a fine mist rose from the still waters and cast shadows over the ground and trees, she likened it to silken gossamer.

On the soft breeze that wafted in through the window, she could hear the rhythmic creaking of the porch swing below. Immediately, she thought of her own swing where she and Jack would sit and talk for hours. To say that their relationship had changed over the past weeks was an understatement. If it were possible to go back in time, she would alter so much.

Just as she was readying to rise and join the rest of the party downstairs, voices came in from the outside. Glancing out the window, she spied Jack and Darlene walking several yards away, along the dock. The sight of them together, talking so earnestly, made her feel exceedingly jealous. It appeared that her best friend had found another to share his thoughts and dreams.

As she sat and watched the two of them, there was a soft rap at her bedroom door. "Sandra?" It was Lee.

"Why are you up here sitting alone in the dark?"

Still facing the window, she quickly patted her eyes and prayed that he wouldn't notice the tears that threatened to fall. Evading his question, she replied, "Oh, I was just enjoying the sunset."

Without comment, he walked over to the window and made himself comfortable. Looking out, he too caught sight of Jack and Darlene. Stealing a perceptive glance over at Sandra, he turned back towards the window and in a voice as calming as the quiet they shared, he asked, "What's the rest of that poem you were reciting this afternoon?"

"Um...let's see, there's a passage that fits this sunset perfectly...

...softly the evening came. The sun from the western horizon
Like a magician extended his golden wand o'er the landscape;
Twinkling vapor arose; and sky and water and forest
Seemed all on fire at the touch, and melted and mingled together.

"I'm amazed that I remembered so much of that narrative."

"It is beautiful. Do you know the Cajun version of the tale?" As she shook her head no, he supplied, "Even though it still ends tragically, it's a bit more realistic. According to lore, the young woman was named Emmeline Labiche, not Evangeline. And her beloved Gabriel was actually named Louis Arceneaux. The pair, like Evangeline and Gabriel, were separated when the Arcadians, the Cajuns—were exiled from Nova Scotia. The two vainly searched everywhere for one another. Emmeline, like Evangeline, came close to finding her love several times, but always just missed him.

"Now here's where Longfellow departs from the Cajun version. He has Evangeline and Gabriel finally meeting in Philadelphia. The young woman, who by this time had become a nun, stumbles upon her love dying in a charity hospital, and stays by his side until he dies."

Interrupting, Sandra whispered, "Maybe if Evangeline had just waited long enough, she would have been reunited with Gabriel when he came back for her."

"That's exactly what Louis did. He gave up his quest and returned home, where he eventually met and fell in love with someone else. When Emmeline finally arrived, it was too late...no 'happily ever afters'."

With a trace of cynicism, Sandra quipped as she looked out the window down at Jack and Darlene, who now were making their way towards the house, "Well, we both know about 'happily ever afters'...even from the start they're usually an aberration."

Surveying her profile, he shrugged, "True, but quite often, if we have the courage, God gives us an opportunity to pen a happy ending."

His words, along with the phantom shadows of dusk, filled the room and hung heavy.

"Maggie! If you can't make yourself useful, you might as well leave and join the others," Lavania admonished as she swatted her hand.

Laughing as her good friend devilishly snapped up several of the andouille puff pastry appetizers that Lavania had just placed in a chaffing dish, Sandra guided Maggie to a chair far removed from the food.

"With all of this food, it's so hard not to eat," groaned Maggie. "Besides, I thought that part of the reward for helping you cook was being able to sample."

"It is. But the rate that you're 'sampling', there won't

be anything left for anyone else. Now, lick your fingers and sit there like a good girl. Dinner will be ready as soon as Alphonse brings the roast in from out of the smoker." Looking up at the clock, she surmised, "And that should be any minute now."

As if on cue, Al walked in from off the back porch carrying a wooden board laden with a 20-pound roast. Just the smell of the seasoned cut of meat made Sandra's mouth water.

Lavania expertly slid the roast onto a serving platter and directed Maggie and Sandra to load the serving cart with an array of appetizing fare. Along with the roast and sausage appetizers were pot au feu or soup meat, rice au gratin, okra and tomatoes, snap beans au vin, mirliton and crab meat casserole, baked sweet potatoes, dinner rolls and cracklin' cornbread. According to Maggie, Al never thought a meal complete without his cracklin'.

With some amusement, Sandra wondered how the old couple stayed so thin. She knew cracklin' was nothing more than fried pork rinds, and just from observing Lavania prepare the meal, she realized that there was hardly a dish to which the older woman didn't add salt pork, bacon, eggs or oil of some sort.

As they sat down to eat at the huge mahogany dining room table, she quickly slid into the chair next to Alphonse, who was sitting at the head of the table. Expecting Lee to sit on her other side, she was surprised when Jack pulled up the chair alongside her. When she flashed him a sharp disapproving glance, he simply offered an especially boyish grin and asked, "You don't mind, do you?"

"No, suit yourself, though I'm not the one you should be asking. Your girlfriend doesn't seem the type to take all of this attention too kindly."

Nodding his head towards the direction in which Darlene and Lee had just taken their seats, Jack smiled as his date leaned in towards Lee and exaggeratedly gushed at something he said. "Oh, I don't think that she minds too terribly."

With Sandra still glowering, Jack took her bowl and asked if she would like him to ladle out some of the spicy soup.

Sandra, determined not to allow him to ruin her meal, saw little choice but to accept his attentiveness. Gradually, despite all of her efforts to remain aloof, she found herself responding to his light conversation, and was soon laughing along with the others at his humorous comments. He proved, not to her surprise, to be a very delightful dinner guest. Several times when she was certain that his attention was distracted she would mentally trace the faint crinkles that broke out around his eyes whenever he laughed. Once to her embarrassment, he turned towards her and caught her studying his face. Not appearing to be in any hurry to break her gaze, he locked his eyes with hers and gave a seductive wink.

The meal went along beautifully, the food tasted as wonderful as it smelled, and Alphonse colorfully peppered the table talk with tales of the bayou.

After she was certain that everyone had eaten their fill, Lavania suggested that they move into the parlor while she cleared the table and prepared for dessert. Both Sandra and Jack rose and simultaneously insisted that Lavania join the group while they cleared the table. As they expected, she wouldn't hear anything of the kind.

"Don't be silly. You two are my guests, besides I now where everything goes. I appreciate the offer, but whenever you leave someone else in your kitchen, they only wind up making a bigger mess."

Jack, with the practiced appeal of an attorney, responded with relaxed ease. "Miss Lavania, I don't blame you. No one knows your kitchen better than you do, but it'll make us feel so much better if you allow us to help at least. Besides, we've got to do something to work off this wonderful meal that we have just eaten, or else we won't have room for any of Maggie's birthday cake."

"Or the homemade ice cream that Maggie keeps telling me about," Sandra added as she took her cue from Jack.

Chuckling, Lavania caved in. "All right you two, grab a plate. Don't let it be said that I stopped you from enjoying your dessert."

In the kitchen, Jack and Sandra stacked the dishwasher while Lavania stored the leftovers, made a fresh pot of coffee and put the final touches on Maggie's cake.

After everyone sang "Happy Birthday," they settled down to watch her open her gifts.

David gave his wife an intricately engraved gold 'poesy' or poetry ring. So called because of the words of love etched around the band. Admiring the antique band, Maggie read its old French inscription out loud, "Por tous jours".

"For always," Jack translated as he turned to look into Sandra's eyes. Feeling her cheek warm, she quickly looked away.

Maggie tore into the remainder of the gifts. Sandra gave a pair of emerald cut amethyst earrings set in sterling silver. She received an exquisite magenta batik silk scarf from Darlene and Jack, and Lee presented her with a handsome hand-hewn rocker, similar in design to the "Lodge" furniture that filled the bedroom upstairs.

The final package to unwrap was a gift offered by the Fontenots. To Maggie's delight, inside the box, carefully wrapped in an antique lace handkerchief, was a silver locket that dangled from a delicate chatelaine.

"Oh, Miss Lavania...this is beautiful." Turning over the locket, she read the inscription, "S.C. 1959".

Fondly explaining the date, Alphonse asked, "You remember that trunk up in the attic, don't you?"

"Yes, it was mother's."

"Well, earlier this week, Lavania was poking through it to find a picture she wanted to give you. When she took out the photo album, the locket fell out. Your mother had wrapped it up in a handkerchief for safekeeping.

"Open it up," Lavania softly suggested.

Silently obeying, she gently pulled at the clasp. Inside was a baby picture of herself, Lee and her dad.

First showing David and Lee, she then gave the elderly couple a warm hug and kiss before sharing the precious keepsake with the rest of the guests.

After several more minutes of conversation, the Fontenots headed upstairs to retire for the evening. On their way up, Al paused and mentioned to Jack that he and Sandra should take advantage of the warm evening and enjoy a walk.

Feeling her face go warm once again, Sandra quickly glanced over at Jack. "I'm sure Jack and Darlene have..."

"My mistake," Alphonse interrupted as he leaned over the banister. "I thought I heard Lee promise to walk Darlene on over to the old school house."

"Is that dilapidated thing still standing?" asked Maggie. "It looked like it was on its last leg twenty years ago."

"It's still there. I was just going to suggest that we head on over before it gets too late." Turning to the rest of the group, he extended an invitation, "Anyone else who's up for the walk is more than welcome to come along."

"You're talking about at least a one mile walk, one way through the swamp!" Maggie exclaimed," No thank you." Snuggling up under her husband's arm, she suggested, "Why don't we sit this one out and help ourselves to some more of that ice cream? We can take it out on the porch."

Smiling down into his wife's face, David gave her shoulders a loving squeeze. "Lee, you heard my wife. It looks like we're going to sit this one out."

"Well, Sandra and Jack, that leaves you two."

Sandra, looking over at Darlene all snuggled up next to Lee, wondered if it was just her imagination, or did Jack and she seem to be on the outs.

"What do you plan on seeing in the dark?" asked Sandra.

Darlene, exchanging glances with Lee, answered, "Nothing much. It's just something we used to do when...when we were younger."

Looking first at Lee, then at Darlene, Jack smiled and turned to Sandra and suggested, "Well, what do you say to walking with them halfway? Maybe to where the road ends? After that, we can play it by ear."

Seeing little choice, she looked quickly over at Maggie and David. If she stayed behind and enjoyed ice cream with them, she would definitely feel like a third wheel, especially since the Fontenots had already retired. Shrugging her shoulders, she agreed.

Within fifteen minutes, the group was heading away from the house, down the sloping path towards the swamp. Lee suggested that they follow the dirt path towards the narrow clamshell road that meandered with the swamp several yards away from the water. After several minutes of swatting mosquitoes, Darlene commented that she hoped someone had thought to bring along insect repellent.

Chuckling, Jack answered, "Lee and I put some on while you girls were up changing your shoes. I'm sorry, I just assumed that you were going to do the same."

"Typical male!" Sandra teased. "Only thinking about yourselves."

Looking very put out, Lee quipped, "That's not true. I brought along the flashlights and Jack has his gun."

"Gun?" cried Sandra. "Why do we need a gun?"

"Lions, tigers, and bears!" chuckled Jack as he mimicked the popular line.

"Lions, tigers, and bears! Oh my!" Sandra playfully retorted.

Impatiently interrupting, Darlene griped, "While you all play, I'm getting eaten up by these mosquitoes."

Laughing, Lee took hold of her hand, pulled her along as if she were a spoilt child. "Well, there's nothing much we can do now sweetie. Just keep moving and the mosquitoes won't seem so bad."

As the foursome continued along the path making easy conversation, they all stopped short when it became apparent that the insects were still bothering Darlene.

Feeling truly sorry for her, Sandra surveyed the grass and asked, "Is there any lavender around?"

"Lavender? It's the middle of the night, and you're thinking about picking flowers?" complained Darlene.

Flashing a patient smile, Sandra overlooked the woman's sour mood and explained, "The oil from the lavender flower makes a wonderful repellent. I thought that if there were some close by, we could use it to help with the bugs."

Making a grimace as she scratched at her arms and legs, Darlene stood silently as Jack directed the beam of the flashlight across the thicket and further in the woods,"Well, there's no lavender here, at least none that I can see."

Beginning to become irritated by the pesky bugs herself, Sandra offered, "Listen, I don't mind running back for the repellent. The house is just a little ways back, Besides, I forgot to take my allergy medicine, and if I don't take it soon, I'll regret it later on tonight."

Anticipating that Jack would balk at her offer, she quickly lifted the flashlight from his hand and started back down the narrow trail. Turning around, she directed, "It will only take me a few minutes. Keep walking and I'll catch up in no time."

Not exactly happy with the idea of her walking back alone, Jack called for her to stop before she could take more than a few steps."Sandra, wait a minute. Let me walk back with you."

"Don't be silly. I can still see the house, just give me five minutes."

Well aware of how tenuous their relationship was, he decided not to push. "If you're sure. We'll go on ahead and stop when we reach the road. You can't miss it. Just stay on the path. It winds a little, but with the flashlight, you should be able to follow it easily."

Flashing him a smile, Sandra turned back down the trail.

Jack, before rejoining Darlene and Lee, stood and watched until she had safely reached the back porch.

Once inside the house, it took longer than she had anticipated. Lee and Jack hadn't put the repellent back where Lavania usually kept it, and even with Maggie helping, they had to search around a bit before finding it.

Sandra, waving away Maggie and David's offer to walk to the road with her, ran down the slope back towards the trail. The wind, which had picked up, made the balmy night a bit breezy. As the tall grasses bent over the narrow dark path, she soon found the trail difficult to follow.

Several times, she cautiously stopped to make sure that she was heading in the right direction. Thinking that she heard voices close by, she picked up her pace. Suddenly a fallen branch caught her off guard, causing her to trip and fall, dropping the flashlight in the process. To her dismay, not only did the light go out, but it rolled into the midst of the tall grass when it hit the ground.

Quickly picking herself up, she frantically patted the

ground for the flashlight, willing the beam to come back on. No such luck. As she furtively felt around the grass, she looked up and noticed that the sky had become increasingly overcast, thereby blocking out much of the light from the moon.

Now in almost complete darkness, it was impossible to see the house. Even the upstairs bedroom light that had been so clear before was difficult to distinguish. Refusing to panic, she quickly decided that it would probably be easier to find the road than to pick her way back to the house. Besides, she was certain that she had just heard her companions moments earlier.

Calling out, "Jack...Lee!" she strained to hear an answer. Stopping when she thought she heard a response, she realized that because of the wind, it would be difficult to determine from which direction the voices were coming.

After walking several more minutes, she noticed to her dismay that thick fog was rolling in from the swamp. The further she walked, the denser the fog became, and now without the flashlight, it was impossible to see the house, let alone the dirt path. Feeling the ground grow wetter under the rubber soles of her leather shoes, she panicked as she realized that ever since she had taken the fall, she had been walking towards the water.

"Jack...Jack!" No answer. With all of her senses on edge, she detected every rustle of the trees overhead and stirrings from the swamp, which was now only several feet away.

As the wind began to blow harder, the light patter of rain could be heard as it struck the thick canopy of trees. Soon, especially as the rain grew heavier, the drops would find their way to the ground and soak through her light summer sweater.

Taking advantage of the temporary shelter of the trees, she racked her brain for any forgotten bits of knowledge that could assist in getting her safely back to the house. Once again looking up at the overcast sky, she realized that it would be impossible to regain her bearings from the stars. There was no way to signal for help; besides, the rainfall, which was now growing heavier, would only drown her calls out. Staying put until Jack could find her seemed to be the best thing to do.

Glancing down at her watch for the tenth time, she was growing increasingly worried. A full hour had passed since she started back from the house. Surely, they would have begun looking for her by now. When what Sandra hoped to be only a raccoon or opossum scurried past, she nervously sat down on a tree stump and fervently prayed for an early rescue.

The next hour felt more like three. At her wit's end, she prayed constantly that she wouldn't see any of the wildlife that she knew made their home in the bayou. Realistically, she knew that the alligators and snakes could be a real threat, and the knowledge that Jack felt the need to carry a gun didn't help. Soon her imagination began to take over and all she could think of were the stories that the *Picayune* carried on occasion of bayou sightings of bears and cougars. Nervously glancing around, she hoped that they hated being out in the rain as much as she did.

The rain, which had picked up in intensity, now fell through the leaves and moss with a vengeance. Shuddering every time a wave of thunder would roll across the sky, she remembered Lee's earlier comment about the aftermath of lightning strikes. But it was impossible to escape the potential danger that the trees presented, because they were everywhere. With a deep breath, she reminded herself that she wasn't totally helpless.

With a road relatively close by, perhaps there was a boathouse used by area fishermen as well. Reasoning that if she walked as close as possible to the swamp bank, she would stand a pretty good chance of finding some type of shelter, she began sloshing through the murky water. After quickly scanning the ground for a long sturdy tree limb to use as a walking stick, she was soon on her way.

Water was everywhere. In less than an hour, the bayou was filled with brand new lagoons. What was dry land only an hour before was now ankle deep muck. Even with the aid of the stick, it was difficult not to slip on the muddy forest floor. Just as she was beginning to question the wisdom of her decision to seek shelter instead of staying put, the sky overhead flashed white and filled the swamp with an ear-splitting crackle. Several seconds later, an enormous bald cypress several hundred yards away toppled to the ground.

Speechless, she found herself rooted to where she stood. As a second wave of thunder filled the air, she broke out into a blind run. No longer poking cautiously through the waters for poisonous snakes and alligators, she ran clumsily through the chilly water, which was now up to her calves. It was only after falling face down that she forced herself to stop.

Lord please! As she combed through the gray darkness, she suddenly became acutely aware of a sound that she hadn't heard earlier. Closing her eyes, she remembered what Lee had taught her on the drive down, the woods and the swamps had a way of speaking. All she had to do was to listen.

So, she forced herself to concentrate. Within moments, she heard what sounded like rain hitting a tin roof. As her eyes pierced through the darkness, her heart caught when she picked out what appeared to be a narrow boathouse several yards off. It was sitting on stilts surrounded by water several feet from what used to be the shore.

Braving her fears of alligators, Sandra, still gripping her walking stick, stepped out into the watery depths. By the time she reached the base of the stilts, the water was waist deep. Mustering up the remainder of her strength, she pulled herself up onto the porch's overhang. Tugging at the door, she scrambled inside and offered up words of thanks.

Slowly, as her eye's adjusted to the dimness, she realized that her newfound shelter was not a boat house as she had first thought, but one of the jerry-built fishing and hunting shacks that were common in the area. As another roll of thunder filled the sky, she looked upwards and thanked God again for keeping her out of harm's way. Thinking that she might find a flashlight, or at least a candle and matches, she poked through several cupboards. Jumping for joy, she pulled out a container that held a box of candles and a book of matches, finally some light.

The lit candle cast eerie shadows against the windowless slatted walls. The small room was stripped of all furniture, except for a broken chair that leaned useless over in a corner. The wooden floor was littered with old newspaper, empty tin cans and fishing line. It was obvious that the shack hadn't been put to use in quite a while. After having assured herself that there were no snakes lurking in the corners, she sat down. Using the leg of the broken chair to prop open the door, she settled in the musty darkness and stared out at the gloomy swamp. She had a feeling that it was going to be a long night. Already, her trek through the swamp had taken close to three hours and the rain showed no signs of lightening up.

Chapter Twenty-two

For well over thirty minutes, Jack, Lee and Darlene waited at the road for Sandra's return. Sensing Jack's growing concern, Lee suggested that they retrace their steps to the house. "Knowing Miss Lavania, she probably predicted rain and made Sandra stay put. Why don't we head on back."

Jack, without comment, slowly followed the couple but continuously peered into the woods.

Darlene, still oblivious to everything except her insect bites muttered, "Lee, it wouldn't make sense for Sandra to have stayed. She knows that these mosquitoes are killing me. Besides, how can she just assume that we know it is going to rain?"

Though neither said anything, the same thought had run through both men's minds. Halfway up the path, the fog began to roll in, prompting Jack to call out, "Sandra...Sandra..."

No answer. Several times, they thought that they had heard a voice, but the wind made it impossible to tell for sure.

Once again, Darlene verbalized the men's fears. "You don't think that she's gotten lost, do you? Well, I pity her if she did. It'll be next to impossible to find her in all of this fog."

Jack and Lee glanced nervously at one another as they shined their flashlights into the woods.

"Damn," whispered Jack, as heavy fat raindrops

began to fall. "I pray to God she's waiting back at the house."

As they scrambled up the porch, Lee called out for his friend.

Puzzled, Maggie rose from the swing, "Sandra left out of here almost an hour ago. You mean, you haven't seen her?"

Darlene, whose stinging bites were more of a concern than Sandra's disappearance, trooped in the house. "I'm waking Miss Lavania to see what she can put on these bites."

Worried, Maggie desperately scanned the woods, "We offered to walk her to the road, but she seemed pretty sure of knowing the way back. We just can't leave her out there! What do you think we ought to do?"

Stepping back out into the now pouring rain, Jack glanced up at one of the house's turrets. "Let's go in and turn on all of the lights upstairs. If she's lost, maybe she'll be able to get her bearings."

"There are binoculars inside. Maybe we can spy her from one of the windows," Lee suggested.

On the staircase, they were met by Alphonse, who was visibly worried. Slipping on his shirt, he calmly took charge. "Darlene told us what happened. Lavania is in there now calling the sheriff. More than likely, he'll put together a search party of some kind. Maggie, you and Darlene take the binoculars on up and see if you can spot her from the windows. Don't forget to turn on all of the lights. Jack, Lee, and David, follow me."

The younger men followed Al into the kitchen. Silently they watched as he took out lanterns, batteries, flare guns, compasses and several small first aid kits. The men understood that when you lived in the bayou, it was essential to be prepared for any sudden disaster.

As they donned the rain slickers and thigh-high rubber boots that Alphonse had handed each of them,

Lavania came into the kitchen with several wool army blankets. "The sheriff's rounding up a search party now. He said for you to leave word with me where you're headed and he'll meet you out there." Looking over at Jack's pinched face, she smiled, "Don't you worry none, we'll find her. She couldn't have gotten far. Let's think positive. This area is filled with all types of jerry-builts, so there's a good chance that she even found shelter somewhere."

But they all knew that for those unfamiliar with the bayou, things could turn treacherous fast, especially in the rain.

Alphonse, grabbing paper and pen from a drawer, walked over to the large oak table and sketched out a quick map of the area where they expected to find Sandra. "Now bear in mind that with all of the rain that's been falling, this is real rough. At this point, it'll probably make more sense to skiff the waters, and when we hit land get out and search on foot. Jack, do you think that you can still find your way around in one of the pirogues?"

"It's been a while, but I think that I'll do fine."

"Good." Pointing to the map, Al gave out assignments. "Jack, you start out here, off to the west. Lee, it'll be hard, but try to stay to the east of the fork. David, you come with me. Lavania, go fetch my shot gun and bring down a couple of revolvers."

Down at the boathouse, the men each headed off in their assigned direction with arrangements to fire a flare twice if they found Sandra, and three times, if they needed assistance.

As Jack expertly skimmed through the water in the narrow cypress log, he was grateful that the pirogue could carry him through the numerous waterways, some no more than two to three feet wide. Shining his flashlight into the dense foliage that burgeoned along the shore, he slowly scanned the woods for any sign of her.

Desperately trying not to imagine the worst, he called out her name as he remembered the last smile she flashed him before she turned to walk down the path. With a breaking heart, he remembered that she was only wearing a light sweater. Already the rain, which was still falling steadily, had turned the night air cooler than what had been predicted, and he knew that she must be feeling the damp coldness.

"Sandra! Sandra!" Nothing. His calls were met only with the pattering of rainfall. As a flash of lightening lit the sky, he caught sight of the telltale yellow of a copperhead. The poisonous snake was a night feeder and more than likely was scrambling to find drier ground, away from the rising water. Slowly reaching for his revolver, he took aim and fired at the snake, killing it instantly. Ordinarily, if it were of no immediate threat, he would have let it be, but just in case Sandra was close by, he didn't want to take any chances.

As he inched his way upstream, he berated himself for the hundredth time. What did she know of poisonous snakes and alligators? Instinct had warned him not to allow her to return to the house alone, but he had been too intent on not pressuring her, for fear of losing her. Now he might have lost her for good.

Sardonically laughing at the irony of it all, he vowed to end the months of madness that they both had been enduring. By week's end, there would be little doubt in her mind of his love. But first, he had to find her. It was now more than four hours since she had last been seen. Combing the beam through the underbrush, he whispered, "Sandy, I love you."

"The bayou, once it's in your system, it is impossible

to shake." Well, it will be impossible to shake this all right; Sandra grimaced as she remembered Lee's words. This experience will permanently be etched in my mind.

Shifting to a more comfortable position, she picked up the candle, which she had placed in one of the tin cans and tried to warm herself as much as possible. The rain, it seemed, had no intention of letting up, so for now she had to sit tight. Steady it fell, lulling every creature quiet, or so she hoped. As she looked out the door, she felt as if she really wasn't a part of her surroundings, but a spectator. The surreal view before her was every bit as mystical as the dreams that seemed to always accompany her sleep. Gray vapors rose from the waters and clung as dewy droplets to all that they touched. The air, heavy and still, enshrouded the moss-laden trees that stood moodily against the night sky like silent sentries.

Closing her eyes, she prayed that God would take away her fear, keep her safe and provide a rescue. Feeling very tired, but no longer fearful, she allowed herself to be carried away by the sweet lull of the willows, cypresses, live oaks and water ash. As the rain melted into the deep languid water, she, herself now a shadow of the bayou, drifted to sleep.

Her slumber moved from being peaceful to restive as she dreamed of the forest being brilliantly lit in glorious color.

Slowly the prism of light begins to dance in and out of a heavy cloud of mist...

After tethering their pirogue, Robert takes her hand and leads her onshore. Together they walk purposely towards a tall figure that is beckoning them to hurry. Not knowing quite why, Robert takes her hand and urges her to walk a little faster.

Just as she is able to make out who it is that they are hurrying to, a wisp of moss flutters in front of them. As it grazes the ground, it transfigures into a beautiful woman. With a gasp, she is certain that her eyes are deceiving her. Upon first glance, the woman is Darlene, and then suddenly the cemetery sylph-'Might-Have-Been'. Her evil smile and piercing eyes are unrelenting. The combination sends a fear through her soul that roots her steps.

Robert, seemingly unfazed, gives her hand a tight squeeze before letting it go. Wordlessly, he reaches out to the sylph and leads her away into the woods. The woman, flattered by the attention, smiles into his face and follows without a backwards glance. Slowly the pair dissolves into bits of moss and fly away on a phantom breeze.

Continuing her trek towards the beckoning figure, she suddenly recognizes it to be Jack. As she runs to him, she feels his warmth even before she reaches him. Falling into his arms, she is awash with a perfect sense of security. There is no doubt; this is where she is meant to be. Not only is his warm embrace welcoming, but also it is also sensuously exciting.

Lifting her face upwards, she feels her heart race as his darkening hazel eyes spark with tender passion. Passionately covering her mouth with his, he kisses her with wonderful abandon. As his fingers become lost in her silken curls, instinctively his tongue seeks hers. Urging her head closer towards his, his strong hands trace the hollow of her back until they come to rest upon her round hips.

With her breasts standing full and firm under the thin gauzy fabric of her dress, she arches her shapely body against his hard chest. Unaware how the transparent drape of her gown beautifully accentuates her silhouette, she steps away from her love and gently pulls him onto a fragrant bed of rose petals, grass, pink orchids and honeysuckle.

With boldness she isn't aware that she possesses,

she sensuously undoes his shirt, slowly...button by button. Molding her soft curves to his toned muscles, she feels his lower body hardened. With a mischievous smile, she allows her hands to wander and tease. First, her fingers tantalize their way down to the hollow of his back, and then they travel across his stomach and under his waistband, until they run across the metal zipper of his pants. Stopping, she suggestively taps her manicured finger as she feels him harden even more. Slowly pulling the zipper down, her fingertips lightly caresses the object of their teasing.

Inhaling sharply, he gently rolls her onto her back. As she looks skyward towards a canopy of fluttering Spanish moss, she turns her head and soak in the beauty of the colorful water hyacinths that lazily float along the nearby lagoon.

Jack's strong hands take their time as they appreciatively glide over her every curve. Slowly he unlaces the satin ribbon front of her gown. His hands, surprisingly agile, start first at the bodice, pause teasingly at her breasts and continue down to the beautiful round of her stomach. With his teeth, he unfastens a short row of satin covered buttons and allows his tongue to brush past the dark triangle of soft hair, downward to her firm thighs.

His task now complete, he slips off her gown. Groaning plaintively, she wraps her hands around his waist and pulls his warm body towards hers. Taking his time, her lover slowly runs his tongue with feather like strokes along the nipples of her breasts until they are pinpoint hard.

Nuzzling her face against the rough hairs of his chest, she feels her hips match the rhythm of those pressed against her. Feeling her lower being suddenly flash from simply hot to molten liquid, she closes her eyes and moans, "Jack..."

Just when all of her anticipation is to be delightfully

met, a cold breeze rushes across her body, a bit of moss flutters from the canopy and he is gone. Sobbing out his name, she pleads, "Jack, please don't leave me...not again."

"Honey, I'm not going anywhere."

Rubbing her eyes in disbelief, she saw Jack standing over her, black rain slicker dripping wet. Was she still dreaming? Jack?

With a deep chuckle, he quickly pulled off his slicker and placed it around her shoulders. Basking in its warmth, she closed her eyes and allowed herself to be cradled in his strong arms. His chest was just as warm as she dreamed.

Suddenly, without quite being aware of what she was doing, she buried her head against his neck and cried into his shirt with long sobs, of both happiness and joy. Not only was she safe, but also she was with her man, Jack.

Gently wiping away her tears, he let her weep and assumed that she was just scared and tired. When it was apparent that all her tears were spent, he studied her face and gently kissed her forehead. "You're safe and sound now, Sandy. Let me help you out of here. We'll be home before you know it."

There was so much that she wanted to tell him, but her emotions were in such a state that words were impossible. Like a father soothing a helpless child, he lifted his charge into the pirogue, cooing soothing words as he wrapped her in several warm blankets. But despite the layers of fabric, he couldn't warm her up enough to stop the shivering. Anxiously eyeing his found love, he signaled to the search party and quickly made his way back to the Fontenots'.

Chapter Twenty-three

The evening following her adventure, Sandra was temporarily seized with panic. Had she really been rescued, or was the whole adventure just a horrible nightmare? Desperately trying to get some bearing, she frantically searched the darkened room for a clock and was stunned to find that it was well past 8:00 p.m.. She closed her eyes as she began to remember the past twenty-four hours. It was as if the experience in the swamp, the dream and her rescue were all one long blur.

The last thing that she fully recalled was Jack carrying her into the house and up to the bedroom. But from that point on, it was difficult to remember all of the household's comings and goings. There was Lavania who constantly came in and out, mothering her with tea, soup, and extra blankets. Followed by Al, Maggie and Lee with their hugs and words of concern.

Then, if her memory was correct, Jack came in and introduced her to the doctor, a woman, Dr. Debonet or was it Deveraux? The one thing that stood out in her mind about the doctor's visit was Jack's attempt at supervising the exam. Smiling, she thought of Jack. After shooing everyone out of the room, she last remembered him giving her the sleeping pills that the doctor had prescribed, and kissing her gently on the forehead before wishing her sweet dreams.

Suddenly eager to see him, she slipped from under

the covers, stepped onto the cold floor, and searched for her robe and slippers. Just when she had shrugged them on, there was a quiet knock at the door and with a motherly smile, Lavania bustled into the room. Noticing Sandra in her robe, the woman's voice grew stern, "Just where do you think you're going, young lady? Get back in that bed." Without waiting for an explanation, she took hold of her elbow and led her across the room.

"It's 8:00 in the evening...I just wanted to see what everyone else was up to."

Lavania, tucking her snugly under the blankets, firmly remarked, "Don't you worry about everyone else. They're up and doing just fine. You, on the other hand, have had quite an ordeal. Dr. Delcambre left strict orders for you to stay in bed and rest. Picking up the thermometer from off the nightstand, she continued as if speaking to a wayward child. "Now, you are to stay in bed. The only reason I should see you out is if you need to go to the bathroom. Have I made myself clear?"

Playfully obedient she answered, "Yes, ma'am."

Smiling down at her charge, Lavania smoothed back her hair and softened her tone. "We just want to make sure that you are indeed all right. I don't think that you fully realize the scare you gave us last night."

Before relating the previous day's events, Lavania slipped the thermometer under Sandra's tongue and fluffed up the pillows. "When Jack brought you in this morning, you had a temperature of 103. He was convinced that you needed to go directly to the hospital, but the sheriff had already called Doc to come on over when word got out that you had been found."

Pushing the thermometer aside, Sandra, genuinely surprised at all of the 'to do' asked, "The sheriff was out here?"

"Sandra, like I said, you gave us quite a scare. Getting lost out there in that swamp is serious business.

There's too much that can happen, especially if you don't know the area...and with it being dark and raining...like I said, you don't realize the scare you gave us."

"Oh, Miss Lavania, I'm so sorry. Here I am, supposed to be a guest, and I've caused so much trouble."

"Hush, it wasn't your fault. It was just one of those things...Fate." Pulling up the rocker, Lavania thoughtfully studied the young woman's face. "You know, you're one lucky girl. After hearing Jack describe how he stumbled upon you, all I can say is that God must've sent an angel to watch over you, that's for sure."

"How...how did Jack know where to look for me?"

"Sh!...No talking until I take that thing out of your mouth." After reaching over to adjust the blankets, Lavania answered the question. "It seemed that he saw the light from your candle. He called out, and when he didn't get an answer, he just assumed that you were a fisherman waiting out the storm. Just when he was about to continue on, a gale of wind, from out of nowhere pushed the door open and he saw your white sweater." Reaching over to take out the thermometer, Lavania seemed satisfied that the fever had broken.

"Miss Lavania, where is Jack now?"

Quietly placing the thermometer back on the nightstand, she paused momentarily to choose her words. "Oh, he ran into town with Darlene, Maggie and David. They should be back shortly."

Feeling tears well up in her eyes, she asked, "Um...Lee didn't go with them?"

"No, he drove out to his workshop. When they get back, I'm sure they'll be up to check on you. Are you hungry?"

Shaking her head no, she swallowed hard before softly commenting, "I guess I ruined Jack and Darlene's romantic weekend."

Chuckling as if the notion was farfetched, Lavania felt

her forehead with the back of her hand. "On the contrary, I think that your little adventure stirred up quite a bit of romance. I have a feeling that Jack and Darlene are each going to get what they want. But, right now young lady, you look like you are in want of a bit of sleep. You're still looking a little peaked." Smiling, Lavania rose from her chair. "I'll be back up shortly to check on you. Al's in our room reading, so if you need anything, go to the stairs and holler."

Sandra, desperately struggling to keep her emotions in check, forced a smile and choked back tears, "Yes, ma'am."

As soon as the woman closed the door, Sandra let out several long sobs. No longer able to ignore the emotional turmoil that had been raging inside, she closed her eyes and tried to block out the picture of Darlene and Jack. She had been a fool to think that their relationship could return to the way it was, too many hurtful words and time had been allowed to pass.

Closing her eyes, she remembered the evening Robert introduced her to Jack. Robert had twisted her arm to come along to a party thrown by his fraternity. She hated their get-togethers and usually found a way to keep from going. But that evening, Robert was insistent. He told her that he wanted to show her off to his "frat" brothers. But knowing Robert quite well, she knew that she wasn't the one he wanted to put on display, it was the $2000 engagement ring that he had just given her.

After about an hour, growing tired of the noise and juvenile behavior, she started inching her way across the packed room towards the door. Just seconds short of freedom, Robert grabbed her from behind and introduced her to one of his frat brothers, Jack. There were very few of Robert's friends that she actually liked, and she assumed that Jack would be no different. Out of politeness, she offered a faint smile and indulged in sev-

eral minutes of half-hearted conversation. Robert, growing bored, asked Jack to keep an eye on her while he
went to get a beer. As soon as Robert disappeared into
the crowd, Jack had turned towards her and flashed that
charming smile of his. "Let's get out of here while we still
have a chance." Taking his hand, she followed him on out
the door.

Once outside, the two of them sat and talked for well
over an hour. From the start, she felt as if they were true
soul mates. They shared a similar sense of humor,
enjoyed many of the same cultural activities, and appreciated one another's proclivity for spending time alone.
As the three of them spent more time together, Robert,
who thrived on people and the bustle of activity, would
often tease that they were their own best company.

Jack's personality was a pleasant contrast to that of
most of the students she met on campus. Not only was
he very focused and quite responsible for his age, but he
always seemed to know what he wanted from life, and
was willing to do whatever it took. Not only was he taking
the maximum load of classes, but he was also juggling a
full time job.

Realizing his situation, she began to notice that he
always seemed pressed for time. So, she began to offer
to do small things like type term papers and pick up
needed books from the library. Jack, not wanting to feel
as if he was taking advantage of her, agreed to the
arrangement, but only with the stipulation that he tutor
her in two of her weakest subjects, math and economics.
Together they worked out a schedule to meet every
Thursday at her apartment. It was during those late
evening study sessions that she fell in love with him.

After working on her assignments, they would often
wind up talking way into the night. Thursdays quickly
became her favorite evening of the week. The evening of
her last spring final, Jack had dropped by to see how she

made out. He was on top of the world, exams were over and done with, and graduation ceremonies were the coming weekend. Jack, wanting to thank her for all of her help, offered to treat her to dinner. Fully aware of his tight budget, she insisted that instead, he cook one of his favorite pasta dishes.

The evening went wonderfully. After eating, they finished off the wine, listened to music and talked. After the meal, he presented her with a beautiful antique watch that had belonged to his mother, the same watch that a few weeks back, she had stumbled upon in her dresser drawer. Insisting that she take it, he explained that he couldn't have made it through his last year without her help. As he fastened the watch on her wrist, he further explained that the watch was symbolic of not only the time she had given him, but also of how much he enjoyed their time together.

Smiling, she had walked to her bedroom and brought out her own gift. Handing it to him, she explained that it was his graduation present. As usual, the two of them were on the same wavelength, for inside the box was another watch.

Sitting back on the sofa, they both fell into one another's arms as they shared a hearty laugh, and then suddenly out of the blue, he leaned over and gently touched her lips with a light kiss. Remembering the scene as if had happened the night before, she recalled how she without hesitation laid a hand on his chest and returned the kiss. Suddenly the room had filled with a tingling intenseness. Though he didn't utter a word, her instincts told her that his heart was pounding just as fast as hers was. The few seconds that transpired before the inevitable felt ten times longer than they actually were. As Jack's arm hungrily encircled her, his warm mouth covered hers. This second kiss was unlike the first; it was full of fire and emotion. Looking back on that distant night, she realized that not once did she feel any trepidation or pangs of guilt. Indeed she was engaged to Robert, but Jack was the one she desired, the one who she enjoyed spending time with. Staring up at the ceiling, she remembered how he effortlessly lifted her into his arms and carried her into the bedroom. The feel of his muscular body against hers, as well as his warm musky scent, left her emotions in shambles. Jack, who had already captured her soul, that night, captured her body.

It was at this point that the memories became almost too unbearable. Rising, Sandra wiped away the tears that spilt onto the pillow, and walked over to the window seat. Peeking out from behind the heavy drapes, her eyes grazed the dark treetops and settled on the brilliant glimmering reflection of the bayou moonlight. Oh, when was it going to sink in that she and Jack were only meant to be friends. Hadn't she learned her lesson that long ago night?

Sobbing quietly in the dark, she remembered how she cuddled in his arms and willed that wonderful night to last forever. The following morning, her happiness turned to disappointed despair. She had awakened to an empty bed.

Stunned, she had frantically searched for a note, something that would offer a clue as to why he left or more importantly, if he was coming back. The only thing that she could find was the watch that she had given him the previous night. Feeling foolish and used, she took a long shower with the hopes of washing away the memory, but to no avail. As she finished dressing there had been a knock at the door. Thinking it was Jack, she hurried to open it, but to her dismay, it was Robert.

Unaware of her betrayal, he was all smiles, happy that the semester was over and wanting to take her to breakfast. Not knowing how to wriggle out of the invitation, and angry with Jack, she kept silent and accepted.

She didn't hear from Jack again until the graduation ceremonies. And then, Robert was present.

Several times during the months that followed, she had been tempted to give him a telephone call. Not knowing whether it was foolish pride, deep-seated hurt, or simply the fear of hearing what she had already suspected, she always stopped herself from calling. Then he went away, and she forced him out of her mind. That is, until he returned to New Orleans. Funny how Fate works her often times evil hand. Just when she had "forgotten" him, he reappeared as Robert's new FBI partner. She wasn't even aware that he worked for the U.S. Treasury Department. When the three of them would socialize, as they often did, she would sit in infuriated silence and wonder how he could carry on as if they had never shared any type of intimacy. As time wore on, she convinced herself that she had read much more into their one night of lovemaking than what was actually there, for Jack's actions made it clear that it was little more than a one night stand.

Hearing footsteps on the stairs, she quickly ran over to the bed and slid beneath the covers. Purposely turning her back to the bedroom door, she closed her eyes and silently waited for it to open.

"Sandy..." Jack softly whispered.

When she didn't answer, he quietly walked over to the bed and pulled up the rocker. How long he stayed there, just watching, she had no idea. All she knew was that she wasn't yet ready to face him, so she forced herself to fall to sleep.

Several hours later, Sandra rose to the carefree chirping of the nightingales. Hastily glancing out the window at the dark morning sky, she sighed a breath of relief when she spied Jack's sports sedan parked at the end of the driveway. So far, so good. If she could make it to the car, she would be home free. Before falling asleep, she had decided to leave the Fontenots' before any of the household woke. It would be close to impossible to hide her feelings for the reminder of the weekend. She had made the mistake of opening herself up to him once before. She sure in hell wasn't going to do it again. Time apart would give her the chance to regain a mature, non-emotional perspective on their relationship.

Quickly stepping out of the bed, she walked to the door and quietly inched it open. Just as she had hoped, the house was still deep in slumber. As noiselessly as possible, she pulled her clothes from out of the chifforobe and packed them hurriedly into her overnight bag. After throwing on a pair of jeans, blouse and blazer, she haphazardly drew her hair into a ponytail, and quickly scrawled the Fontenots' a note.

Before grabbing her bag, she checked her purse to make sure Jack's spare keys were still on her key ring. She needed his car to drive back to the city. Carefully opening the door, she tiptoed over to the staircase. At the top of the stairs, she could hear Jack softly snoring in the other bedroom. Against the stillness of the morning, it took on a very pleasant quality. It took all of her resolve to walk down the stairs. Quietly setting her bags down, she walked over to the Fontenots' door and slid her note underneath. Then as quickly as she could, she continued down the remainder of the stairs, and on out the house.

The traffic into New Orleans was light, and she was able to make it home in record time. Running into the house, she hurriedly packed a suitcase, grabbed her charge cards and made several phone calls, one of them to Millie Ceasar. Just as she had hoped, her assistant was more than willing to run the shop for a little while longer. If the rest of her plan worked as easily, in two hours she would be winging her way to Florida.

Just as she was leaving, the phone rang. Letting the answering machine pick up the call, she impatiently waited by the door.

"Sandra..." Glancing down at her watch, she muttered an oath. Jack had discovered that she was missing sooner than she had intended. In a harried voice, he continued, "If you're there, stay put. We really need to talk. I've borrowed Darlene's car and I'm headed over to your place. I'll be there in a little while..."

Before the answering machine clicked off, she was out of the door. With him just leaving the Fontenots' she had more than enough time to take care of a bit of unfinished business and make her flight.

Quickly deciding to take Jack's car, she reasoned that it would delay him in guessing her plans. In light of his message, it was obvious that he fully expected her to be home. If he arrived and saw her car still parked, he would have no way of knowing if she ever returned.

Pulling down the drive, she headed for his condo at breakneck speed. Just as Fate would have it, she was stopped by a traffic cop. With her heart pounding rapidly, she handed over her driver's license as she nervously lied as to why she was driving a vehicle not registered in her name.

"Officer, my car is in the shop, so my friend loaned me the use of his."

Sarcastically the police officer commented, "Your friend must not be aware of your driving habits."

Feeling a lecture brewing, she looked down at her watch and wished that he would hurry and write the ticket.

Noticing her impatience, the officer dryly inquired,

"Am I holding you up?"

Smiling, she took note of his graying hair and badge number. It was obvious that he had been with the police department for a while. Desperate to speed along the process, she read his nameplate aloud, "R.S. Millay...you look familiar."

Oh..."

"Yeah, weren't you one of the officers who came to pay respect at my husband's funeral? You probably don't remember Robert was killed several years ago."

With renewed interest, the officer studied first the license, and then her face. Putting the two together he asked, "Robert...Robert Petain? Wasn't he the FBI agent killed a little while back over on Abundance and Metropolitan?"

Mutely nodding, she swallowed. Having gone this far, she might as well continue. "In fact, this car belongs to his partner, Jack Thibodeaux. He was nice enough to lend it to me while mine is in the shop. I'm sure if you called his home..."

Interrupting, the officer took off his hat, "Mrs. Petain, that won't be necessary. I apologize for not immediately connecting the names. How are you and your family doing?"

After a full 20 minutes of small talk and a promise to slow down, she was finally able to go on her way. Grimacing, she wondered if it would have been quicker if she had gotten the ticket. Well, at least she was out of having to pay a $65 fine.

Dashing into the condo, she paced as the elevator made its laborious journey down to the lobby. Normally she would have taken little notice of the wait. But this morning was different, time was of the essence. Just as she had decided to take the stairs, the elevator doors opened. After what felt like an eternity, she let herself into his apartment.

Usually Jack kept his quarters as neat as a pin, so she wasn't prepared for the mess that greeted her. Fearful that someone had burglarized the place, she turned on a lamp as she cautiously stepped into the living room. Taken aback at the disarray, a look of puzzlement crossed her face as she took in the rumpled clothes carelessly thrown over the back of the sofa, a pile of clean laundry that was in need of folding, and the newspaper that littered the room.

It was obvious that the place had been neglected for some time. Placing her handbag on the sofa table, she walked into the kitchen and immediately noticed the stack of unwashed dishes in the sink. Temporarily forgetting the purpose of her visit, she pulled open the refrigerator door. The shelves were bare except for a couple of eggs, several half-eaten containers of take out, beer and a quart of milk. From the smell of things, she was certain that it had soured. Hurriedly picking up the carton, she kicked the door closed, and poured the milk down the drain.

Not to her surprise, the rest of the apartment was n similar shambles. It was obvious that Jack had not been his usual self for quite some time. Concerned, she wondered what had so disrupted his life. She couldn't help wondering if Darlene was the culprit. Everyone handled love differently. Perhaps Jack was so in love that he spent most of his time over at her place and only used his apartment as sort of a way station, a place to run in for a quick change of clothes.

Taking a small narrow box from her blazer pocket, she walked down the hallway and into the master bedroom. With the drapes drawn, the usually bright room looked dark and shadowy. As her eyes adjusted to the dimness, she caught sight of one of Whitney's drawings stuck in between the mirror frame that hung over the chest of drawers. Taking the picture down, she felt her eyes tear up as she thought about how much Whitney and Jesse loved their Uncle Jack. Their love for him was pure and unsullied by disappointment, sad memories, or unexpressed words. Wiping her eyes, she took the box she had been clutching and gently laid it on top of the drawing.

"What's in the box, Sandra?" came a low cool voice.

Gasping, she turned with a start and gripped the edge of the dresser as she noticed the masculine frame that barred the doorway. "Jack...what are you doing here. I...I didn't hear you come in."

"That's obvious," Jack commented in a deceptively calm tone. "I'm sure that if you had, you would have what...hidden under the bed until you were sure I was gone?" Shaking his head, he stuffed his hands into his trouser pockets, and menacingly rocked back and forth. "No, on second thought, I think running is more your style. You would have crawled out the window."

Jack, with contempt plain, stood silent and waited patiently for the astonished woman to respond. Pursing her lips, she bit back a retort as she studied his face. His words were cold and cutting, but even in the shadows of the room, she could see that his eyes were that of a man haggard, worn, and sorely in need of rest.

In a very dismissive tone, she attempted to gain control of the conversation, "Jack, I'm, not going to argue with you, I have a plane to catch."

"A plane to catch...so you've proven me right. Your style is running." From the nasty chuckle, his feelings were more than clear.

As he slowly crossed the room to stand a little more than a few inches away, she found herself unable to drag her eyes away from his face.

"Are you running from this?" Jack angrily demanded as he pulled her into his arms, and kissed her with rough passion.

Choking back tears, she let out a stifled sob as she dragged her lips away. "Jack, why are you doing this to me? Just let me go."

As she walked towards the door, he made no move to go after her. Instead, he stopped her in her tracks by quietly asking, "So I should let you go, just like that, just like before...let you leave without explanation?"

Suddenly her tears ceased and daggers of anger flashed from her eyes. Turning, she walked over to the bureau and picked up the box she had set down earlier. Thrusting it into Jack's hands, she exhaled audibly as she seethed with years of repressed emotion. Finally she demanded, "Just who left without explanation, Jack?"

Sincerely baffled, he looked down at the box and slowly opened it. Inside was the same watch that Sandra had given him that fateful night, years ago. Anxiously waiting a reaction, she noticed a shuttered expression seep across his face and a dewy glisten come to his eyes.

Fully expecting a storm of stammering apologies and quickly made up lies, she was stunned when he raggedly answered, "True, I left that morning without explanation. But, I was coming right back! I wanted to surprise you with breakfast in bed, so I went out to pick up a few groceries. Sandra, what was your reason?"

"My reason?"

"Yes, your reason. By the time I got back, I saw you walking hand and hand off into the sunset with dear sweet moneybags. What did you do? Call him as soon as I had left?"

Stunned and washed with disbelief, she could not believe that her life had been forever altered by a simple misunderstanding. Suddenly, the lines from the cemetery tombstone came to mind.

In a torment of relief, Jack was finally able to fully bare all of the disappointment and pain he had stoically carried for over a decade. "Sandra, you know, I could have taken it a whole lot better if you had at least had guts to tell me that our night together had been a mistake...a..."

"Jack, no, it wasn't a mistake..."

"You know, I would have understood if you had told me that you still loved Robert." Filling the room with a broken laugh, he corrected himself. "No, let me take that back. I wouldn't have understood. I can finally say it: I honestly think that I was the better man. For one, I sure in hell wouldn't have put you through all of the crap your 'dearly departed' put you through. Robert was only about himself. He was that way before you married him, and he was pretty much that way when he died. Sandra, you knew that I was the better choice...that I would have cherished and loved you faithfully. I guess that's what made everything so hard to take."

"Jack...I..."

"Sometimes I would look at you and wonder how a woman so bright, could judge someone so poorly. I guess that old adage, love is blind, is true."

"So why did you let me marry him?"

"For the same reason I didn't pressure you to leave him when you found out that he had been cheating on you. You had to make that decision for yourself. Things would not have worked out between us if I felt that you were with me only because it was convenient, or were using me as some sort of handy spare. I had to know that you loved me for me."

"Oh, but I did...I..."

"But not well enough to break off your engagement, or to leave Robert. With all of the playing around he did, he gave you plenty of opportunity."

"Jack, don't you understand?" Sandra implored. "I thought that you were the one who left me. That morning, I didn't know where you had gone. When you never showed up, or even mentioned our night together, I assumed that I had read too much into our relationship. After Robert and I married, there were the kids...I was just doing good to get from day to day. Each time Robert was unfaithful, he took a little more of my self esteem and confidence." Her voice trailed off as silent tears began to flow.

As she wiped at her face with shaking hands, she continued, "If the truth is to be told, I did begin to look at you as a...a spare, but only because after a while I began to feel that no one could possibly love me, least of all you. True, you were always around, willing to be that shoulder to lean on, a surrogate husband...but all the while, I would look at you and wonder what kind of fool you thought I was to put up with all of Robert's garbage."

Sounding just as wretched as Sandra, Jack looked steadily into her eyes and shook his head. "I never thought of you as a fool, quite the contrary. As you said, I was there the whole time, and it was obvious that you were putting the well being of the children ahead of your own." With disparaging scorn, he remarked, "I'll give the man credit. Aside from everything that he wasn't, Robert was a good father."

Chuckling bitterly, Sandra turned and faced the mirror. "He knew my Achilles heel, all right. Whenever I would make up my mind to leave, he would tell me that I was punishing the kids just to get back at him." As she mocked her deceased husband, she looked down and fingered the wristwatch that was lying on the dresser top, "Why did I want to make the kids suffer for something they had nothing to do with?" he would ask. "It was as if he knew that we had slept together."

"So you stayed."

"So I stayed," Sandra forlornly answered as she met Jack's gaze in the mirror. Turning to face him, she took in a deep breath and in a strong voice heavy with emotion careened on. "But Jack, you must believe me. When I told you that I loved you over ten years ago, I meant it." Reaching over, she kissed him first tentatively, and when he responded by wrapping his arms around her tightly, she kissed him again with all the pent up ardor of over a decade's worth of unexpressed love."

Winter Park, Florida
Two days later

Finally!" laughed Maureen as she gave Sandra and Jack each a warm hug. Looking over at the children playing out in the yard, the older woman continued, "When Whitney and Jesse hear that you are getting married, I know they will be on top of the world. Now, you've filled me in on the swamp adventure and Sandra's mad flight back to the city, but Jack, you haven't told me how you finally got her to say yes."

Settling back onto one of the cedar chaise lounges that decorated the lanai, Jack grinned as he reached over and took hold of Sandra's hand. "Maureen, it wasn't as easy as we had planned. Sandra definitely made it quite difficult."

Pouring a glass of iced tea, Maureen gave her daughter a teasing wink. "Would my daughter make it anything but? I'm guessing that you've told her everything."

With mock disapproval, Sandra answered for Jack, "Yes Mom, I know everything. But I have to hand it to both of you. I was blind sided and duped. I still can't believe that Lee and Maggie were able to pull off their end of it so well. Not to mention, Mr. and Mrs. Fontenot. They should win an Oscar. How Jack ever convinced all of you to go along with his plan, I'll never know."

Pulling Sandra into his lap, Jack gave her a loving

kiss before answering. "They know how much I love you. To be honest though, I can't take all of the credit. Maggie clued me in on the fact that you had plans on spending the weekend with the Fontenots'. Remember that afternoon that we ran into one another at the restaurant, I don't know if you recall, but she asked for my business card. In order to get everything set up, she called several times.

"She even spoke to Lee. It seemed as if he knew that you were still, as he put it 'hung up on me', so he wouldn't stand in the way of the two of us getting together. His sudden interest in you as just a 'friend' worked to my advantage in that I didn't feel so bad dumping Darlene."

"So, did you really know the Fontenots from before, or was that just a story made up for my benefit?"

"No, honest to God, it was the eeriest thing. My father introduced me to them years ago. Talk about Fate." Shaking his head, he continued, "You don't know this, but Al was the one who woke me right after you drove off. It seems that he had been up reading the newspaper."

"I wondered how you got over to your apartment so quick."

Laughing, he explained, "I called your place from my cell phone. Now, I have to admit, you threw me for a loop when I arrived at your place and saw your car still parked. I couldn't figure out why you would stay in my car and not take yours."

"I wanted to confuse you, maybe buy a bit more time. I didn't expect you to come back to your place. I thought maybe you would drive by Mom's or the shop."

Jack, planting a kiss on her cheek, laughed. "Well my little car thief, you couldn't have gotten far. When you weren't at your house, I decided to head on home and report my car stolen. I figured on catching you one way or the other."

Stunned, Sandra playfully swatted his shoulder, "You

were going to have me arrested?"

"All's fair in the game of love."

"Now one more thing, why did you, Darlene, and Maggie run off into town that last evening?"

Chuckling, Jack took her hand, "Buying your engagement ring of course."

As Jack explained, Sandra, wide eyed, looked down at the antique white gold, marquis cut ruby ring that adorned her hand. "We drove over to an antique shop that Lee knew about. Maggie wanted to help pick it out of course, and Darlene simply wanted a ride into town to pick up a few toiletries."

Gently taking her hand, he softly continued, "Sandy, I was out of my mind with worry when you were lost. I made up my mind when I was searching that I would ask you to marry me before we returned to New Orleans. I don't know how well you remember the day you were found, but after I got back from town, I went up to your room and sat by your bed. I had planned to ask you to marry me as soon as you had awakened. As the night wore on though, it became obvious that you were going to sleep through, so I decided to wait until morning."

Sighing Sandra mumbled, "But then I left..."

"Exactly."

Thoughtfully smiling, Maureen studied the pair for several seconds, and in her characteristic no-nonsense tone, offered words of wisdom. "Let me give the two of you some simple words of advice, make your lives a whole lot less complicated by learning how to leave a simple note."

The End

ORDER FORM

Mail to: Genesis Press, Inc.
315 3rd Avenue North
Columbus, MS 39701

Name _____

Address _____

City/State _____ Zip _____

Telephone _____

Ship to (if different from above)

Name _____

Address _____

Telephone _____ Zip _____

City/State _____

Telephone _____

Qty.	Author	Title		Total

Use this order form, or call 1-888-INDIGO-1	Total for books	_____
	Shipping and handling: $3 first book, $1 each additional book	
	Total S & H	_____
	Total amount enclosed	_____
	MS residents add 7% sales tax	

2000 INDIGO TITLES

Romance, African-American Style.

Soul to Soul	Donna Hill	$8.95
Picture Perfect	Reon Carter	$8.95
Best of Friends	Natalie Dunbar	$8.95
All I Ask	Barbara Keaton	$8.95
Path of Fire	T.T. Henderson	$8.95
Bound by Love	Beverly Clark	$8.95
Sin	Crystal Rhodes	$8.95
Midnight Magic	Gwynne Forster	$8.95
And Then Came You	Dorothy Love	$8.95
So Amazing	Sinclair LeBeau	$8.95
A Dangerous Love	J.M. Jefferies	$8.95
Midnight Clear	Leslie Esdaile	
(Anthology)	Gwynne Forster	
	Carmen Green	
	Monica Jackson	$10.95
Cypress Wisperings	Phyllis Hamilton	$8.95
Forever Love	Wanda Y. Thomas	$8.95
Chances	Pamela Leigh Star	$8.95
The Missing Link	Charlyne Dickerson	$8.95

*You may order on-line at www.genesis-press.com, by phone at
1-888-463-4461, or mail the order-form in the back of this book.*

INDIGO BACKLIST

A Lighter Shade of Brown	Vicki Andrews	$8.95
A Love to Cherish (Hardcover)	Beverly Clark	$15.95
A Love to Cherish (Paperback)	Beverly Clark	$8.95
Again My Love	Kayla Perrin	$10.95
Breeze	Robin Hampton	$10.95
Cajun Heat	Charlene Berry	$8.95
Carless Whispers	Rochelle Alers	$8.95
Caught in a Trap	Andree Michele	$8.95
Dark Embrace	Crystal Wilson Harris	$8.95
Dark Storm Rising	Chinelu Moore	$10.95
Everlastin' Love	Gay G. Gunn	*OUT*
Gentle Yearning	Rochelle Alers	$10.95
Glory of Love	Sinclair LeBeau	$10.95
Indescretions	Donna Hill	$8.95
Interlude	Donna Hill	$8.95
Kiss or Keep	Debra Phillips	$8.95
Love Always	Mildred E. Kelly	$10.95
Love Unveiled	Gloria Green	$10.95
Love's Decption	Charlene Berry	$10.95
Mae's Promise	Melody Walcott	$8.95
Midnight Peril	Vicki Andrews	$10.95
Naked Soul (Hardcover)	Gwynee Forster	$15.95
Naked Soul (Paperback)	Gwynne Forster	$8.95
No Regrets (Hardcover)	Mildred E. Riley	$15.95
No Regrets (Paperback)	Mildred E. Riley	$8.95
Nowhere to Run	Gay G. Gunn	*OUT*
Passion	T.T. Henderson	$10.95
Pride & Joi (Hardcover)	Gay G. Gunn	$15.95
Pride & Joi (Paperback)	Gay G. Gunn	$8.95
Quiet Storm	Donna Hill	$10.95
Reckless Surrender	Rochelle Alers	*OUT*

INDIGO BACKLIST

Rooms of the Heart	Donna Hill	$8.95
Shades of Desire	Monica White	$8.95
Somebody's Someone	Beverly Clark	$8.95
The Price of Love	Sinclair LeBeau	$8.95
Truly Inseparable (Hardcover)	Wanda Y. Thomas	$15.95
Truly Inseparable (Paperback)	Wanda Y. Thomas	$8.95
Unconditional Love	Alicia Wiggins	$8.95
Whispers in the Night	Dorothy Love	$8.95
Whispers in the Sand	LaFlorya Gauthier	$10.95
Yesterday is Gone	Beverly Clark	*OUT*

All books are sold in paperback form, unless otherwise noted.

You may order on-line at www.genesis-press.com, by phone at 1-888-463-4461, or mail the order-form in the back of this book.

Shipping Charge:

$3.00 for 1 or 2 books
$4.00 for 3 or 4 books, etc.

Mississippi residents add 7% sales tax.